Anc

I waded through tl. ...adow where weeds competed with wildflowers for air and precious light. The scarf had landed in a tangle of white blossoming vine. It was oblong in shape, the color of orange sherbet, and as light as the air. Far too pretty to lose in a country meadow, but the woman in the balloon obviously wasn't coming back for it.

Stuffing the scarf in the pocket of my denim skirt, I made my way to the path that led to the kitchen door. A bit of debris lay amidst the tulips. I picked it up, recalling, as I did, the white object that had fallen from the balloon with the scarf.

Limp and damp with dew, it contained a single word, written with what appeared to be deep rose-red lipstick. *Help.*

How strange! An SOS from the sky. If that's what it was. Strange and melodramatic.

Things like this didn't generally happen. Except in Foxglove Corners, headquarters for mysterious and untoward occurrences and an occasional ghost.

This message had to be a joke.

In the kitchen, I bestowed grateful pats on the heads of Halley, my first collie, and Sky, my gentle blue merle rescue, and sat down to examine the missive more thoroughly. It appeared to be a piece ripped from a paper napkin and folded in two, suggesting desperation and haste. The red smear at a corner could be strawberry or raspberry jam.

A napkin from breakfast, most likely.

But what if it wasn't a joke?

I filled the teakettle and reached for a blueberry muffin. Who needed help and why choose this bizarre method to ask for it? The hot air balloon was long gone, and the family with it. I assumed they were a family. A traditional nuclear family on an unconventional Sunday outing in the sky.

"I don't know what I could do," I murmured.

What They Are Saying About

Another Part of the Forest

You know it's a good day, when a new Dorothy Bodoin book is released. ***Another Part Of The Forest*** is Bodoin's thirteenth book in her Foxglove Corners Series and it's a winner—exciting, suspenseful and a story that will keep you rapidly thumbing through the pages to find out what happens next.

Another Part Of The Forest will delight Bodoin fans as you clear the day, hunker down and settle in for a great read all about your friends in Foxglove Corners, Jennet, Crane, Camille, Leonora and Lucy, to name a few. Not to mention the stops at Clovers Restaurant for some tasty meals and delicious baked goods. After ten books, you will feel that you, too, live on Jonquil Lane with Jennet, her husband Crane and their four collies and can't wait to hear about their new adventures.

Suzanne Hurley.
Author

Other Works From The Pen Of

Dorothy Bodoin

Darkness at Foxglove Corners—February, 2007

Foxglove Corners offers tornado survivor Jennet Greenway country peace and romance, but the secret of the yellow Victorian house across the lane holds a threat to her new life.

Cry For The Fox—July 2005

In Foxglove Corners the fox runs from the hunters, the animal activists target the Hunt Club, and a killer stalks human prey on the fox trail.

Winter's Tale—December 2004

On her first winter in Foxglove Corners, Jennet Greenway battles dognappers, investigates the murder of the town's beloved veterinarian, and tries to outwit a dangerous enemy.

A Shortcut Through The Shadows—March 2005

Jennet Greenway's search for the missing owner of her rescue collie, Winter, sets her on a collision course with an unknown killer.

The Witches Of Foxglove Corners—May 2006

With a haunting in the library, a demented prankster who invades her home, and a murderer in Foxglove Corners, Halloween turns deadly for Jennet Greenway.

The Snow Dogs Of Lost Lake—November 2006

A ghostly white collie and a lost locket lead Jennet Greenway to a body in the woods and a dangerous new mystery.

Treasure At Trail's End—November 2005

The house at Trail's End seemed to beckon to Mara Marsden, promising the happy future she longed for. But could she discover its secret without forfeiting her life?

Ghost Across The Water—March 2006

Water falling from an invisible source and a ghostly man who appears across Spearmint Lake draw Joanna Larne into a haunting twenty-year-old mystery.

The Collie Connection—March 2009

As Jennet Greenway's wedding to Crane Ferguson approaches, her happiness is shattered when a Good Samaritan deed leaves her without her beloved black collie, Halley.

A Time Of Storms—November 2009

When a stranger threatens her collie and she hears a cry for help in a vacant house, Jennet Greenway Ferguson suspects that her first summer as a wife may be tumultuous.

The Dog From The Sky—March, 2010

When Jennet Ferguson rescues a collie who has been abused and left in the woods to die, she vows to find the person responsible for this outrage.

Spirit of the Season—October, 2010

Mystery mixes with holiday cheer as a ghost ice skater returns to the lake where she died and a collie is accused of plotting her owner's fatal accident.

Wings

ANOTHER PART OF THE FOREST

Dorothy Bodoin

A Wings ePress, Inc.

Cozy Mystery Novel

Wings ePress, Inc.

Edited by: Cheri Jetton
Copy Edited by: Karen Babcock
Senior Editor: Pat Evans
Executive Editor: Marilyn Kapp
Cover Artist: Pat Evans

Wings ePress Books
http://www.books-by-wings-epress.com/

ISBN 978-1-59705-558-1

Published In the United States Of America

Wings ePress Inc.
3000 N. Rock Road
Newton, KS 67114

Dedication

To Maximillian Bodoin, my nephew.

One

The dogs began to bark before there was any reason for canine agitation. At least none I could perceive. One jet-black collie and one whose coat brought together all the colors of the autumn leaves, they dashed through the daffodils that lined Jonquil Lane, effectively shattering the Sunday morning silence. When they reached the lane, they froze, tails held high and long noses pointed skyward.

"Candy!" I shouted. "Gemmy! Come!"

They didn't even turn their heads to look at me.

Dogs, I knew, could see things invisible to the human eye. Whatever had captured their attention was above us.

I scanned the sky, expecting to see a marauding hawk, a flock of feathered terrors, or perhaps a cloud shaped like a velociraptor. Instead I saw an endless expanse of azure and shreds of cottony fluff moving languidly to the south.

"Nothing's up there," I said.

But I was wrong. A moment later a hot air balloon glided into view. The magnificent flying object had wide bands of bright red, yellow, blue, and green. It flew low over Jonquil Lane.

So low that I could see its four passengers clearly. Two rosy-cheeked, tow-headed children, a young woman in a green sundress whose long auburn hair struggled to escape from the confines of an orange scarf, and a man with his hands resting protectively on the shoulders of the two youngsters.

So low that the people in the balloon could conceivably jump to the ground without harm. Apparently arriving at the same realization, Candy leaped up into the air, jaws open to fasten around the flying machine and pull it down to earth. With her black fur blown back, she was a vision of beauty in motion.

Entranced by her antics, the children laughed and waved. The little girl yelled, "Lassie!" a cry echoed by the boy at her side.

Lassie isn't black, I thought, but I waved back and repeated in my sternest tone, "Candy, Come!"

Gemmy looked at me but decided she wasn't included in my latest command.

I made another attempt to regain control of the situation. "Both of you! Come!"

Not a chance. The lure of the colorful UFO was stronger than the voice of their mistress. The little girl leaned over the edge of the balloon, and the man thrust her firmly back to the center.

It was the kind of day for man and beast to go slightly wild with joy, the first truly warm day of spring with a fresh, sweet breeze and new green leaves on every tree and plant. A day to fly through the air far above the ground where no evil thing could get you.

But that didn't give the dogs a free pass to wretched behavior.

Halley and Sky, my good, docile collies, were barking in the house where they had gone when I'd issued the order that should have ended our long play session. Wanting my canine family all together, I reached for Gemmy's collar, but she danced saucily away before I could grab her. Candy, who knew better than to come close to me at a time like this, kept her distance.

Thwarted, I glanced up at the balloon. A single detail in the sky scene had changed. The orange scarf, having come untied, was on its way to the ground, fluttering gaily in the breeze. The young woman's long hair blew freely, obscuring her features.

As I watched, something small and white broke free from the orange folds and fell in its own direction. The balloon sailed over the old yellow Victorian across the lane, then on above the woods. Skimming the treetops, it vanished from sight.

"All right," I said. "Excitement's over."

But not for Candy and Gemmy. They bounded after the balloon. Foolish, deluded dogs, thinking they could catch a balloon that rode the airways by running through the woods. I could hear them barking, already far away. Should I even bother to call them?

No. They'd chosen not to listen to me today. At any rate, they could outrun me. We all knew that.

At times like these I had to admit that four collies were three too many for a busy high school English teacher and the wife of a deputy sheriff.

During the months after I'd rescued Gemmy, she had learned dozens of new tricks from the incorrigible Candy. Candy would come home without her flying prize when she was ready, and Gemmy would follow Candy. I, Jennet Ferguson, would relax on the porch with a cup of tea and a mid-morning muffin.

But first I wanted to retrieve the orange scarf.

I waded through the meadow where weeds competed with wildflowers for air and precious light. The scarf had landed in a tangle of white blossoming vine. It was oblong in shape, the color of orange sherbet, and as light as the air. Far too pretty to lose in a country meadow, but the woman in the balloon obviously wasn't coming back for it.

Stuffing the scarf in the pocket of my denim skirt, I made my way to the path that led to the kitchen door. A bit of debris lay amidst the tulips. I picked it up, recalling, as I did, the white object that had fallen from the balloon with the scarf.

Limp and damp with dew, it contained a single word, written with what appeared to be deep rose-red lipstick. *Help*.

How strange! An SOS from the sky. If that's what it was. Strange and melodramatic.

Things like this didn't generally happen. Except in Foxglove Corners, headquarters for mysterious and untoward occurrences and an occasional ghost.

This message had to be a joke.

In the kitchen, I bestowed grateful pats on the heads of Halley, my first collie, and Sky, my gentle blue merle rescue, and sat down to examine the missive more thoroughly. It appeared to be a piece ripped from a paper napkin and folded in two, suggesting desperation and haste. The red smear at a corner could be strawberry or raspberry jam.

A napkin from breakfast, most likely.

But what if it wasn't a joke?

I filled the teakettle and reached for a blueberry muffin. Who needed help and why choose this bizarre method to ask for it? The hot air balloon was long gone, and the family with it. I assumed they were a family. A traditional nuclear family on an unconventional Sunday outing in the sky.

"I don't know what I could do," I murmured.

Halley nudged my hand with her nose. A whimper that might have been sympathy but more likely was a reminder that she and Sky were past due for their snack. I opened the Lassie tin and set three heart-shaped biscuits alongside each dog's water bowl.

While they crunched the treats, I tried a few scenarios on for size. The mischievous little boy had seized his chance to play a trick on his elders. One of the passengers was afraid the balloon would spring a leak. The auburn-haired girl had blotted her lipstick on the napkin, creating a stain that only looked like a word.

That last was ludicrous.

Crane, my husband and Foxglove Corners' favorite deputy sheriff, was currently on duty patrolling the roads and byroads of Foxglove Corners. He would know what to do about the message from the sky, if anything. Probably he'd tell me to ignore it, as the unorthodox plea for help sounded suspiciously like a mystery.

To Crane, mystery was synonymous with danger. Although he lived with danger every day, he wanted me to be safe; and neither one of us wanted our happy, peaceful lives disrupted any more than necessary.

So forget the balloon for now. Most likely there's no real emergency. Think of something ordinary and down-to-earth like lesson plans and Sunday dinner.

And I did. For the moment.

~ * ~

With my schoolwork finished and a chicken roasting in the oven, I took Halley and Sky out to the porch and sat in a wicker chair gazing across the lane where the yellow Victorian house that belonged to my, neighbor, friend, and aunt by marriage, Camille Ferguson, baked in an unseasonably warm sun.

Vacant ever since Camille's winter wedding to Crane's uncle, Gilbert, the house had quickly reverted to its previous state. Desolate and lonely. Almost haunted. The way it had been when I'd first come to Foxglove Corners and wondered what secret it held.

Tall grasses and weeds pretending to be flowers grew unchecked amidst the giant foxgloves in Camille's once-pristine perennial beds. It was every plant for itself until Camille came home in June with her husband and restored the gardens to order. But that wasn't now. I missed her more than I would have thought possible.

If she were across the lane instead of in her new home in Tennessee, I'd tell her about the message that had fallen from the sky while we sampled her latest nut bread or sponge cake. And I'd confide my worry about Candy and Gemmy. They hadn't come home yet. I wished I'd been more assertive with them, wished I'd followed them into the woods.

I reminded myself why I hadn't done that.

They were probably safe. There was little traffic on the country lanes that surrounded Jonquil Lane, but people tended to drive fast and might not see a dog in the road until it was too late to stop.

I willed this heartrending scene to dissolve. If I lost one of my dogs today, it would be the fault of the hot air balloon.

They'll come home in time for dinner, I told myself. Like most dogs, Candy and Gemmy loved to eat. Almost as much as they loved to explore in the woods.

If they were home now, I could never have set the chocolate meringue pie I'd baked for dessert on the kitchen table to cool.

There were too many if's in my thoughts today. Too much anxiety with members of my canine family missing.

Candy and Gemmy, come home.

~ * ~

Crane locked his gun in its special cabinet and kissed me again. A light, outdoorsy scent enveloped me. Woods and air, a touch of balsam soap, and a new shaving cologne. His fair hair was damp from the shower, and his frosty gray eyes sparkled.

Next Sunday was the day of our first wedding anniversary, and he still had the power to unsettle me with a touch or a word. Definitely with a kiss. It was corny, but true.

"Need any help with dinner, honey?" he asked.

"No, but thanks," I said. "Everything's ready."

And so was I, serviceable denim traded for a pink cotton dress with a flattering square neckline and a vase filled with wildflowers on the table.

I took the chicken out of the oven and reviewed the other items on my Sunday dinner menu. Stuffing, salad, vegetables, and biscuits. Halley and Sky had eaten already and settled down to wait for leftovers from our plates. Neither Candy nor Gemmy had come home yet.

I tried to make every meal Crane and I shared a special occasion, and we'd both agreed to forego any school or sheriff conversation until after dinner. So I made my one serious observation before we sat down.

"Dogs always give you grief," I said. "They've been gone all day."

He answered in a comforting *I'm-in-charge* tone. "They're probably chasing rabbits or deer. After dinner, we'll drive around and look for them."

"Through the woods?"

"I was thinking of Squill Lane. We'll start there and branch out in every direction."

The orange scarf and the piece of napkin lay on the buffet in full view. Earlier, I'd told Crane about the hot air balloon that had precipitated the dash into the woods and, of course, about the SOS.

"That's odd," he said. "Just ignore it."

I knew him well.

"It was the balloon that distracted them," I'd said.

"Still, they should have obeyed you."

"They listen to you." I tried not to sound envious.

"Yes, but you're with them more than I am. Maybe you should enroll them in obedience class this summer. No dog should make its own decisions. Running free can be a death sentence."

"That's a good idea."

Halley had a diploma from obedience school, and Sky, quiet and inclined to be clingy after a traumatic experience, wouldn't dream of disobeying her humans. But Candy and Gemmy wouldn't hesitate to do so; they were wild cards.

I lit the tall white tapers in the heirloom candlesticks that had once belonged to Crane's Civil War ancestress, Rebecca Ferguson. That was the signal to end all talk of domestic troubles.

"I've wanted to go up in a hot air balloon ever since I saw one on my first morning in Foxglove Corners," I said. "Cameron Lodge was riding in it to advertise Skyway Tours. He said, 'Come fly with me.'"

"You never told me." He winked at me. "Maybe we can celebrate our anniversary in the air."

"That would be unique. But we could wait until fall and make it a color tour."

I passed him the platter of chicken in a surround of his favorite bread stuffing. Yes, fall was the perfect time for a memorable air ride. The woods of Foxglove Corners would be ablaze with color; the air would have a gentle bite. Then we'd come back to earth to celebrate properly in a restaurant like the Adriatica, where we'd had our first date.

"We'll do it," he said.

Halley started barking, and Sky lifted her pretty blue head moments before I heard an ominous grating sound at the door. Nails raked the wood, creating an appalling sound reminiscent of a hand scratching desperately at a coffin lid.

That was another trick Candy had taught Gemmy.

"It looks like the wanderers have returned," I said.

Two

"Bad, bad dogs," I said, attempting a grave, wounded tone. "To worry your mistress! For shame!"

Gemmy flattened her ears and offered me her paw to shake, while Candy made a beeline for her water bowl and lapped loudly.

"Just look at your fur!" I added. "I'll have to cut all those tangles. Your coats will be ruined."

My rebel collies, freshly brushed this morning, must have tangled with every burr-bearing weed and bush in the woods.

Crane gave Candy a few rough pats on her ribcage. "That's another bullet dodged."

He'd been worried about the runaways, too. I'm sure Crane loved all of our collies, but Candy was his special pet. She had once saved his life.

"I think I'll have another piece of pie," he said. "How about you, honey?"

"That sounds good. I'll get it."

Her thirst sated, Candy stuck her nose in the empty food dish and looked up at me, an unbelievable hint of reproach in her dark eyes.

"You ladies missed dinner," I informed them as I opened a new bag of kibble. "Luckily your sisters didn't eat it all up."

What was the point of lecturing to unhearing ears? I refilled our coffee cups, cut two more pieces of pie, and moved the rest to the top of the refrigerator. Candy was home.

Now that the specter of death on a country road didn't hover over our household, this second dessert would taste better than the first. I realized that I hadn't enjoyed the roasted chicken. The knots in my stomach were as tight as those in Gemmy's tug-of-war toy. Still, in spite of today's happy outcome, I knew there would be additional incidents in the future.

"I wonder how far they went," I said.

"More to the point, did they do any damage along the way?"

I'd fielded more than one complaint about Candy's activities. She considered the whole of Foxglove Corners her playground and my neighbors' ponds superior to the ones found in the woods. One time a stranger had threatened to shoot her for disturbing his turkeys.

"If she did we'll soon know about it," I said.

But, for awhile, I would be unreachable, and tomorrow, while I was at school, the dogs would stay inside until Crane had an opportunity to stop home and let them out. Camille had served as faithful collie sitter until her move to the South, which was one more reason to miss her.

I wasn't quite ready to end my lecture. "I hope you girls enjoyed your day of freedom. You're both headed for summer school."

Halley and Sky searched my face, trying to decipher my words. Candy was already half sleep, and Gemmy was extracting a twig that had stuck to the fur on her hind leg.

"I'm sure they're impressed," Crane said with an amused twinkle in his eye. He took his dessert into the living room and settled down on the loveseat. I joined him, thankful, as always, that he was safe at home. One more day; one more bullet dodged.

Chocolate pie and coffee had a wondrous restorative effect on me, as did the prospect of an uninterrupted evening with Crane and the knowledge that I was as well prepared for tomorrow's classes as possible.

Now I was going to be a wise wife who knew when to let sleeping dogs lie. Forget the four collies who were at present taking their after-dinner naps. Forget mammoth grooming sessions and a parade of irate homeowners demanding Candy's head in a gathering basket. Forget every extraneous thing. It was still the weekend, and my husband deserved attention too.

~ * ~

Alas, the newest member of the Lakeville Collie Rescue League can't forget about collies for long. Later that evening the league's founder, Terra Roman, called on my cell phone apologizing for bothering me on a Sunday.

"It's no bother," I lied.

"I have a new collie for you to rescue," Terra said. "This one is a four-month-old puppy named Sandy."

Puppy? Envisioning chewed woodwork and shredded slippers, I reached for the pad of paper reserved for Rescue assignments.

"It's on North Arden in Lakeville," Terra said

I knew the street; it was in a quiet, pleasant section of town, as I recalled.

"The present owner, Mrs. Nell Lawson, will be expecting you. Just give her a call ahead of time."

"I can pick the puppy up tomorrow after school, but…" I glanced at Crane, his fair head bent over the evening newspaper. "I can't possibly keep a fifth collie at my house."

"That's okay," Terra said. "I'm at my limit myself. You can take her to Mrs. Palmer or the Woodville sisters."

It would be Foxglove Corners Animal Shelter, I decided. Lila and Letty Woodville, who ran the no-kill shelter in an old white Victorian turned haven for unwanted dogs, had opened what they referred to as a collie wing. Wafer, one of my winter rescues, was still there waiting for a new home.

"Who doesn't want an adorable little collie pup?" I asked.

"Mrs. Lawson. Her daughter won Sandy in a charity raffle. It was an unpleasant surprise for Mrs. Lawson, who doesn't like dogs, especially females."

I remembered a book by Albert Payson Terhune that began with a collie being rejected because of her sex. That story had angered me, as did the idea of a similar occurrence in real life, to say nothing of the raffle.

"What idiot thinks a live puppy is a suitable prize?" I demanded.

"As to that, I can't say."

Our veterinarian, Doctor Alice Foster, had once mentioned that unspayed purebred females were desirable commodities. They often found themselves stolen and sold to puppy mills. The very thought made me shudder. Little Sandy deserved to be rescued from that fate as soon as possible. Every dog should be in a home where she's loved and wanted.

I only wished I didn't have to go to school tomorrow.

"Oh, and, Jennet," Terra said, "don't argue with Mrs. Lawson. Don't try to convince her to change her mind or even mention raffle prizes. She's already made her decision. Just remove the pup from the house."

I'll try, I thought. Aloud I said, "I'll let you know how it goes."

~ * ~

My tenth-grade World Literature students stormed into the classroom the next day with an unseemly display of noise and disorder. The warm, sunny weather continued, inspiring a demand for all the windows open, a session outside on the grass, or at the very least a free day.

That we'd just had a tornado drill intensified their boisterous behavior.

The windows were already open, allowing delicious air to flow into the stuffy room. I wasn't foolish enough to defy Principal Grant Grimsly's directives and lead my students outside to chronicle signs of spring, as they suggested.

Which wouldn't have been a bad idea with a more malleable class and a lenient administrator.

Instead I'd planned to analyze three spring poems, beginning with *in just* by e e cummings. Naturally I'd anticipated their confusion and outrage. If a poet with his work published in their textbook could abandon rules of capitalization, why did I circle *their* errors with red ink?

Why indeed? First know the rules; then you can break them.

I stood at the blackboard in a blue shirtwaist dress that felt too warm for the day, listing signs of spring as students shouted contributions from their desk. They were loud but enthusiastic and involved.

By the end of the hour, we had the ingredients for a group poem of our own. Inspiration struck. Write a poem of your own imitating Cummings' style. That would be tomorrow's lesson plan in my two-tenth grade classes.

The bell rang, and the class came to life. They trooped out of the door before I remembered to remind them that they'd need pens for tomorrow's class work.

As I wrote *Do Not Erase!* on the board, hoping the custodian would read it, Leonora, my longtime friend who taught English in the next room, appeared in the doorway. She carried her beige raincoat and her purse. Nothing else.

"Nice," she said. "I'd copy your idea, Jen, but I started *Julius Caesar* today."

"Ah, Shakespeare. We should have studied him in January."

But Grimsly insisted that the English Department followed the syllabus.

Since Leonora's move to a pink Victorian house in Foxglove Corners, we'd shared the hour-long commute to Marston High School in Oakpoint, Michigan. Sometimes we shared ideas for making literature fun for our classes.

"Are you ready?" she asked. "I'm in a sort of hurry."

"Just a minute." I locked the windows and gathered my own folders and grade book.

"I have a dinner date tonight, and my hair looks like a haystack," Leonora said.

It didn't, of course. "On a Monday?" I asked.

"It's Jake's day off."

"Jake," I said.

I waited until I locked the door and we were on our way to the parking lot to comment further. I'd thought Deputy Sheriff Jake Brown had lost his chance with Leonora when he had tried to date her and my sister, Julia, at the same time, going so far as to give them matching presents. In matters of the heart, however, there's no place for assumption.

"We're going to the Pheasant and Ale," she said. "I want to find the perfect dress and wash the chalk out of my hair."

"It looks lovely," I said.

With her breezy blonde pageboy and turquoise dress, she could have stepped into an upscale restaurant this moment without changing a thing. Just the clunky leather shoulder bag.

"Thanks. But there's always room for improvement." She seemed glad that I wasn't going to offer an opinion about Jake. And

I didn't intend to. Leonora already knew that Jake was a handsome, charming philanderer and apparently didn't mind.

"Dinner at the Pheasant and Ale is a bit more elegant than my usual frozen entrée in a country kitchen," she added.

The frozen entrée surprised me. A one-time home economics teacher, Leonora was almost as accomplished in the kitchen as Camille.

"I'm in sort of a hurry myself," I said and told her about my new rescue assignment in Lakeville.

"If Sandy is a nice puppy without any major problems, could I see her?" Leonora asked.

She had been talking about adding a collie to her household ever since she'd bought a house with acreage.

"Sure. She'll be at the animal shelter."

"And as soon as school is over, I'd like to help you with your rescue work, too. Do you think they'd have me?"

"I'm sure they will," I said. "But I'll ask Terra."

"I know I don't have your qualifications, but it breaks my heart to think of sweet, loving collies like Halley and Sky without homes."

We'd reached my new black Taurus, its sleek body streaked with Foxglove Corners mud. "That's all you need, Leonora," I said. "Heart."

~ * ~

There were other desirable qualities, though, and after six months and eight rescued collies, I was still fine-tuning them. After I took Leonora home and turned in the direction of nearby Lakeville, I reflected on the advice I might have given Leonora.

A member of Collie Rescue had to remain cool and detached when faced with a nightmarish situation. She couldn't become emotionally involved in her cases. If a person chose to surrender a pet, she shouldn't try to change his mind. When coming across an abandoned or hurt collie, she needed to anticipate every eventuality, including a bite from a traumatized animal.

Possibly, and most important of all, she ought to be able to resist adopting her own foundlings.

My greatest shortcoming was refraining from inflicting my personal views on the people I dealt with. That was going to be the challenge in the coming rescue.

The address Terra had given me was a Spanish-style ranch on a double lot. A white pine surrounded by spring flowers formed an island in the front yard. The house had a deep, green backyard but no fence to keep an adventurous puppy from roaming.

I parked in a circular driveway and followed a yellow brick walkway to the porch, suddenly anxious to end this particular assignment.

The person who opened the door was a diminutive young girl in jeans and a floaty white top. With thick brown braids and streaks of mascara under her blue eyes, it was difficult to judge her age, but she must be at least in her teens.

"Hello," I said. "My name is Jennet Ferguson. I'm from the Collie Rescue League here to pick up Sandy."

"I'm Josie Lawson." The girl's voice broke on the words. "You're too late, Mrs. Ferguson. She's gone."

Three

"I don't understand," I said. "Gone where?"

From the back of the house came a shrill, petulant voice. "Is that the rescue lady? Josie?"

"My mom," Josie said with a faint blush. She tugged at one of her braids. "You'd better come in."

I stepped into a vestibule the size of a room. A small table topped with a pitcher of purple tulips dominated the vast space. Beside the flowers lay a small pink collar and a short show lead. "Where's the puppy?" I asked.

Josie shrugged. "I don't know. She ran away."

"And good riddance!"

The owner of the voice came through an archway and dropped a stack of towels on the nearest surface, a red sofa filled with plump needlepoint pillows. She reminded me of a housewife on a fifties sit-com. A crisp blue dress with a Peter Pan collar open at the neck, the requisite string of pearls and a yellow gingham apron tied around her slender waist. Every wave in her dark blonde hair looked as if it had been glued in place.

"I'm so sorry you had to make the trip for nothing," she said. "My name is Nell Lawson. This is my daughter, Josie."

"I'm Jennet Ferguson." I addressed my next comment to Josie. "Why would Sandy run away?"

Nell shrugged. "Why do dogs do anything?"

"She knew she wasn't welcome here," Josie said.

Nell gave her daughter a frosty look. "You know I can't abide dogs, Josie. Why you even brought her into this house I can't fathom."

"What was I supposed to do? Leave her there at the bazaar?"

"Yes."

Josie said. "I won her fair and square. She's mine. I have her pedigree papers and everything. She has the prettiest registered name. It's Mallowmere Drift of Sand."

Nell gave an exasperated sigh. "Yeah, well now she's gone. Sorry again, Mrs. Ferguson. Josie should have called you earlier."

"I have a few questions," I said. "How did it happen?"

Nell looked at her daughter. "Josie?"

"I took her outside to the backyard this morning," Josie said. "She sniffed around a little, then took off running. That way." She pointed east.

"Without a leash or collar," Nell added. "Don't forget that."

And without a fence. The need to run free must be ingrained in every dog's psyche. When Halley was a puppy, my recurrent nightmare was her loose on a busy city street. Poor Sandy could be dead by now, run over by a car or picked up by one of those vile puppy mill procurers. She was young, purebred and an unspayed female. In other words, a dog collector's dream.

"I ran after her, but she got away," Josie said.

"You're not responsible enough to take care of a goldfish."

"Why does it matter to you?" Josie demanded. "You wanted to call the dog pound. They'd kill her there." She turned to me, obviously seeking an advocate. "I'm the one who phoned you. I saw a story about the Collie Rescue League in the paper and figured you'd find Sandy a home where someone else would love her."

"I'm glad you did," I said.

"I wanted to put up 'Lost' posters, but she wouldn't let me."

"What's the point?" Nell demanded. "To get back a dog you're going to give away?"

"To make sure she ends up safe and in good hands," I said.

"She *was* in good hands." Josie tugged on her braid again and confronted her mother. "There's no reason why I can't keep her."

I detected a slight furtive note mixed in with Josie's defiance. Her eyes kept shifting from our faces to the floor, and she'd used the present tense as if Sandy were in the next room.

I suspected I wasn't hearing the entire story and that wasn't likely to happen today.

Having desperately wanted a collie myself when I was Josie's age, I truly sympathized with her. How sad to have your possession of a cherished collie puppy vetoed by a higher authority, in this case an unfeeling woman in pearls and an apron. The situation wasn't uncommon, but inevitably, it would have long-lasting repercussions, further damaging the fragile relationship between Josie and her mother.

Be patient, Josie, I wanted to tell her. *In ten or fifteen years, you can have your own place and another puppy. Just not this one.*

That assurance wouldn't have satisfied me when I was a child. Spoken now, it would only add to the anger that swirled around us, and I couldn't appear to be taking sides in this conflict. Terra would be horrified.

I wanted this sad episode to end. My own dogs were waiting for me. Crane would be home soon, and I wanted to be there to greet him. At this time, on a normal day, I would be starting dinner. Now I felt as if I were trapped in an escalating domestic scene that should have nothing to do with me. Still, I was involved because of my position in the Rescue League.

Mother and daughter were glowering at each other. The air was so thick with tension that the purple tulips were drooping.

I had one more question. "You said you won the puppy, Josie. Where was this?"

"At the Spring Bazaar at Saint Emerentiana's Catholic Church. I bought two dozen raffle tickets."

At a possible dollar apiece, Josie had paid twenty-four dollars for her treasure. An astounding price for a purebred puppy; a sizable amount for a teenager.

I made a mental note of the church's unusual name. "I didn't realize anyone gave away live dogs as bazaar prizes," I said.

"They do it every year. Isn't that neat?"

"I don't think so."

"Yesterday was my birthday," she added with a poignant sniffle.

It seemed that I had stepped into Albert Payson Terhune's book, the one that had left me angry. *Bruce*, I believe, was the title. The boy in the story had bought Lass with his birthday money. He'd been promptly ordered to take the nasty female dog back. Past or present, fiction or reality, some mothers never change.

"Won't you come in, Mrs. Ferguson?" this one asked. "Sit down? Have a cup of coffee or tea? For your trouble."

There wasn't the tiniest shred of welcome or sincerity in her voice.

There was, also, no reason to linger, without a collie to rescue. Except, as long as Sandy's whereabouts were unknown, Terra wouldn't close the case. I'd come to Arden Street to pick up an unwanted puppy who might still need saving. I wasn't going to accomplish that here.

"Thank you, Mrs. Lawson," I said, making a show of consulting my watch. "But I'm running late today. The fact remains…" I slipped with ease into lecture mode. "Josie accepted Sandy. Until you turn her over to me, she's still your responsibility, like it or not."

Nell bristled at that. "I don't like it, and really, what can I do? The dog is gone. She won't find her way back to this house; she was only here for an afternoon and overnight. Just long enough to bite me and make a mess on the carpet." She sniffed the air. "That's my pork chops burning. If you'll excuse me…"

She swept out of the room without a backward glance or word of farewell.

"She's so hateful sometimes." Josie swiped at her eyes, creating larger smudges on her cheeks. "If you find Sandy, Mrs. Ferguson, will you take care of her, please? She's so little."

"I promise," I said. "If I find her."

But where would I look with only a direction, east, for a clue? Sandy had been gone for a whole day.

"She's the color of a butterscotch sundae, all golden and soft. She has white on her chest and the tip of her tail."

"She sounds pretty," I said.

"She's beautiful. The most beautiful collie ever."

Josie's teary plea, combined with my certainty that Sandy had already met with an unfortunate accident or fallen prey to an unscrupulous opportunist, should have brought tears to my eyes. Why didn't it?

As I walked back to my car, I answered my own question.

Because Josie's story didn't ring true.

~ * ~

Even after I passed the Lakeville city limits, I kept watching for a collie puppy with fur like butterscotch padding along the road or hiding in dense foliage. Of course all I saw were rabbits and deer and once a mother duck leading her ducklings across a narrow lane, confident there was no danger to her family.

By now I was more than halfway home. Could four little puppy legs have taken Sandy this far from Lakeville?

Probably not. It became more and more likely that Sandy was indeed gone. Still I kept looking. I'd learned to do that anyway ever since joining the Collie Rescue League. And, as I drove down the quiet country roads, I formulated a plan. Even if I didn't find Sandy, I could investigate the outrageous practice of offering puppies as raffle prizes. A plush toy collie would have been an appealing alternative.

St. Emerentiana's church was the place to begin, and thanks to Josie, I had the name of Sandy's kennel. Mallowmere. A lovely word, fanciful and poetic. I'd never heard of it. Nonetheless, both church and kennel should be easy to find. Blame, in this case, didn't stop with the organizers of the bazaar.

When I turned onto Jonquil Lane, the air blowing through the open windows seemed sweeter. The daffodils that appeared every spring along the lane were at their peak, all shades of yellow to the palest creamy white. They were incredibly fragrant.

My yellow brick road, I though fondly, and the green Victorian farmhouse where anger and resentment would never destroy the serenity.

Crane's Jeep was parked in the drive, and Candy's and Gemmy's faces were at the kitchen window, side by side. But Halley was the first collie to greet me when I opened the door. Sky emerged from her place of safety under the oak table and stretched.

Crane was drinking orange soda. He was still in his uniform, still had his gun belt strapped on. I wasn't that late then.

"Hello, honey," he said, opening a bottle for me. "Where's the new puppy?"

I dropped my schoolwork and purse on the nearest catch-all, the counter. Candy jumped up to investigate them.

"Heaven only knows. Apparently she ran away this morning."

"That isn't good. How old did you say she was?"

"Four months."

"Just a baby then."

I put two strip steaks in the broiling pan and brought out ingredients for a salad. While I rinsed and chopped and tossed, I told him about my visit to the house on Arden Street and my suspicion that a chunk of the story was missing.

"Josie's keeping a secret," I said. "I'll bet anything on it."

"Do you think she got the puppy some other way?" he asked.

"I don't know. Her story is easy to verify, though. It's heartbreaking to see a young girl separated from her dog."

"That sounds like one of those tearjerker movies for kids," Crane said.

That was true. *Old Yeller*, *Lassie Come Home*, so many others. I must have seen them all.

"If I ever have a daughter, I'm not going to crush her dreams," I said.

"What if she wants a kitten? Or a horse?"

"Even then."

"If we're lucky, she'll want a collie of her own," he said. "Come here and kiss me, Jennet. It's been hours since I've seen you."

I did as he asked and ran my hand through his hair. He had more gray now, silver streaks shining in the gold. "We have the whole evening together."

"Did you hear the news about the hot air balloon?" he asked. "I wonder if it was the one you saw yesterday."

I looked up from the basket of cherry tomatoes. "What happened?"

"It crashed on the other side of the lane. Not only that; the people who were riding in it disappeared. It's on all the stations."

"They must be somewhere."

"No one knows where. The balloon is in a heap on the ground, totally disabled. There was nobody in sight."

My mind filled with images of a magical flying machine, torn apart on its descent to the ground, its multi-colored pieces scattered on a rocky terrain.

"If it's the same balloon I saw, there were four people in it." I abandoned the salad and sat down, taking a long sip of my soda. "Two of them were little children, about eight or ten. They all looked so happy up there in the sky. The little girl waving, calling out 'Lassie'..."

Then, the orange scarf fell and I found the napkin with *Help* written in lipstick on it.

"I guess I can't ignore that SOS now," I said.

Four

"That's only half the story," Crane said. "The tour guide was found shot. Eric Abbott was only nineteen." He snapped his fingers. "Just like that, a freak accident turns into a homicide."

I reached for my bottle of orange soda and found it was already empty. Opening another, I said, "That's terrible. Who do they think shot him?"

"That's another mystery. Eric was working alone at the Skyway Tours office yesterday. Nobody missed him until a farm couple called in to report a downed balloon in their cornfield. About the same time, someone else came across his body dumped on Spruce Road. That's close to the launch site."

"Nobody should work alone these days," I said. "It's way too dangerous. Let's recreate the scene. Someone has the idea to rob the office. Eric resists and is shot. In the meantime the balloon has already set sail. I don't know how Eric's body ended up on Spruce Road, but the shooting and crash must be related."

"Eric had his dog with him, a black shepherd. He was wandering around the Skyway area."

"A collie would have gone for help," I said, thinking of Candy, Crane's faithful guardian. "Being a German shepherd, Erik's dog must have attacked the shooter. In which case, he'd have scratch marks or bites."

"And be easy to identify. Amazing the dog didn't get shot, too."

"It's too bad he can't talk," I said. "Be sure and pick up the *Banner* tomorrow. I'll see if there's anything more in the *Free Press*."

As the only journalism teacher at Marston High School, I had access to two copies of the Detroit newspaper during the school week. I often used provocative articles in my lessons and always encouraged the students to read more than the Sports page and comics. This story, for example, would be one to follow closely.

"I wish I could be sure the balloon that crashed was the same one I saw," I said.

"It must have been. I understand only one tour was scheduled for yesterday. It carried four people."

"Were two of them children?"

"At this point, that's unknown."

"If the people had any inkling the balloon was about to go down, you'd think they'd be shouting for help, not dropping a paper to a casual observer. And they wouldn't have looked so calm and happy."

Crane uttered the words reluctantly. "It's a mystery."

"And I'm in it."

"Again." He didn't look pleased. Slivers of frost gave his gray eyes a dangerous glitter.

"I was on our own property playing with our dogs," I pointed out. "Minding my own business."

"I know, honey. You can't help attracting mysteries, but I sure wish you could. If you saw those people, they saw you."

I'd thought of that, of course. And they'd seen my collies and the house.

Crane didn't mention the SOS, but I could tell it preyed on his mind. Now that there appeared to be a connection between the hot air balloon and me, he couldn't help worrying. Neither could I, especially since a young man had been shot to death.

"I'll take the message and scarf to Mac at the FCPD after school tomorrow," I said. "In the meantime maybe they'll find out what went wrong with the balloon."

"Or find the bodies."

"There don't have to be bodies. Couldn't the family have just dusted themselves off and gone on their way? Assuming no one was hurt."

"Possible but unlikely. Even from a low-flying balloon, that would have been a dangerous plunge."

Like a fall from the roof of a three-story house, I thought. The sky riders had to be dead.

"The balloon had a name," Crane added. "The Sky Princess. Skyway Tours owns other balloons. They all have the word 'sky' in the name."

Our own Sky glanced at him shyly, no doubt wondering if we were talking about her. She looked so concerned that I reached over to pet her and assure her she was a good dog.

"Skyway Tours is one of Cameron Lodge's side enterprises," I said.

The owner and publisher of the *Banner* lived up north in Maple Falls. I'd met him a few times and called to ask for his help on another occasion. Possibly he would drive down to Foxglove Corners to investigate the accident personally. I'd like to see him again.

"Whatever happened, for whatever reason, it was a tragic end to a perfect spring day," I said. "And to at least one life."

Crane nodded. "And we don't know what else may have happened."

~ * ~

The next day, during my conference hour at school, I scoured the *Banner* for news of the crash. The major story had been written by Jill Lodge, Cameron's reporter cousin whom I'd met when Winter, my first foundling, received a medal "For Valor" after saving a child from drowning.

Coverage of the Sky Princess crash was sketchy. The passengers seemed to have dropped into a black hole, but their names had been dutifully recorded in the Skyway Tours' log: Peter, Wendy, Janie, and Johnston Holliday.

Were Peter and Wendy the children?

The wreckage had been cleared from the cornfield, and, in another part of Foxglove Corners, Eric Abbott's body taken away for an autopsy. How unnecessary, I thought. Cause of death was obvious. A single shot in the heart. He must have died instantly.

The weapon was missing. Abbott's black shepherd, Charger, was grieving for his young master. Eric's brother was taking care of him. One surprise fact set me reeling.

Skyway Tours, until recently owned by *Banner* publisher, Cameron Lodge, had been purchased last month by Brent Fowler, our friend and the celebrated fox hunter of Foxglove Corners who had money to spare and a well-hidden boyish streak.

Brent felt responsible for Eric Abbott's death. "I've known him since he hired on at my stable," Brent had told Jill. "Eric was saving money for college. He wanted to be an archaeologist."

Like so many young people who yearned for an adventurous career. Horses and hot air balloons. Challenges and death.

Brent had offered a generous reward for information leading to the shooter's capture.

Would that be the same person who had sabotaged the Sky Princess?

If that was what had happened. Although what reason could anyone have for wanting to destroy a beautiful hot air balloon? Perhaps the people were the target and not the balloon.

Surely not. Surely not those two happy little children.

I recalled all the times I'd imagined myself sailing above the countryside I'd come to love. Not once had I worried about escaping gas and plummeting to the ground. Not once could I remember hearing of a similar accident in Michigan.

The paper included a sidebar intended to convince fearful readers that hot air balloon excursions were comparatively safe. Airplanes crashed. Boats sank. Cars slammed into each other every day. Still… I wasn't so eager now to take a color tour over the changing leaves of fall.

~ * ~

I came across Brent Fowler in the New Deli eating a sandwich and drinking his favorite beverage, root beer, from his own mug. He wore a hunter green shirt. The color complemented his dark red hair and coaxed green flecks to appear in his eyes.

I'd expected to find Brent in a somber, reflective mood but should have remembered that wasn't his way. He was his usual blustery, jovial self, a man who kept his deep feelings to himself. He rose when I approached his table and gestured toward one of the vacant chairs.

"You're feeding the Sheriff deli tonight?" he asked with a trace of his old teasing humor, or what passed for humor, reminding me of the days when he fancied himself a serious contender for my affections. He used to bedevil me by using the wrong title to address Crane.

My answer never varied. "Crane didn't win an election yet. He's still a deputy, and yes, we're having corned beef sandwiches and coleslaw tonight. It's too hot to cook."

"It's only eighty-five degrees."

"In the shade. But it feels wonderful in here."

For the first time all day, except for my commute, my dress didn't feel as if it were made of flannel.

Marston High School didn't have air conditioning in the classrooms. My car did, but it had been a long, sweltering trek from my parking place to the deli.

"I thought when a man got married, he could count on having a home-cooked meal every night," Brent said.

"Fortunately Crane doesn't share your views. Sometimes he brings a pizza home for dinner. Sometimes he even barbecues ribs or steaks."

"But you still bake, right? Pies, cakes, cookies…"

"And muffins and biscuits," I assured him. "But only when it's cool outside."

I placed my take-out order and sat down opposite him again. "I'm sorry about Eric and the Sky Princess," I said, instantly changing the atmosphere at the table.

"That was one of my rare mistakes," he said. "If I'd never had the idea to buy Skyway Tours, Eric would still be alive, working at the stable. He was a good kid. Good with the horses. Good all around."

"Why *did* you buy the company?" I asked.

"On a whim. Lodge wanted to unload it. It was a steal," he added. "But look at the price we paid."

"Did they find the family?"

"Not yet, and that's a puzzler. I think one of them knows what happened to Eric. Maybe shot him, for all I know."

"I saw the Sky Princess as it flew over Jonquil Lane," I said. "Candy and Gemmy went chasing after it. They were gone all day."

"They could tell us something."

"My thought exactly—and so could I."

I told him about the orange scarf that had come floating down from the hot air balloon to land in my wildflower vine and about the SOS scrawled in rose red lipstick.

"The police have them now," I said.

Brent's eyes widened. "That could be a real clue, Jennet. It practically shouts out, Danger! Now, if we just knew what's going on. Damn!" He slammed the table. People sitting nearby turned to stare at us.

"It had to be the woman who threw the paper out of the balloon," I said.

He frowned. "How do you figure that?"

"Elementary, my dear Brent. It was wrapped in her scarf. The writing in lipstick… Need I say more?"

He nodded. "Oh, yeah. Too bad Crane won't let you work for the Force, Jennet. You're a natural."

"I already have a job," I reminded him.

From across the deli, the waiter called my name and pointed to a large white bag.

"I'm a part of this mystery even though I'm not officially involved. Let me know if there's anything I can do, and keep in touch."

"I always do," he said.

"Can you come to dinner some night next week? I'll call you."

He smiled. "Any night."

"And oh, here's something you could do for me, if you will."

"Just name it."

I told him about Sandy. "One of my rescues escaped before I could save her. Would you post a notice at your barn? *Lost collie puppy. Four months old. Answers to the name of 'Sandy'. Last seen on Arden Street in Lakeville.*"

"Sure will, Jennet, and I'll look around myself. Is she black, blue, brown, or white?"

How could I have forgotten that detail?

"She's the color of a butterscotch sundae with white markings," I said. "Think whipped cream and marshmallow."

"Now I want dessert," Brent said.

"So do I."

I hadn't ordered any, having a whole lemon meringue pie at home.

Curiously, in spite of the shadows that had fallen on the spring day, I felt suddenly encouraged about Sandy. Brent had a reputation for accomplishing what he set out to do. If anyone could find Sandy, it was he. Unless it was too late.

Five

Not being one to expect others to do my sleuthing for me, the following Saturday morning I set out for Saint Emerentiana's Catholic Church in nearby Spearmint Lake. Afterwards I intended to visit Mallowmere Kennels.

Ellen Grove of Colliegrove Kennels had given me the name of Sandy's breeder, Marvel McLogan, and the kennel's location. Ellen had met Marvel at a dog show last year. She couldn't believe that a Mallowmere collie had ended up as a raffle prize.

"Something's wrong there, Jennet," she'd said. "If you weren't investigating the matter, I'd do it myself."

Fortunately Ms. McLogan lived on the outskirts of Spearmint Lake. With luck I could visit both church and kennel, have lunch at Clovers, and be home shortly after noon.

The spring heat wave had passed, and the temperatures dropped to a pleasant seventy degrees. I drove with the windows open, savoring the scent of spearmint wafting from the fields that bordered the lake.

The church was a tidy brick structure landscaped with evergreens and young, blossoming trees. Wild violets bloomed in the lush green lawn, currently being trampled on by four youngsters pouring out of the heavy front doors. Across the street was the school, built with the same light yellow brick.

Some day when I had time I planned to research the life of the saint with the unusual long name. I knew nothing about her except that she was a Christian martyr living or, rather, dying in early Roman times. I didn't think she, being a saint, would condone cruelty to animals.

Saint Emerentiana, help me find a little lost puppy, I prayed.

Keeping to the stone walkway, I bypassed the church's main entrance looking for the rectory. Once I learned the names of the bazaar organizers, I could figure out how to contact them. Perhaps in this case subterfuge was unnecessary. Why not simply ask who they were and state my mission?

I hadn't mentioned these visits to Terra but didn't doubt she'd cheer me on.

The rectory was unlocked. I opened it and found myself in a small, dim hall with one open door at its end. In a light, airy office, a middle-aged woman wearing a navy polka dot dress was frowning at a computer screen. She looked up, squinting in a shaft of sunlight that crossed her desk, and pushed her glasses back on her spiked blonde hair. A plaque identified her as Nancy Allen, Secretary.

"Good morning." She gave me a cheery smile. "How can I help you?"

"My name is Jennet Ferguson," I said. "I've come about the Spring Bazaar."

"Oh, I'm sorry. It was last weekend. But there'll be another one in the fall."

"Will you have another raffle too?" I asked.

"We plan to. Would you like me to send you a book of tickets to sell when they're ready?" She took a pen from a seashell-embossed mug and reached for a pad of post-it notes. "A couple of books maybe?"

"No," I said. "I don't belong to the parish, but I'll buy a raffle ticket—in the fall."

"Then I don't understand."

Because you didn't give me a chance to explain.

I took a deep breath and delivered my rehearsed opening. "I'm a member of the Lakeville Collie Rescue League. I was appalled to find out you gave away a collie puppy as a prize."

She dropped the pen back in the mug and looking down, possibly in an attempt to hide the blush that spread over her face or to summon her composure. Obviously she hadn't expected this bit of unpleasantness to come through her door on a sunny spring morning. However, she rallied quickly.

"But we always do," she said. "It's our tradition."

"So I've heard."

"No one ever complained before."

"If there isn't a law against it, there ought to be."

It occurred to me I should have done my research, but all I'd thought about was the lost puppy and time running out.

She started to rise. "Maybe I'd better call Father Horace."

"There's no need. I wanted you to know that Sandy, the puppy you raffled off, ended up in the home of a woman who didn't want her. She was going to call the dog pound when her daughter intervened and got in touch with the League instead. Before I could rescue Sandy, she ran away."

Nancy blanched at the word 'rescue' but retaliated immediately. "That puppy was well treated. I kept her in my own home before the bazaar."

"I'm sure you did," I said. "It's what happened afterwards that's so wrong."

"That girl who won the pup was happy."

"But her mother doesn't want a dog in the house."

"I didn't know that. Yes, maybe I should have, but the money we raised will go toward replacing the school's old playground equipment."

"A good cause, I'm sure."

"And meals for hungry children during summer vacation. So many kids get only one good nutritious meal a day—their school lunch. When school's over, so are the free lunches."

I sighed, steering the conversation back to the puppy. No one could argue against hungry children, but I was on another mission this morning.

I brought out every big gun I could think of, emphasizing the killing of surplus pets and the horrors of puppy mills. "A dog running loose could be crushed by a car on the road," I said. "That's a horrible way for a dog to die. It may already have happened to Sandy."

"Well, I don't know… Aren't you being a little pessimistic?"

"I'm being realistic. Every dog deserves to be in a home where her owner truly wants her. Every puppy deserves a decent start in life."

The ticking of the wall clock seemed unnaturally loud, reminding me time was indeed running out for Sandy while I stood here, trying to drive home my point to a woman who obviously preferred to hold on to her own views.

"The winner can always decline the prize," Nancy said. "We'd have given this Josie twenty-five dollars in cash if she'd preferred."

"What girl who desperately wants a dog would accept money instead? And, in that case, what would happen to the puppy?"

Her answer came quickly. "We'd find it a home, of course." Her eyes narrowed. "We're not monsters here, Mrs. Ferguson. What exactly do you want?"

"For you to consider offering an inanimate prize in the fall and in any future bazaars," I said. "A life-sized plush animal, perhaps. A Sandicast collie if you like. Anything that doesn't breathe."

She seemed so relieved I wondered what she'd been expecting.

"I'll speak to Father Horace and the committee. Now if that's all..."

"There's just one more thing," I said. "Could you tell me who donated the puppy to the bazaar?"

The blush returned, along with the defensive stance. "Well, if you must know, I did."

~ * ~

Nancy Allen was glad to see me leave her office. She all but hustled me into the hall and out the door.

Outside the church, I stood on the walkway breathing fresh spring air and a scent of lilac drifting across the grass from a stand of trees. I hoped my visit had done some good, if not for Sandy, then for future unfortunates.

Had I been too accusatory? Too combative? I didn't think so. My cause was just, my solution sensible. Come fall, I intended to see if Nancy Allen, her committee, and Father Horace had implemented my suggestion and offered an alternate prize.

Apparently thinking it would strengthen her case, Nancy admitted that she'd paid four hundred dollars for Sandy, using money from the parish's slush fund. She hadn't cared for my pointing out that, with the price of the puppy, they'd only made a two hundred dollar profit. Hardly enough to buy a swing set and feed needy children through the summer months.

I could only hope that Sandy's breeder, Marvel McLogan, had been unaware of the church's plans for the puppy when she'd sold her.

Now, on to Mallowmere and the second part of my day's project.

The kennel was three miles from the lake on a scenic dirt road. The kennel sign was new and shiny; the farmhouse old and white with peeling paint. Close to the house a new-looking frame outbuilding was enclosed with high chain length fencing divided into six runs.

All of them were empty except for the one closest to the house, which contained two puppies, a tricolor and one the color of butterscotch. An older tricolor, a gorgeous animal whose black coat had a blue cast, must be their mother. All three dogs were barking and leaping at the gate.

I parked the Taurus in the gravel driveway and walked over to the run. The puppies tried frantically to claw their way through the fence and into my arms while the older tri wagged her tail joyfully.

Collies. They were so friendly they'd give away the farm if you asked them politely.

A screen door slammed. I turned to see a young woman clad in jeans and a white shirt walking toward the run at a brisk pace. Unlike the collies, she looked anything but friendly.

"If you came about the ad, I only have one pup left, the tri male," she said. "But I wish you'd have called first."

Oh, no. Another tense encounter.

"I'm sorry," I said. "But I came for a different reason."

She smoothed her hair that didn't need smoothing. It was styled like mine in a shoulder-length pageboy with wispy bangs and was the same shade of dark brown. She stood with one hand pressed on the fence, scrutinizing me with cornflower-blue eyes.

"I'm Marvel McLogan," she said. "You look so familiar. Have we met before?"

"I don't think so."

"Maybe I saw you at one of the shows. I don't usually forget faces."

I knew why Ms. McLogan thought we'd met. On occasion my picture had been in the *Banner*, a few times with Halley at my side. I didn't feel like enlightening her at this point but wasn't quite ready to launch into my story. So I said, "They're beautiful puppies. Was it a large litter?"

"Jess had six pups, but I lost two of them." She turned to her small survivors. "The little girl is Brandy; the boy is Andy."

And there was Sandy. The names rhymed. *How cute*.

"I have a Candy," I said.

I tried to reach Andy's head to stroke it. Brandy poked her small paw through the space in the fence and licked my finger with a tiny pink tongue. Andy shoved her out of the way, and she yipped indignantly.

"Are you a collie person?" Marvel asked.

"I have four adults; three of them are rescues," I said. Here was my opening. "I'm Jennet Ferguson of the Lakeville Collie Rescue League."

"Jennet—Greenway! That's where I saw you. In the *Banner*."

I smiled. "It's possible. I've been there a few times." Not elaborating, I said, "I've come about one of your puppies, Sandy. I thought you'd like to know…"

My heart twisted at her stricken look as I told her what had become of Sandy since leaving Mallowmere. Her blue eyes filled with tears.

"My little baby. I want her back."

"I'm looking for her," I said. "So are my friend and my husband. Crane is a deputy sheriff. He covers a lot of territory every day."

"I thank you, but Sandy is my responsibility." She wiped her eyes with her hand; her voice took on a razor-sharp edge. "That woman, that Mrs. Allen, didn't say anything about a church bazaar. She just said she wanted a nice collie puppy."

"Well that was true."

"Now my poor baby is out there somewhere, hungry and frightened with no one to take care of her." She clenched her fists. "I'm going to find her."

Marvel didn't appear to realize that this might not be possible. Not wanting to be the bearer of still more distressing news, I didn't remind her.

I shared Marvel's determination. It was my job to rescue collies, and I would have done so in any event. But I thought that finding Sandy would make up a little for not responding to the SOS from the hot air balloon in time to help the people inside.

Maybe I couldn't have saved them, but Sandy was a different story. And if or when she was found, she already had a place to go. Home to Mallowmere Kennel. Many breeders, I knew, would take back a puppy they'd sold if the transaction didn't work out.

"I need to think." Marvel moved toward the porch where five rockers sat in a row, with pots of red geraniums between them and on the ledges. She beckoned me to join her. "Can you help me at all, Jennet? Tell me where to look? Tell me where you've looked."

I settled myself in a wicker rocker very much like the ones on my own porch. "Sandy was last seen running east on Arden Street. That's in Lakeville. I'm going to notify my friends at the Foxglove Corners Animal Shelter. People are always bringing them dogs. They're keeping rescued collies for the League."

The country silence settled around us. There were no clocks nearby to tick. But I felt time's passage as if it were a tangible entity pushing away the comfort.

"What can I do?" Marvel addressed her question to the geraniums. I didn't think she expected an answer.

"Things just keep getting worse," she said with a sigh. "This was supposed to the perfect breeding. A champion stud dog out of Ohio. My pretty Jess... Now that I know what happened to Sandy, I'm convinced this is an unlucky litter. That terrible woman put a curse on me."

Six

I stared at Marvel. A curse? Surely she wasn't serious?

"Do you mean Mrs. Allen?" I asked.

"No, I was talking about Barbara, my former friend. She tried to talk me out of building my kennel or even buying Jess, come to think of it. She said there were enough collie breeders in Michigan already and too many dogs in the world."

"Good friends don't crush your dreams," I said.

"Barbara was always critical and pushy even when we were in school. But all I ever wanted was to raise collies. I've been to all the shows and read every book and article I could find. I studied hard and saved my money. Then a wonderful opportunity came along, and I grabbed it."

She glanced at the rolling acreage north of the house. For the first time I noticed the two barns in the distance and a long section of white plank fence.

"This used to be a horse farm, Mallow Brook, but the owners lost it to foreclosure. The price was unbelievable for the house and land together."

"It's beautiful," I said, and it was. Even without landscaping or trees.

"I think so. I found another job close by and moved myself and Jess. The house needs loads of work, but I can manage."

"This friend of yours might have disapproved, but she couldn't have put a curse on you," I said.

"Barbara wished me ill. She said I'd never succeed, that I wasn't cut out for country living and didn't have any business sense. I haven't talked to her since. Then two of my puppies died when they were a day old. Such tiny, precious lives. They were black like my Jess."

"Did something else bad happen, besides Sandy ending up as a raffle prize and losing two of the litter?" I asked.

She nodded. "Just yesterday. It's Mandy."

"Do you want to tell me about it?"

I needn't have asked. Of course she did, although why she would confide in a stranger, I couldn't imagine. Except in the article she'd read, a reporter who tended to exaggerate had referred to me as a talented sleuth. It had already brought me unwanted attention.

Marvel said, "No one else knows, so please keep this to yourself."

I promised to do so, and she continued. "Mandy was the pick of the litter. The lady who owns the sire is taking her in place of a stud fee. To someone who doesn't know how to evaluate collie puppies, Mandy looks like Brandy, the little female out there in the run. The differences are in markings. Mandy has more tan on her right foreleg and more white in her collar. She's a little sturdier, more outgoing."

Out in the run, Brandy and Andy began yipping as a blackbird swooped down and perched on the fence for the merest moment. When it flew away, the pups started running frantically in circles and chasing their tails while their mother watched them calmly.

Sandy, Brandy, Mandy, Andy. What had possessed Marvel to give her puppies rhyming names? They were swimming around in my head.

"Yesterday two women drove in from downstate to buy a puppy," Marvel said. "They'd seen my ad in *Collie Vistas*. The younger one, Suzette, chose Brandy right away. It was such an easy sale, and everything happened so fast. I gave her Brandy's papers and a package of her food and they left, saying they had a four-hour drive home. It wasn't until the puppies' dinner that I realized they'd taken Mandy instead of Brandy."

"Oh no! What a mix-up! But I'm sure that kind of thing has happened before."

"I'm sure it hasn't," Marvel said. "I've been telling myself it really wasn't my fault, but it was. I should have checked more carefully instead of letting Suzette take Mandy. What kind of breeder doesn't know one of her puppies from the other?"

"But this mistake is fixable." Honesty compelled me to add, "Probably."

"Now I've only got one puppy left to sell, and so far nobody wants him. One prospective buyer called him a scarecrow."

"How unkind. Couldn't he have said 'ugly duckling'?"

Her smile was forced. "I may end up keeping him. Maybe he'll turn into a swan."

"He's a little beauty now," I said, regretting the implication of the duckling remark. "You got in touch with the buyer, didn't you?"

"That's the problem. I haven't been able to contact Suzette. She gave me her cell phone number, but my messages go straight to her voice mail; and it's someone else's mail. I was so excited and flustered I forgot to ask for her address. That was only my second sale."

"Well, you know her last name."

She shrugged. "Just Suzette. She called her friend Loreen."

Marvel's situation was shaping up to be a major dilemma. Now I could understand her wary reaction when I'd appeared unannounced at her dog run. Searching for an encouraging comment, I said, "Suzette isn't the most common name in America. And that was yesterday. Maybe she has already discovered the mistake."

"That's too much to hope for. She hasn't called me."

Marvel seemed determined to see only the dark side. "Suzette has Brandy's paperwork—and she has Mandy. What can I tell Willa Bradstone? Mandy was supposed to be her puppy. She's driving up to Michigan next week to take Mandy home, and I have no idea where she is."

"Don't tell her anything," I said. "By then, Suzette may call you or come back with Mandy and you can switch the puppies. Willa Bradstone never has to know."

"But what if I can't reach her? Maybe she made a mistake when she gave me her cell number?"

Not wanting to give Marvel anything more to worry about, I didn't suggest that Suzette might have given her the wrong number on purpose—and taken the wrong puppy deliberately, seeing those qualities that made Mandy the pick of the litter.

But Marvel must have told her Mandy was reserved for someone else. Besides, the scenario I was spinning seemed unlikely. Most breeders would be sharper than this novice. A prospective buyer wouldn't be foolish enough to try to trick them.

"Didn't Suzette mention a city or town in passing?" I asked.

"No, only that it was a long drive and they were going to stop for fast food on the way."

Four hours from Spearmint Lake. Downstate, Marvel had said. South. But then, southeast or southwest? There was no way of knowing.

"You may have to tell Willa Bradstone what happened," I said. "Would she be willing to take Brandy instead of Mandy if you can straighten out the paperwork?"

"I don't know; I don't think so. Mandy is a show prospect worth more than Brandy."

"You'll have to pay the stud fee then," I said.

"Yes, but that isn't the point. When word gets around about my rookie mistake, everyone in Collies will know how inept I am. Willa is a well-known, respected breeder. People listen to her."

"You can hope she's also discreet." I leaned back in the wicker rocker, feeling suddenly tired, although it was still morning. Too much had been happening in too few hours. "You both made a mistake, Marvel. It doesn't have to be the end of the world."

"Just the end of my career."

"I wish I knew what to tell you. I never heard of something like this happening. I still think confiding in Willa Bradstone is your best option."

She sighed. "As a last resort, maybe. Jennet, in that article I read about you, the reporter said you'd trapped a killer. Are you a detective or a private investigator?"

"Oh, no, I'm an English teacher who occasionally finds herself in trouble. Quite often because of collies," I added.

"But you *did* solve that mystery last year? The one in the paper?"

"Guilty," I said.

She paused and leaned eagerly forward. "Do you think you could help me?"

I knew what was coming. It was on course. Inevitable. I couldn't stop it. Still, I said, "Help you find Sandy? Sure. I'm already looking for her."

"Yes, and to find Suzette so I can get Mandy back and give her Brandy. And do it in the next few days. Then I don't have to tell Willa."

"I'm not a miracle worker," I said.

"I know it's asking a lot, but I'd be forever indebted to you. I'll pay you any price you ask."

"I couldn't take your money," I said.

"Then you'll do it! Oh, thank you!"

That wasn't what I'd said. Had I?

Well, no matter. How could I refuse to try? I'd made more than a few mistakes myself, just recently by not responding immediately to the SOS from the hot air balloon. Besides, I couldn't believe Suzette was untraceable. Realizing I'd overlooked an important detail, I said, "Didn't she give you a check for Brandy? Her address might be on it."

Marvel shook her head. "She paid in cash, all twenties. She joked that this was her household money for two weeks, that she'd be eating soup for dinner."

"But you gave her a receipt—with her last name and address. Right?"

Marvel shook her head. "I'm hopeless, Jennet. Suzette didn't ask for one, and I didn't remember. We were both so excited about the puppy."

Marvel's friend was right in one way. Marvel had to work on her business sense and set up an ironclad procedure for future sales.

I said, "Suzette from somewhere downstate. A four-hour drive. I wouldn't know where to start. In Ohio, maybe?"

"I'll give you the cell number," she said. "Let's hope it's the right one. In the meantime I'll keep calling."

"But if there's another person's voice mail on the phone…"

"I'll be right back," she said, leaving me alone on the porch.

Marvel had unwittingly transferred her anxiety to me. I tried to center myself by looking at blue sky, white clouds, green grass, and the frolicking puppies in the run. All of the world's loveliness in my view. Its power was immeasurable. Something was wrong with the picture, though. It should be Mandy in the run, not Brandy.

I'd set out this morning to right a wrong and now had another mystery to solve. It was a strange one. A ludicrous mix-up; a woman, last name unknown, in unlawful possession of a valuable puppy; and, with the breeder's imminent arrival, a time frame. Not to mention little lost Sandy. It sounded as if Marvel's ill-wishing false friend had indeed cursed the new enterprise.

The key question was, can *curses be real?*

Marvel came back to the porch and handed me a slip of paper with the questionable cell phone number on it. I heard myself promising to do all I could to trace Suzette and retrieve Mandy, heard my wise Inner Self mention my already overloaded schedule. But it was too late to back out now. In any event, I didn't want to. Marvel needed all the help she could get, and I'd taken on the impossible before.

Also, this mistake had set in motion a chain that would be difficult and painful to break. Assuming Suzette had made an honest mistake, she had spent a first night with a whining, homesick puppy. Mandy and her new mistress had begun to bond with each other. Mandy was getting used to being called Brandy and growing accustomed to her new home and toys, while Brandy remained at the kennel, the property of an absent owner.

In all, the puppies had almost as much at stake as Marvel.

"You're a life saver, Jennet," Marvel said as I dropped the paper with the cell phone number on it in my shoulder bag. "With a little bit of luck, maybe we can break the curse."

Seven

Leaving Mallowmere Kennels behind, I headed for familiar territory and Clovers, the picturesque little restaurant on Crispian Road. Here I hoped to find something different and tempting on the menu and perhaps an update on local gossip from the charmingly outrageous young waitress, Annica.

Anything but another tale of woe. Anything but another mystery.

Although it wasn't yet noon, I felt a trifle guilty about being away from my dogs for so long. I tried to talk myself out of it, as finding Sandy and helping Marvel to unravel her tangle were both connected to the welfare of the canine race. As for stopping at the animal shelter, that would have to wait for another day.

The glossy green clovers that bordered the restaurant always seemed real to me. Once in a high wind, when two of them had blown down, I'd discovered they were indeed real. That is to say, they were real decorations with painted dewdrops on their leaves.

Once inside, I smelled cinnamon. The dessert carousel near the entrance was filled with pies today. And there was Annica as I'd hoped she'd be, flitting among her tables like a butterfly in a gaudy shade of yellow, her long coral earrings a perfect accent for her red-gold hair.

She waved and beckoned me to an empty booth toward the back. "I've been hoping you'd come in one of these days," she said. "You'll never guess what I know."

She bought me a tall glass of ice water and a menu.

"But you won't need to look at it," she said. "We have your favorites on special today. Country ham on rye and apple pie."

These weren't my favorites, but they sounded good. I placed my order and asked, "What's going on?"

She glanced around, and, apparently assuring herself the lunch crowd was well attended to, said, "I have some new information about the hot air balloon that went down in your backyard."

Annica loved to embellish a story. For this one, she was several acres off.

"It crashed on the other side of the woods," I said. "But it flew over Jonquil Lane."

Her eyes took on a hungry glimmer. "Really? You saw it?"

"Yes, and so did two of my dogs."

"No kidding." She called across the room to her fellow waitress, "Hey, Marcy, I'm going to take my break now!" Setting her order pad aside, she sat down.

"What happened then?" she asked.

"They ran after it. The silly creatures thought they could catch it."

"Did the balloon look like it was in trouble?" she asked.

Deciding not to tell Annica or anyone else about the message written in lipstick, I said. "On the contrary. It was gliding along like an airborne sailboat. The people inside looked happy. Like anyone would on an excursion in the sky."

"You got a good look at them then."

"From the ground," I reminded her. "But they were flying low."

"Could you describe the people, do you think?"

"Why?"

"I'll tell you in a minute. The paper didn't have their pictures, so you're probably the only one who saw them."

I hadn't thought of that, and it didn't cheer me.

"That is, you and Eric saw them, but he can't tell us now," she added.

"It sounds like you knew Eric," I said.

"We went out a few times. He was such a sweet guy. I don't know why he had to die that way except he was in the wrong place at the wrong time."

"Yes," I said, thinking of Brent. "At his job."

"Tell me, Jennet, what did the people look like?" she asked again.

It was easy to call the memory back; it hadn't gone far, those colorful moments in the sky when the balloon flew by and over the woods. "There were two young children, a boy and a girl, with rosy cheeks. They were dressed like kids, wearing tee-shirts with comic book characters, I think. The woman had long auburn hair and an orange scarf. The man… I don't know. He was good looking, I guess. He had a mustache."

Annica scoffed. "This from the great detective? You said they were flying low."

"I didn't know it would be important," I said. "The little girl waved and called Candy Lassie when Candy tried to catch the balloon."

"That doesn't make any sense. Isn't your Candy black?"

"Sure, but she's a collie. So—Lassie."

"Mmm," Annica said. "The woman's red hair is the only detail that helps."

"Why all the interest in their appearance?" I asked.

"Because they're missing, and I think I saw them at Clovers the same day the balloon crashed. But darn it all, I can't remember what time it was. You know how it goes. You get busy and distracted. I didn't know it was going to be important either."

"Did you tell this to the police?"

"No, I wanted to tell you first."

I suppressed a smile. Lieutenant Mac Dalby would love to hear that. Fortunately for us, he wasn't here today.

Annica frowned. "Actually, we had two parties who could fit that description: a man and woman, two children. They came in an hour or so apart. Would you believe both women had long red hair? Dyed, of course. I could tell." She touched her own cascading tendrils. "One wore her hair straight, the other had curls."

"You should contact Lieutenant Dalby," I said.

She shrugged. "Even if I can't be sure what time they were in?"

"Even then. He may be able to use the information."

"I remember the second party especially because the kids were so whiny and bratty. They started throwing pancake pieces at each other. One landed on Marcy's apron. The man yelled at them. The woman just looked embarrassed."

"I should think so. Did you hear any names? Say, when the man yelled at the kids?"

"You mean like 'Cut it out, Timmy' or 'Eat your breakfast, Tammy'? No."

"The children in the balloon were named Peter and Wendy," I said.

"Yeah, I remember. The kids in *Peter Pan*." She drummed her fingers on the table. "Neither woman had an orange scarf, though. They must be the wrong people."

"Well, by then she would have lost it." I did some rapid calculating. "They must have come into Clovers after I saw them.

Sometime after noon. So they'd be the second party. Apparently they walked away from the crash and went straight to Clovers for a bite to eat. How odd."

"Wait! Lost it where?"

Remembering that I didn't want Annica to know about the SOS message, I said, "Somewhere. It blew away in the wind. If it's the same woman."

"Why couldn't she have folded it up and put it in her purse? She had one of those large straw bags with rainbow stripes on it. She kept it on her lap."

"She could have," I said, hoping to lay the matter of the scarf to rest. "You're very observant, Annica."

What seemed significant to me was a purse kept on a lap during breakfast. Most women would have set a handbag on the table, a spare chair, or even the floor.

"Do you think those balloon riding people killed Eric?" Annica asked. "Not the kids. I'm thinking of the man."

"I don't know, but you have to tell the police, Annica. Promise you will."

"Oh, all right," she said, a shade too quickly. She wasn't going to do it.

"Jennet, I was thinking. Maybe you and I could team up and solve the mystery. Put what I saw together with what you saw and—"

"No," I said. "You just wondered if the man in the balloon killed Eric. Don't you realize how dangerous he could be?"

"But what if we found them? Think of the notoriety. Our pictures in the paper. The reward. There's bound to be a reward." Her eyes were shining. "Even if we split it, I could take an extra summer class instead of working."

She wasn't going to let this go.

"None of that appeals to me," I said. "Besides, I'm already looking for a lost collie puppy and a woman named Suzette. You can help me with that, if you'd like."

"How?"

"By putting a lost dog notice on Clovers' board. I'll bring one by tomorrow."

"I'll be happy to."

"And whenever you have a chance, listen in on your customers' conversations. Let me know if anyone calls her female companion Suzette."

She tossed her head and the coral beads tinkled. "Oh, sure. Nothing easier. I'll get your sandwich now," she said.

~ * ~

Home at last. I felt exhausted, but anyone who has four collies doesn't have the luxury of taking a nap in the daytime. The dogs all gathered around me, delighted that I'd returned and was henceforth available for play and outings.

I had the top half of the house to dust and vacuum, dinner to cook, and a test to write for my American Literature class. Everything but the dogs could wait.

The answering machine was blinking. Bringing my message up, I heard a familiar voice:

It's Jill Lodge, Jennet. I'll be in Foxglove Corners this afternoon around three. If it's okay, I'd like to stop in. It's half business.

And half pleasure? How like a reporter to be vague. Jill was covering the balloon crash story for the *Banner*. She might want a quote from me, although how she'd found out I'd seen the balloon before it went down was a mystery. Reporters had their methods, I remembered, and Jill was especially resourceful.

The dogs were reminding me in various ways that their walk was late. I leashed Candy and Gemmy and took them outside, with Halley and Sky padding along proudly at my side. I'd swear they were lording it over their sisters because they didn't need to be attached to leashes.

Up Jonquil Lane, past the new houses that would acquire historic status before they were finished or found a buyer. Past the shortcut through the woods that led to the cottage at Lane's End. Right on Squill Lane and down to the horse farm.

All familiar places. The dogs knew the route well. Along with enjoying myriads of scents that were always new, Candy and Gemmy occasionally glanced skyward. Waiting, anxious, hopeful, and, incredibly, whining.

Candy was especially vocal, her cries and whimpers at times almost desperate.

What caused their agitation today?

I'd learned to take canine signals seriously, even when I didn't understand the language. But today I didn't see anything to disturb my lively collies, either in the sky, or on the ground. Which didn't mean all was well. They could hear and see things beyond my ken.

There were the woods and the haunted fields between Jonquil Lane and the horse farm where spring wildflowers were beginning to emerge. Danger in a dozen different forms. From the sky, more likely on the ground.

Still, I resolved not to let the dogs' unease affect me. Scanning the clouds, I said, "The giant balloon is gone, girls."

And the other hot air balloons weren't flying. Brent had voiced his intention to keep the fleet grounded until every balloon could be thoroughly inspected and pronounced safe. Besides he had lost enthusiasm for Skyway Tours and turned his attention and resources to finding Eric's killer. It wouldn't surprise me if the company changed hands again.

Then, all but the most confirmed daredevil would be leery of sky cruising until the memory of the crash faded.

So Candy and Gemmy could look elsewhere for their diversion, and I could look elsewhere for the source of their strange behavior.

Eight

An hour later I sat with Jill on the front porch, while the dogs, having soaked up enough attention from Jill to last them for a week, napped in a shaded area of the front yard. They had biscuits and a large bowl filled with cold water; we had lemonade and sugar cookies.

In her lavender linen suit, Jill managed to look crisp and cool despite the heat from the molten sun that sent its rays in our direction. After tramping up and down the lanes with the dogs, I felt like taking a bath in lemonade.

While commenting on the lovely spring weather, Jill took a black notebook and pen out of her purse. Opening it, she explained the reason for her visit. It was her story, of course, and a startling new development in the hot air balloon mystery. In truth, it was a dead end.

"There's no record of the Holliday family in Holland Ridge, Michigan," she said. "The people who vanished into the thin air never existed in the first place."

"That sounds like a tale from the *Twilight Zone*. Visitors from the future travel in time to observe the denizens of Foxglove Corners from the air."

Her soft laughter caused Candy to wake up and survey the edge of the woods across the lane. She had been the last of the four collies to settle down after our walk. This preoccupation with her surroundings set a faint alarm bell ringing in my mind. But Jill didn't appear to notice anything amiss, and after a moment, Candy laid her head on her paws and closed her eyes.

"Can you think of another explanation?" she asked. "One that's reality-based?"

"Sure," I said. "Their names aren't Holliday, and they don't come from Holland Ridge. Is there such a place by the way?"

Jill nodded. "About fifty miles north of here. Population sixteen hundred. What happened after that raises suspicion. The way they dropped out of sight, leaving a dead body behind."

"You're assuming they were responsible for shooting Eric?"

"They were on the scene. The time was right."

"Someone else might have been there too. But they *do* make good suspects."

"The man," Jill said. "Not the others."

"Those names… It's possible that parents would name their children after characters from *Peter Pan*, but now that I think about it, they sound like aliases. I should have realized that."

"And Jane and John. What names are more common?" Jill said.

"Janie and Johnston. Clever variations. How about that last name, Holliday? Were they thinking of their holiday in the sky? And why did they need to use made-up names?"

Eric had recorded these names in the log book, together with the balloon's time of departure and their address which, according to Jill, didn't exist.

Neither Jill nor I had a plausible answer to our questions, and our speculation was taking us nowhere.

"This is my most intriguing story in months," Jill said. "Since you saw the people in the balloon, I hoped you could shed some light on it."

"How did you know that?" I asked.

"I was talking to Brent Fowler yesterday. He mentioned it in passing."

To a reporter? Albeit a pretty, persuasive one? I made a note to myself to have a word with Brent about confidentiality—mine. Annica craved publicity, but I kept trying to keep a low profile while Fate insisted on shining her spotlight on me.

"Brent says he doesn't trust the police," Jill said. "He's so determined to find Johnston Holliday, or whatever the man's name is, that he hired a private investigator."

"He can afford to," I said. "Brent feels Eric's death is his responsibility. Does he know about the fake address?"

"I told him yesterday. Let's go over it again. Janie and Johnston Holliday hire a balloon that goes down. Then they disappear along with their children—if Peter and Wendy belong to them—and we find out they're not who they said they were. Where does that leave us?

"With a mystery," I said.

"Which I'm going to solve. Cameron still gives me all the fluff pieces. I need a challenge."

"This should be it."

Knowing that Jill was someone I could tell about the scarf and the message on the torn napkin, I gave her the part of the story she didn't know and added the tossing of pancake pieces that Annica had witnessed. Jill would keep it quiet if I asked her to. In other words, out of the paper. I didn't think the police would appreciate important details being released to the public without their approval.

"Lieutenant Dalby has them now," I said. "At the time I thought the woman—we'll call her Janie—might have untied the scarf and it blew away in the wind when I wasn't looking, just for a second. But that doesn't explain the SOS."

"Janie wanted to let you know something was terribly wrong and probably didn't want Johnston to see what she was doing. But he must have seen the napkin fall out of the scarf. Did he react?"

"Not that I noticed, but it happened so quickly. Then they were gone. Besides, I was looking at Candy and Gemmy. I just knew they were going to take off after the balloon."

Jill frowned and tapped her notebook. "I wonder. What were you supposed to do from the ground?"

Brent had asked the same question; I still didn't know the answer. "I couldn't very well call the police. But I've been wishing I'd done something."

"Well, you couldn't have stopped the crash," she said.

"No."

Jill sat back and let her hand trail through Candy's snowy ruff. Candy, awake again, had climbed up the stairs to sit at Jill's side. Her eyes were on the dessert plate where three cookies and a mouthful of crumbs lay waiting for a certain collie who was still hungry.

"At this point Janie couldn't have known the balloon was going to crash," Jill said. "Maybe the man was threatening her."

I nodded. "He still had the gun. But later they were all having breakfast together and the kids were showing signs of strain."

"Little kids don't need to be stressed out to be bratty," Jill said. "Maybe that's how they always act."

"True." I thought back on the scenario we'd begun to create. A menacing man, a frightened woman, misbehaving children. "Offhand, I don't see how Peter and Wendy fit into the picture."

"But they must," Jill said. "They were part of it."

"All I know is that wasn't a typical family party Annica saw at Clovers that day."

Jill opened her shoulder bag and slipped the notebook and pen inside. It was cream-colored leather, expensive-looking with shiny brass hardware. To my dismay, Candy thrust her long nose inside. Jill merely laughed, nudged Candy aside, and snapped the bag shut.

"Annica is the redhead who works at Clovers, right?" she said. "That flashy young girl?"

This was a fair description of Annica, but there was more to her than Jill's words suggested.

"She's working her way through college," I said. "And she's the one whose stories I take with a whole shaker of salt. Remember that when you talk to her."

"She might have seen more than she thinks. For instance, could Janie have left another message for help at Clovers?"

"Easily, but likely to go unnoticed and be discarded with other after-breakfast debris."

"A little visit to Clovers is next on my list," Jill said. "Care to come along?"

I shook my head. "I can't. Not today."

Annica would be happy with a reporter's attention, especially if it led to her picture showcased in the *Banner* and ultimately a share of Brent's reward money. But what could she tell Jill? That she'd witnessed a food fight and an exasperated father whose hold on his patience had snapped? She'd admitted she was so rushed waiting on the lunch crowd she hadn't noticed the time.

I pointed this out to Jill, but she had already considered it. "Even if it's a will-o-the-wisp, I'm going to follow it. Don't worry. I have a built-in truth-o-meter."

As she rose, swinging her purse up to her shoulder, the other three dogs woke from their naps. I glanced at the plate that had held the uneaten cookies. It was empty. Now when had Candy done that? I knew the culprit was Candy because she was closest to the refreshments and couldn't possibly have looked more innocent.

Well, what had I expected? Leave something valuable unwatched, and it disappears. At times life was like that.

I walked Jill to her car and kept my hand around Candy's collar as we stood rehashing what we knew or suspected.

Her visit to Clovers should be interesting. If I didn't have a roast in the oven, that test to write, the upstairs rooms to clean, and a half dozen or more other chores, all before Crane came home, I'd have joined her.

~ * ~

After Jill left, I hurried through my tasks and set the table for dinner. All the while, my *Twilight Zone* theory played through my mind with amusing variations.

Janie and Johnston Holliday and their offspring were visitors from another planet posing as tourists come to observe earthlings. I'd seen more than one movie with the same premise. This would explain the fictitious address and the vanishing act.

Letting my imagination roam free was fun, but in the end counter-productive, and none of my versions explained a hastily written call for help or a body.

Wherever the balloon people were now, they must have driven to Clovers for their late breakfast. They certainly couldn't have walked from Jonquil Lane to Crispian Road. However, the only car at the scene was Eric's ancient Chrysler.

How does one travel from Point A to Point B without a car?

Could they have hitchhiked? All four of them? Anyone offering two adults and two children a ride would be certain to have read or heard about the missing people from the balloon and would have reported it to the authorities. Scratch hitchhiking then.

I smiled as I fell back on the alien-from-outer-space idea. That would explain traveling without traditional transportation.

I'd love to discuss the mystery with Crane, but he'd think I was getting too interested in it. He'd be right, of course, and there was the worrisome fact I'd seen the people as they flew by. And they'd seen me. If anything nefarious was going on, I was on the fringe of trouble again.

But as of now, only the fringe.

How could they know I'd been so unobservant?

I remembered the children's rosy cheeks. Well, many children would be rosy cheeked when on a carnival ride—or in a hot air balloon. The woman? My mind stalled on long, straight auburn hair and an orange scarf. I couldn't recall her face. As for the man, I'd had a fleeing impression of handsome features and a mustache. No more.

That wasn't enough for even the most talented of police artists to build a respectable sketch on.

But Jane and Johnston couldn't know how little I recalled, if it became important.

I could only hope that would never happen.

Nine

Eventually it occurred to me that the new mysteries in Foxglove Corners could challenge the most talented of sleuths. I was thinking of the canine mysteries since Mac Dalby was in charge of the balloon crash investigation, as he should be.

Sandy, the runaway collie puppy, hadn't surfaced even though Brent had offered a generous reward for her recovery. As for Suzette, without her surname and address, I didn't know where to begin my search—and the clock was ticking away, bringing us closer to the arrival of Mandy's owner at Mallowmere Kennels and disaster for Marvel McLogan.

It felt as if the earth had stalled in its turning.

Enter Annica.

On a day when Principal Grant Grimsly held an especially long teacher's meeting and construction zones tripled in number on the freeway, I dropped Leonora off at her house and drove on to Clovers for take-out dinners.

"I found her!" Annica announced as she rushed to the counter. She was dressed like a mermaid today, all in misty sea green with long seashell earrings.

Sandy, I thought, but Annica added, "Suzette! Two women came in for lunch today. One said, 'They have your favorite soup, Suzette.' It was mushroom barley."

Rapidly I switched gears. "Did they say anything that would help me trace them? Like where they were going?"

"They were talking about antiques and eggs."

"That's a strange combination. Could you describe Suzette?"

"Sure can. This time I knew it would be important. She had wavy dark brown hair, cut short with lots of gray in it and blue eye shadow but not much other makeup. She was kind of pretty for an older lady."

"How old?" I asked.

"Maybe somewhere in her thirties. She wore white slacks, and her blouse had a green and blue floral pattern. She had a pretty necklace with blue stones in two shades and long nails painted a frosty orchid color."

"I guess I could recognize her in a small crowd," I said. "Until she changed her outfit and removed the eye-shadow."

Annica tossed her head. "I remember more than you did about the balloon lady. Oh, I almost forgot. The nail on the fourth finger of her left hand was broken down to the quick. How's that for specific?"

"Very good," I said. *Until she filed them all down.*

But Annica had done an admirable job of cataloging details. I could almost see Suzette running her finger with its orchid frosted nail under the 'Soup of the Day' offerings.

"Did either one mention a place?" I asked. "A town or city?"

"Just Lakeville," she said. "I asked them if they were new in town. Suzette said they didn't live here—they'd just driven up for the day to go antiquing. Her friend didn't talk much."

That narrowed my search down to one small city in Lapeer County. But at the same time, it pointed me straight to the street known as Antique Row because of the antique shops located on that block. Among them was the Green House, my favorite place to browse among treasures from the past and spend money.

How eggs fit into the picture, I couldn't say. An egg salad sandwich or an omelet? Faberge eggs, perhaps?

"Be sure to mention my name when you tell Lieutenant Dalby about Suzette," Annica said.

"Why would I tell him?"

"Because he's handling the balloon investigation." Her eyes lit up. "Unless you're going it alone. Then I can help you."

I tried to remember what I'd told Annica about Suzette. Nothing specific. Only the name, Suzette, as the puppy mix-up was Marvel's personal business.

"That's something else I'm working on," I said. "It's unrelated to the balloon crash. Which reminds me. Did you talk to Jill Lodge about your four customers?"

"Yeah. She's cool, isn't she? I wonder if I should switch my major. I think I'd make a good reporter."

I smiled, recalling Annica's penchant for spinning outrageous tales. "As long as you don't stray from the truth."

"That'll be hard," she said. "But I can do it. Don't forget, Jennet, I'm officially on this case now that I found Suzette for you."

"Then call me if she comes back to the restaurant. Tell her I have to talk to her. It's very, very important, and it has to be soon." I tore a sheet from my small notebook and wrote my cell number on it. "Say it's about Mandy. I mean Brandy."

She promised to do so. Like it or not, I had a partner.

~ * ~

Being already late I wasn't able to visit the shops on Antique Row until the following day after school. By then Suzette and her friend would long since have left Lakeville. In any event I knew my chance of finding Suzette by following a trail she might have made was slim, but I had no other clue. Only a few days remained until Mandy's owner arrived from Ohio expecting to take her puppy home.

Marvel was frantic. She'd called last night to tell me she hadn't been able to reach Suzette. The cell phone number was obviously wrong. She'd tried punching in variations of the number with no success; and Suzette hadn't called her or me. She hadn't been back to Clovers then. The sense of urgency that I'd asked Annica to convey, combined with the mention of her new puppy's name, would surely have solicited a prompt response.

"I'll have to tell Willa Bradstone what happened," Marvel said.

"Maybe, but wait until the very last minute."

Hoping for success in spite of the dismal odds, I went first to the Green House of Antiques, where I knew the owner's niece from past shopping trips. Their charming, evocative window displays always had the power to enchant. This month vintage dolls, stuffed animals, and hobby horses frolicked against a painted meadow background, all of them welcoming spring.

I resisted the temptation to linger outside.

Brass bells gathered in a grapevine swag jingled as I opened the door. Bypassing a stack of old-time books in a series with a similar power to enchant, I walked briskly to the back of the shop. Rebecca, the owner's niece, was arranging vintage storybook dolls on a mahogany Duncan Fyfe table.

The owner and her staff liked to showcase the shop's collection of antique clothing. Usually their skirts swept the floor. Today

Rebecca wore a flapper's fringed dress and long beads. Her hair was short and bouncy with long bangs and strands that curved forward on her face.

I told her what I wanted and added that it was practically a matter of life and death for a friend of mine.

"I remember that lady," Rebecca said. "She and her friend were here for about an hour. They were looking for vintage toys and made several purchases, but they didn't give me their names."

"Let me guess," I said. "They paid in cash."

Rebecca nodded. "I'm sorry I can't be of more help to you, Jennet. But they said they'd be coming back this way again. They didn't have time to visit all the shops in one afternoon. If I see them, I'll be happy to give them a message."

Once again I wrote my cell number on a sheet of note paper. "Please tell her to call me. Tell her it's urgent."

Thanking Rebecca, I moved on to Second Spring. Unfortunately the owner, Colin Springer, whom I knew, was out. As for the other establishments on Antique Row, either Suzette and her companion had skipped them, or they'd entered and left unnoticed. Or possibly the salesclerks wished to protect their customers' privacy.

Because I didn't consider 'eggs' a viable clue, all I had now was the possibility that Suzette would return to Antique Row and the Green House or Clovers. Discouraged, I headed for home. How frustrating to be so close to Suzette and not find her. She was always several steps ahead of me, always seeming to vanish in the shadows just when I thought I was going to catch up to her.

~ * ~

Then, my luck changed. The next day, Suzette called me on my cell phone while I was making dinner. Her voice was soft and pleasant, but it held the slightest trace of anxiety.

"This is Suzette Harwood," she said. "I understand from a young lady named Annica that you need to speak to me about my puppy."

At last. With two days to spare until Willa Bradstone's arrival.

Now that the desired call had come, I realized how strange, how utterly awkward, it would be to relay my message over the airwaves. But it had to be done. Quickly.

"Marvel McLogan of Mallowmere Kennels has been trying to contact you," I said. "You took the wrong puppy home. You have Mandy, not Brandy."

"Is this a joke?" she demanded, her voice not so soft and pleasant now.

"I'm afraid not. There was a mix-up…"

"You must be mistaken. I have Brandy, the puppy I bought and paid for. I have her papers."

"You have Mandy. She was set aside for someone else."

"But I already purchased her." The finality in that statement was impossible to miss. "Incidentally, why am I talking to you and not the breeder?"

"Because I'm helping her; I'm a friend. We've both been trying to get in touch with you."

"Well, Mrs. Ferguson, is it? I don't believe you. Your joke isn't funny. It's cruel. I'm going to hang up now."

"Wait!" I said quickly. "Please call Marvel." I gave her Marvel's phone number, just in case she didn't have it. "There are subtle differences in the two pups. She can explain them to you. The problem is that the other buyer has a prior claim to Mandy."

"And I took the puppy the breeder placed in my arms."

I didn't see the point in going into detail about stud fees and the pick of the litter, nor in pointing out that Marvel had made a mistake. Marvel could do that and convince Suzette that keeping Mandy wasn't an option for her.

But Suzette possessed Brandy. Wasn't that nine-tenths of the law? How would Marvel go about getting the puppy back if Suzette refused to relinquish her? Suzette had disappeared once, albeit unintentionally. She could very well disappear again, although now we knew her last name.

In the long pause that followed, I feared that Suzette would make good on her threat and hang up, and that she'd never contact me or Marvel again.

She said, "Assuming I believe you, which I'm not sure I do, it's too late. We've already bonded. Brandy has a home. Her own toys. I can't just give her away."

I could easily imagine myself in Suzette's place. "It isn't easy," I said.

Not for anyone. Certainly not for little Mandy.

"Then you understand."

"Of course I do, but you can't keep Mandy. Not legally. Not morally."

I hoped I was right about the legal aspect of the matter. I had no idea how a judge would rule if Suzette Harwood chose to pursue the puppy's ownership in court.

But I felt I had fulfilled my promise to Marvel. I didn't know what else I could do or say. Maybe Marvel could negotiate a compromise that would allow Mandy to stay with Suzette.

Never, I vowed, would I let my own affairs become so hopelessly muddled.

"If you take the puppy back to Mallowmere, Ms. McLogan will straighten everything out."

Somehow.

"I will," Suzette said. "I don't want this cloud hanging over me, but I'll tell you one thing. Brandy is my puppy. I have no intentions of giving her up, and nobody is going to take her away from me."

Ten

The ownership of Mandy/Brandy was far from settled. Fortunately it was out of my hands. I'd called Marvel to alert her to Suzette's impending visit. Now I hoped the two of them could reach an amicable agreement with the least pain possible, especially for the puppy, Mandy.

Meanwhile, my other life, the less mysterious one, went on. Our first wedding anniversary went by without ceremony, only a gift exchange, because Crane had to work late. "We'll celebrate later," he'd promised.

I packed away the last of my winter wardrobe and set out a navy polka dot dress for school tomorrow. It was very 'early spring', and the light fabric, combined with my newly trimmed hair, was perfect for cool mornings that would turn into warm afternoons.

On Monday morning I found myself in my classroom waiting for thirty World Literature students to come strolling through the door.

No one was in a hurry at Marston High School these days except for Principal Grimsly, who rushed through the halls on his quest to capture wayward students in his net.

The early heat wave had given way to a string of balmy days that turned thoughts to summer vacation. Absenteeism became a major problem, along with water pistols and outfits that danced lightly around the school's already lenient dress code.

Into this giddy mix of spring and youth and exuberance, I planned to introduce William Shakespeare's comedy, *A Midsummer Night's Dream.* A formidable task, but last week I'd paved the way for it painstakingly and detected a flicker of interest. Background notes covered the blackboard, and a model of Shakespeare's theatre sat on a table in front of the room. Now to introduce the cast of characters and read the first scene.

The second bell rang signaling the official start of class.

My audience was less than enthusiastic. Douglas, one forward-thinking scholar, had counted the pages and informed the class how long the play was.

Amidst grumbles, Linda asked in her signature whine, "Can't we just read *Cliff's Notes* or look the story up on the Internet?"

"Or see the movie?"

I couldn't tell who said that. The voice, feminine and petulant, came from the row by the windows.

"Yeah, the movie, Mrs. Ferguson!" That speaker was Douglas, loudly rallying his troops.

"Did they make a movie out of it?" asked Tracy.

"I think so." Actually I knew so.

"Then why should we bother to read the book?" Tracy managed to project sincere puzzlement.

I seemed to remember having this same argument with the class at the beginning of the course and elected to ignore it.

"We're going to read the play first," I said. "Then maybe I'll find out if I can rent the DVD. You can write a paper on how well the screenwriter adapted Shakespeare's work for the film version."

Fine, Jennet, I thought. *Mitigate the pleasure of movie watching with composition writing. That's not going to inspire anyone.*

But with or without inspiration, we were going to forge ahead.

Our textbook had an abridged version of the play with ample footnotes and color photographs. A generation of video game players should respond well to enchanted woods, magical flowers, lovers, actors, fairies and the kind of zany mix-up they might see on their favorite sitcom. What more could they want?

"Why can't we go back to poetry?" wailed Linda.

"Poems are shorter," Douglas added.

"And they rhyme," Linda said. "I like stuff that rhymes."

"Our play has parts that rhyme."

I know a bank where the wild thyme blows,
Where tulips and the nodding violet grows...

Was there any poetry in our book more exquisite and lush than lines from *A Midsummer Night's Dream*? Such passages had mesmerized me when I was a young girl. But my tenth-grade students weren't like me, then or now. I couldn't help smiling. Was anyone?

I'd let them discover the beauty and magic of Shakespeare's words for themselves. And if they didn't, so be it.

"We read too much in this class," Sally announced.

"Well it *is* a literature class," I said. "You read literature, just like you draw pictures in art class."

Having experience with reluctant English students, I played my winning hand. "This is the last selection of the course," I said. "When we're done, we'll review everything, take the final exam, and you'll be free for the summer."

Sally clapped her hands. "No more English! Yea!"

"Don't forget to bring in the movie," Douglas said.

~ * ~

Another bell rang, and I moved on to Journalism, the one class in which we—teacher and students—were enjoying a rare downtime. The last edition of the school newspaper, celebrating this year's graduates, had been sent to the printer. The last assignments were in my 'to be corrected' folder. I'd chosen next year's editorial staff. It was too early to make posters to advertise the sale of the June paper and take inventory of supplies. Hence, downtime.

"Let's read the *Free Press* today," I said. "I don't mean the comics or sports or puzzles. Look for updates on your articles."

No questions or complaints came my way. I'd brought extra copies of the *Free Press* to class, anticipating this sort of free reading day. With the rustling of paper and murmur of conversation, the future journalists embarked on their task

I hoped Principal Grimsly wouldn't make an impromptu appearance at the door, as he'd be certain to think my class was loafing. In truth they were doing an ongoing assignment.

Each student had chosen one news story to follow from its first appearance through the last article or the end of the school year, whichever came first. Subjects dealt with matters relevant to their lives: the crash of a small plane and subsequent search for survivors, the migration of ugly invasive carp to the waters of Lake Michigan, the latest environmental hazard in our area.

Two boys had chosen the crash of the hot air balloon in Lapeer County, which I considered my story as well.

There was nothing in the paper today about the disappearance of the balloon people, but another story caught my attention. *Children Feared Kidnapped. Babysitter Suspected.*

The facts were skimpy. An Amber alert had been issued for ten-year old twins Briana and Bennett Cooper, last seen the previous afternoon in the company of their babysitter, Sara Hall. According to a neighbor who had talked briefly to Briana, the three were en route to a water park.

The twins had fair hair, blue eyes, and light complexions. They were wearing Disney-themed tee shirts. No photographs accompanied the article, and there was no mention of an attractive male companion or the babysitter's hair color.

As I read the article, I made an inevitable connection, and as I had done on previous occasions, called back the memory of the children in the hot air balloon. Fair hair, rosy cheeks. Eye color impossible to determine from the ground. A little girl who liked collies enough to call out to one who was leaping high in a futile attempt to catch the strange flying object.

Briana and Bennett. Could they be Wendy and Peter? And was the auburn-haired woman with the orange scarf the babysitter, Sara Hall? Or were there two sets of children, both of them in danger?

I could hardly wait for the school day to end so I could discuss the new development—if development it was—with Leonora and Crane, in that order.

"What do you think?" I asked Leonora as we entered the freeway and merged into smoothly flowing traffic.

"That these children have been missing since yesterday morning. How long ago did the hot air balloon fly over Foxglove Corners?"

I counted back to last Saturday morning. "A week and a day."

"Then how can these be the same kids if they're just now being reported missing?"

"It's possible, but you have a point."

"You should be able to identify the balloon children," Leonora said.

"If I saw their picture, maybe, and I could compare them with pictures of the kidnapped twins."

And what would I tell the authorities?

I might have seen Briana and Bennett Cooper with Sara flying over Foxglove Corners in a hot air balloon. On their way to Oz. Oh, no, they crash landed north of the yellow brick road.

"Don't forget," I told Leonora. "The woman with the auburn hair sent down a message for help. And if these are the kidnapped kids, they're doubly missing."

~ * ~

Twins disappearing while on an excursion with their babysitter. Two children vanishing after a hot air balloon went down. The free reading day in Journalism class had further complicated my life.

Crane knew more about the abduction than the *Free Press* reporter, no doubt because the balloon disappearance was Lieutenant Dalby's case, and, like me, Mac had made an inevitable connection. Mac and Crane were friends who usually met during the day for coffee. That evening after dinner, he filled in the missing pieces.

The time frame that had bothered Leonora proved to be irrelevant. Incredibly, the children's mother hadn't known they were missing. She'd been on vacation, having left Briana and Bennett with Sara, a relatively new hire who had come to the family with impeccable references.

The twins' teacher had merely recorded absences, the neighbors hadn't noticed anything amiss, and the whereabouts of the children's father was unknown. He liked to travel.

There was one more significant fact. The children's grandfather was wealthy developer Gerard Zoller, but so far no ransom note had been received.

Absent parents, a mother delegating the care and amusement of her children to a slightly known young woman. Anything could have happened to them. Maybe it had.

"Mac is stopping by with pictures of the Cooper twins," Crane said. "If you can identify them, we'll know where they were last week."

"I'm not sure I'll be able to do that," I said. "Does Mac know if Sara Hall was a redhead?"

"You'll have to ask him, honey. He didn't say."

"Mac can show the twins' pictures to Annica, too," I said. "She thinks the balloon party had breakfast at Clovers. The kids started throwing pancake pieces at each other."

He smiled. "Being a waitress has its drawbacks."

"The man with them… I wonder if he could be the twins' father."

"We'll ask Mac if he knows anything about him."

"I don't want my name to appear anywhere. Annica's the one who craves notoriety."

"I don't want that either," Crane said. "Someone else must have noticed a hot air balloon flying low over Foxglove Corners on a sunny Sunday morning."

"You'd think so. Tell Mac to find them. Really, Crane, I don't want to be the only person who can identify the children from the balloon."

In our cozy familiar living room with four collies on the alert, after their fashion, the specters of Kidnapping and Murder hovered over us. Their presence made our home a little less safe.

Eleven

Mac brought the pictures of the Cooper twins over that evening. The presence of another powerful lawman in the house sent the hovering specters of Murder and Kidnapping running for cover.

I'd made a fresh pot of coffee and thawed a loaf of banana bread. Mac liked to brag about his wife, Joanna Larne, a writer of Gothic/time-travel/cozy books who plied him with an endless stream of hot dinners and homemade treats. One taste of my banana-nut bread and Mac would see that Crane was equally fortunate.

Mac set the pictures on the dining room table and stepped back, hope written all over his rugged face. They were school photographs in color. Very clear, very good.

"Well, Jennet, were these the children in the hot air balloon?" he asked.

He wanted me to say yes; I wanted to say yes. But I couldn't be sure. They looked like Peter and Wendy. Sort of. Briana in a misty blue dress with a matching ribbon in her blonde hair was solemn and dreamy. Bennett wearing a white dress shirt and tie had the grin of a restless imp.

I tried to envision them in Disney character tee shirts, laughing and excited to be up, up, and away.

"The pictures were taken last fall when school started," Mac said. "Jennet?"

"I'm thinking."

In my mind, I stood in front of the house again, watching the giant balloon swoop down low, a bright rainbow burst against the blue sky.

The children's faces were a blur, melting in the molten sun. I'd given them only a cursory glance, my attention caught and held by blowing auburn hair and an orange scarf that drifted down, losing the bit of paper tucked inside.

Rosy cheeks. I remembered rosy cheeks, an impression of bright hair and the wave of a child's hand. The little girl—Wendy? Briana?—calling out to Candy, calling her Lassie. But the children's features eluded me.

Everything had happened too fast. Scarf and paper floating down to the earth; Candy trying to leap up to the balloon, convinced that she could do it; the balloon drifting away over the woods; the dogs giving chase.

"I'm sorry, Mac, but I can't be sure," I said. "They could be Peter and Wendy. They're the right age." I looked away from the pictures, looked back, and was still uncertain. "Did you show them to Annica? She would have had a closer view. They were on her level, I mean."

Mac shook his head but couldn't shake the disappointment. Usually the help I gave him was more substantial.

"Annica couldn't be sure either, but she thinks they're the same children." he said. "You focused on rosy cheeks. She noticed sulky faces, sticky fingers and pancakes flying."

Remembering my earlier concern, I said, "Didn't anyone else in the area see the balloon?"

"About a dozen people. Half of them identified the children as Bennett and Briana. Half are sure they're not or won't commit themselves."

"What's your guess, Mac?" Crane asked.

"That they're the Cooper twins."

I took one last look at the photographs. No, I simply wasn't sure. "Do you have a picture of Sara Hall?"

"No picture. Just a description. She's five seven with a slender build, has long, dark red hair and brown eyes, and wears fancy sunglasses most of the time. She's been described as extremely attractive."

"Janie had long auburn hair," I said. "So did the two women Annica saw at Clovers."

As far as I was concerned, auburn sealed the identification. The color wasn't all that common, and no one but Sara Hall would be with Briana and Bennett. The sunglasses could have been in her purse.

But why wouldn't she be wearing them on a balloon ride that took her close to the sun?

"I didn't realize there were so many red-haired ladies in the county," Mac said. "Why are they all wandering around in my case?"

He didn't expect an answer and didn't receive one.

"What about the children's father?" I asked. "Was he dark and handsome with a dapper mustache?"

Mac smiled. "Blond and homely. But apparently Steven Cooper is a nice guy. Not to his wife, though. She despises him."

Hair could be dyed but homely couldn't turn into handsome except in fairy tales.

"The man in the balloon wasn't Johnston Holliday then," I said.

Mac slid the photographs of the Cooper children back in their manila envelope. "We suspect that Johnston Holliday is a phony name."

"I have to call him something. Not just the man in the balloon."

Crane tightened his arm firmly around my waist. "No you don't, honey. Mac is hot on the trail. You're not."

There was no use arguing. In truth, there was nothing to argue about. I had no intention of involving myself further in a case that involved murder and a possible abduction. My work with the Collie Rescue League kept me busy and sufficiently supplied with mysteries. I was only curious. Who wouldn't be?

I reached for the empty mug that Mac had set on the buffet. "Have another cup of coffee, Mac, and a piece of banana bread. You won't find any better in the state of Michigan. Even at home."

"I'll vouch for that," Crane said.

~ * ~

Mac ate two pieces of banana bread, pronounced it tasty, and left to go home to his clever, nurturing Joanna. Crane took the collies for a long moonlight walk, and I settled down in the rocker with *The Complete Works of Shakespeare* to reread *A Midsummer Night's Dream.*

I didn't remember the book being so heavy or the print so small, and I didn't recall scribbling notes in the margin, but there they were, neatly written in my own hand. I turned the lamp to its brightest setting and began.

Now fair Hippolyta, our nuptial hour
Draws on apace; four happy days bring in
Another moon...

As I started reading, all of the play's magic came back, wrapping me in an enchantment as light and airy as a fairy queen's wing. At the end of the first act, I closed both the book and my eyes, thinking about woods: the fictitious forest near Athens and the wooded acreage across Jonquil Lane that had been part of my view since my move to Foxglove Corners.

I had met Crane on my first morning in the green Victorian farmhouse that I'd purchased in the wake of the Oakpoint tornado. He had been looking for a site for the log cabin he wanted to build. The acres had been for sale all this time, but nobody was buying property these days.

Naturally I regarded the woods across the lane as an extension of our own land.

At least twice a year, in the spring and the fall, I took the dogs hiking there. Exploring the woods was always an adventure; we always found something new. Berries, birds, and strange, lovely flowers to transplant around the house. In spite of the 'No Trespassing' sign, nobody cared.

Woods have a universal appeal.

I found myself contemplating fallen trees, thickets, and the little stream I'd found that first summer when all of Foxglove Corners was new to me. Dark, secret places teeming with wildlife and occasional surprises.

One bitter December day, the snow-white collies who haunted Lost Lake had appeared in the woods just in time to save my life. With the memory of the ghost dogs, my thoughts turned to the runaway puppy, Sandy. I hadn't forgotten her even though she might have run off the face of the earth for all anyone knew.

A frightened young dog on her own could have taken refuge in one of the many wooded areas in the county. And what then? Fallen prey to a predator or turned feral as my last rescue, Wafer, had done? If Sandy had wandered into a woodland, wherever its location, she would be next to impossible to find.

The other possibility was that somebody had found her and given her a home, a person who hadn't seen or didn't intend to respond to my 'Lost Puppy' notices.

In any case, Sandy remained among the missing. I'd have to get in touch with Josie soon. As soon as we resolved the puppy mix-up.

A high-pitched barking outside alerted me to the arrival of Crane and his canine entourage. I set the book aside, consigning woods and fairies to the daylight hours when there was a better chance of seeing clearly.

~ * ~

Marvel's call interrupted our quiet evening. She wanted to thank me again for finding Suzette Harwood. "And you did it in the nick of time," she said. "Suzette is visiting the kennel on Saturday morning. Willa Bradstone is arriving in the early afternoon. With my dismal luck, their visits will overlap."

"Is she bringing Mandy back?" I asked.

"I hope so, but I don't know. Suzette doesn't want to give her up. She offered to pay me more if she could keep her. What she really wants is Mandy's papers."

"It's too bad she's keeping the puppy these extra days," I said. "That's just more time for Mandy to get used to Suzette's home."

"I told her that. She claims she has to work. Last week she was on vacation."

"That could be true. What are you going to do?"

"Keep trying to convince her until I run out of time." In the pause that followed I knew what she was going to say. "Jennet, are you terribly busy next Saturday? I'd like you to be here if you could. For moral support."

"I guess I can," I said slowly. "For a little while."

I *did* want to meet Suzette since I'd invested so much time and effort in locating her. Also I wanted to see how alike litter sisters

Sandy and Mandy were, to see if I could detect those subtle differences that made Mandy a show prospect and Brandy a pet.

But as curious as I was, I knew the scene would be painful or volatile depending on Suzette's intent. Giving up a dog, no matter what the circumstances were, was always a heartbreaking experience. Was it Albert Payson Terhune or Rudyard Kipling who had warned against giving your heart to a dog to tear?

My eyes came to rest on my collies, all of them sleeping after their night outing. I'd given my heart four times over.

Those of us who love dogs accept the inevitability of parting. But maybe—just maybe—Suzette could be spared that pain until sometime in the distant future.

Twelve

A light breeze blew through the windows of my classroom, bringing home that wondrous scent that could only be described as 'May'. The view of the thinly wooded property that adjoined the school's north side was all green-blossoming spring, and the air was warm and luscious, a perfect accompaniment to our play.

I read:

> *Now fair Hippolyta, our nuptial hour*
> *Draws on apace; four happy days bring in*
> *Another moon…*

Douglas raised his hand. "What does that mean, Mrs. Ferguson?"

"Theseus, the Duke of Athens, is telling Hippolyta, Queen of the Amazons, that their wedding is four days away," I said.

"Oh." He made no attempt to conceal the sarcasm. "Now it's perfectly clear."

I had anticipated a torrent of questions but not with the first lines of the play. I thought the class was well prepared for today's reading. I'd reviewed the characters, defined unusual words on the blackboard, and summarized the first act. I would have assigned students to read the various parts but knew they'd stumble over the unfamiliar phrasing. So I'd elected to do all the reading myself.

Carrie didn't bother to raise her hand. "Why doesn't he just say that?"

"Because it wouldn't be poetry then," Nancy pointed out with a superior sniff.

Lori added, "Yeah. Then we might know what they were talking about. Why can't we read something else, Mrs. Ferguson? Something in English?"

How easy it was to drift away into irrelevancy. Five minutes into the lesson, and I was ready to count pages.

But remember, Jennet, you're the teacher. Drift back.

I said, "If no one else has questions, could we please continue?"

We did.

"Hippolyta answers her intended bridegroom:

> *Four days will quickly steep themselves in night;*
> *Four nights will quickly dream away the time...*

By the time we'd finished the first act, the breeze blowing through the window had turned sultry, the class had grown restless, and the cotton material of my blue shirtwaist dress felt too warm for the rising temperature.

At this snail's pace, it would take a month to finish the play. We had two weeks. My goal wasn't merely to read Shakespeare's comedy with my students. I wanted them to love the words and the story, or at least to appreciate them. At some future time, if they attended a professional performance of *A Midsummer Night's Dream*, I hoped they would remember when they'd read the play in their World Literature class.

"Can't we stop here?" begged Janice. "Please?"

With twenty-five minutes left of class time to go? Why not? Hoping that Principal Grimsly was in his office and not roaming the halls in search of wasted time, I said, "That's a good idea. We'll review what we just read."

Fielding a chorus of groans, I embarked on the last phase of the day's work. Identify the characters from the first act. Summarize the story so far. Ask questions. It was sheer drudgery maintaining class enthusiasm with the alluring voice of the outdoors talking over me.

But I was the teacher, the one to lead the way. At the moment I was everlastingly grateful that the World Literature textbook had an abridged edition of the play.

I told myself that covering one act in a class period was respectable progress. Perhaps hearing real actors speak the lines in the second act would hold their attention. Could I buy or borrow a DVD of the play by tomorrow?

As the hour dwindled down to seven minutes, I let my reluctant Shakespearean scholars talk and gather their materials for the next class while I wrote 'Save!!' on the board in orange chalk.

I refused to let my beloved comedy die so soon—or at all. There must be a way to bring it to life in blazing Technicolor. With surround sound.

On the way home that afternoon, Leonora and I bandied about innovative ways of teaching Shakespeare to today's young people.

Our English Department curriculum gave us a choice of two plays to teach for our World Literature classes. Leonora's students were reading *Julius Caesar*. Naturally they thought *A Midsummer Night's Dream* would be more fun, while mine wanted to know why they couldn't read *Julius Caesar*.

"Plays were never meant to be read in a classroom, except by English majors," I said. "They need to be seen and heard with actors on a stage in costumes and eye-catching scenery."

"I agree," Leonora said. "Especially plays with colorful settings."

She steered the car around a row of orange construction barrels to the far right and stepped on the accelerator. "Even actors have to read plays and scripts sometimes."

As co-sponsor of the Drama Club, Leonora was responsible for producing two plays a year. She knew all about reading, memorizing lines, and reciting.

"Actors are already motivated," I said. "Our kids aren't."

"Except the ones who join the Drama Club," she pointed out. "The extroverts and future movie stars."

"Yes..." Suddenly an idea dropped into my mind. "I have it! I know how to make the play more palatable." I fell silent, quickly working out the details in my mind.

"Are you going to tell me about it?" she asked.

"It's simple. I'll divide the class into groups. After we finish reading the play, each group will be responsible for acting out a scene for the class. They can get as creative as they like with costumes and scenery. That'll take the place of a test."

"Wonderful! I'll do the same with *Julius Caesar* and take your idea a step further. Your groups can perform their scenes for my students, and mine for yours."

"Then all we'll need is popcorn and pop for the audience," I said.

"If Grimsly will suspend his 'no eating or drinking in class' rule for one day. He'll love this idea, by the way."

"That's an added bonus," I said. "He's not one of my fans."

"We'll have to make sure he knows what we're doing. Maybe invite him to the performances."

"And hope he doesn't come?"

"Well, yes, but the invitation will be out there."

'I'm going to tell the class about it tomorrow," I said. "This will be a fantastic way to end the school year."

Far better than a composition and a test.

As we neared Foxglove Corners, I realized that I was looking forward to my students' reaction to the idea. In truth, I was looking forward to the next day. Would wonders never cease?

~ * ~

Riding a wave of enthusiasm, I took the dogs outside for their walk as soon as Leonora dropped me off at home.

When we reached Jonquil Lane, Candy froze in her tracks, her head pointed toward the woods. With her blowing black fur, she was exquisite and breathtaking—and ornery.

Being a creature of habit, I usually took the dogs in the opposite direction—to Squill Lane, since I preferred spaces untenanted by humans to proud, remote houses sitting on their ten-acre plots. But Candy didn't want to walk on the lane. She wanted to go into the woods across from it. I could tell.

If only I could make her understand that it was too late in the day for our traditional hike in the woods. If we went her way, her dinner would be late. And she wouldn't like that.

Impervious, she tugged on her new leather leash. Gemmy followed her lead, while Sky busied herself sniffing at a patch of grass and Halley stood patiently at my side, waiting for my decision like the perfectly behaved collie she was.

Suddenly Candy lunged forward in her chosen direction, almost yanking me off my feet. I regained my balance and pulled up hard on the leash. "No! Candy, Heel!"

'Heel' wasn't one of Candy's favorite words, but she obeyed after a protest of desperate whining.

"We're going this way," I said and turned left, away from the woods toward Camille's yellow Victorian house.

One battle won.

As Candy gave a final put-upon whine, I remembered my intention to take her and Gemmy to obedience school this summer. It was easy to forget because I didn't really want to do it. Halley and Sky had spoiled me. I assumed that every one of my collies would naturally adore and obey me.

Candy, my wild card, proved me wrong time and time again. But her days of defiance were numbered. Come summer, I'd have plenty of free time, and it was only right that I devote some of it to my own dogs. First, I'd have to find the right class.

At Camille's house, Candy tried to turn on the walkway that led to the wraparound porch, tried to drag me along with her, whining again.

Why, Candy, why? There's no one there.

No wicker furniture invited a visitor to sit down and exchange neighborhood gossip. No plants grew in hanging baskets or terra cotta pots, except the large container of mixed annuals that I'd placed beside the front door to fool a possible trespasser into thinking the house was inhabited.

By someone who let her extensive gardens grow wild? Well, I hoped there'd be nobody to wonder.

The old yellow Victorian looked more desolate every day, more spell-steeped, more haunted. The vast perennial gardens were thriving in spite of the lack of care they'd received. The grasses and weeds grew tall even though our neighbor, Doctor Linton, kept the small bit of lawn mowed. And Camille's treasured foxgloves towered over lesser plants, as always keeping their secrets.

Sometimes I thought I saw a flicker of light in an upstairs room. Then, when I looked again, it was gone. The interior rooms were dark, broadcasting loss and loneliness to the outside world.

But Memorial Day was fast approaching. After the holiday, Camille would be coming back to the yellow house with her husband and the dogs, Twister and Holly. Coming home, if only for the summer.

I had so much to tell her; so much to hear about her adventures in the South.

There was no light in a window today. I urged the dogs forward, and we walked on, covering several yards before Candy stopped again. This time her gaze fastened on the sky where clouds were breaking apart into fluffy shreds as they moved across a background of pure, rich cerulean. We all stopped with her, and I felt a quiver of apprehension fueled by her strange behavior.

Strange but not unusual. Candy had acted this way before, spooked by the sky or by something in the woods that I could never see. Or by a sound meant only for a dog's super-sensitive hearing. With Candy, who could know?

"What is the matter with you today?" I demanded.

Like a sassy child, she tossed her head, whimpering. Dark eyes bright with intelligence seemed to ask me to see what she saw. Which was nothing, of course.

Was she remembering the hot air balloon that had appeared in the sky one day only to float away over the treetops? I knew dogs lived in the moment. I'd also heard they never forgot. But didn't that last apply to cruel or kind treatment?

I leaned forward to pet her head, hoping to reassure her all was well.

Then a flock of huge black birds winged their way across the sky, catching the attention of all four collies, who promptly began to bark at them.

There was no need for me to read any dark significance into Candy's restiveness. None at all. Not today. Still, I did.

Thirteen

Whenever a phone rang, whether landline or cell, it seemed to bring me unwelcome news or make one more demand on my time. This evening it was my cell, ripples of notes all but lost in the hum of the kitchen ceiling fan.

Josie's voice came over the line, slightly hesitant, a little louder than I remembered it. Darn. And I didn't have good news for her about Sandy, or any news at all.

"Mrs. Ferguson? You said I could call…"

"Yes, anytime. Is something wrong?" I asked.

"You promised you'd help me with Sandy."

It was a plain statement without a hint of reproach, more of a reminder. "I've done everything I could think of to find her," I said. "So far, no luck."

"Well she ran away."

I frowned. "I know."

"She really did run away this time."

I drew in a deep breath as the significance of Josie's statement sank in. *Really? This time?*

"What do you mean 'this time'?" I asked.

"I kind of lied before." She took a deep breath of her own and plunged on. "But I had to. You understand, don't you?"

With a sigh, I stepped over Gemmy, who was lying in the living room entrance, and found a comfortable chair to sit in. "Not really. You'd better explain, Josie. Why did you lie and what happened? Where has Sandy been all this time?"

"You met my mother," she said. "You saw how mean she was about Sandy, but I thought if I could find a safe place for her to live, just for a little while, I could talk Mom into letting me keep her. So my sister said she'd let Sandy stay at her house temporarily."

I had known something was off about the situation but didn't expect this deception. With her tremulous pleas for help that had certainly seemed sincere, Josie had convinced me the puppy was indeed missing.

I thought of all the 'Lost Dog notices I'd posted, of all the times I'd driven down the streets of Lakeville and the country roads looking for a wandering collie puppy. All the times I'd imagined her run over by a car or struggling to survive in the wild. Of Brent Fowler's generous reward and the Woodville sisters' worry. All this effort for a puppy who wasn't lost to begin with. Until now.

Of course from the moment Sandy had been purchased as a raffle prize, she'd been in peril.

I took a firm hold on my temper. There was no undoing what Josie had done and only one direction to go. Forward. At the center of the mystery, there was still a young girl whose desire to keep her collie puppy had been overruled by an unyielding parent. Josie and Sandy still needed help.

"How did Sandy happen to run away from your sister's house?" I asked.

"Kelly had a handyman working inside yesterday. He went out to his truck and left the front door open. Nobody saw her go."

Puppies loved to run free. I imagined Sandy's excitement at finding an open door. A leap and a bound to freedom with no concept of danger. And nobody saw her go? That showed how little attention she'd received from Josie's sister.

We were back in square one, all of us. I would have to inform Terra and Marvel, who was about to deal with the puppy mix-up. The posters could stay where they were but needed an update.

"Where does your sister live?" I asked.

"On Vermont Street in Lakeville. I'm sorry I lied to you, Mrs. Ferguson. I didn't know what else to do." The childish quiver in her voice tempered my annoyance with her. "Will you still help me find Sandy?"

"I'll do what I can," I said. "But you have to promise me something."

"Anything. If you'll just find her."

"Tell your mother the truth and let the chips fall where they may." I said. "Sandy needs a stable home, not one where her welfare isn't a priority. No wonder she's always running away."

"Okay," Josie said. "I'll tell her tonight.'

I hoped she meant it.

~ * ~

It was a joy to turn off my cell phone in anticipation of a leisurely evening with my husband. I went further, dropping it into my purse and pushing it to the bottom. That left the landline, but we had an answering machine; and chances were excellent we wouldn't have unexpected company tonight.

Nothing was going to intrude on the country quiet that had somehow become so elusive for us.

I brought coffee and dessert—the last loaf of banana-nut bread—into the living room, and Crane laid the *Banner* down on the coffee table. I lit the jar candle, moving it away from the table's edge. Finally I relocated the dessert plate to the mantel as far from the collies as possible and sat down on the loveseat beside Crane.

The stage was set.

The drowsing dogs stirred and began to bark. Candy leaped to her feet. On cue, the doorbell rang. Our chances of being alone evaporated.

"Are you expecting anyone?" I asked with a quick glance out the window at an unfamiliar car, a blue Mustang with a fresh-from-the-showroom shine.

"Jake, maybe. He was going to be in Lakeville today."

Jake never announced his impending arrival with a phone call. Neither did my sister, Julia, who had been conspicuously silent lately. I started to rise.

"Sit still," Crane said. "I'll get it."

I got up and tried without appreciable success to convince four excited collies to lie down and be quiet. Or at least to Sit and Stay. I reached for Candy's collar. She jerked her head away, as Sky melted into my side.

Crane opened the door to Brent Fowler. He was beaming, his handsome face alight with suppressed excitement. Raindrops glistened on his dark red hair, and in the distance, thunder rumbled across the sky. A bad omen?

He had a newspaper tucked under his arm.

"Behold the ferocious wolf pack!" he said, undercutting his words with a rough pat for Halley. "I remember when you only had one dog, Jennet."

Crane told the collies to lie down and they did, even Candy, although she grumbled a little first.

"You've been baking, Jennet," Brent said, eyeing the dessert plate on the mantel. "From here it looks like my favorite."

Everything I baked was Brent's favorite. "Come join us," I said. "We're just having some downtime."

I poured another cup of coffee and cut him a large slice of banana-nut bread, keeping it out of Candy's reach.

"Have you seen today's paper?" he asked.

"Not yet," I said.

"Just the front page. What's up?" Crane asked.

"Look on page four. 'Kidnapping Suspect Left Note'. He settled himself in the rocker and began rustling pages, an innocuous move that set Sky trembling. I let my hand rest on her head. She was fond of Brent, but the noise must remind her of something she'd endured at the hands of her abuser.

"Our mystery woman, Sara Jane, left a farewell note for her aunt. What does this do to our balloon case?"

"It adds another ingredient," I said. "Did they just find it or were the police holding it back?"

"Her aunt just came forward with it yesterday."

"What did Sara say in the note?"

"Only that she was going on vacation and not to worry. She didn't say a word about the kids she was babysitting. The aunt, Margaret Travis, never heard Sara mention Johnston Holliday, but she went out sometimes with a boy named Johnny."

He handed me the article, but a quick perusal told me that Brent had already given us the gist of it.

"So she was planning on going away." I recalled Briana's comment to the neighbor about a day at the water park. "Why didn't you know about the note, Crane? Are you out of the loop?"

"I don't think so."

It occurred to me that Brent might be. "Mac is almost certain the children in the balloon were kidnapped. They're Briana and Bennett Cooper."

"I knew that," Brent said, not explaining how. "My P.I., Scott, is concentrating on the man, Johnston Holliday. We think he shot Eric. If he did, I'm going to see to it he pays."

"Did Scott find him?" I asked.

"He tracked him to Traverse City, then lost him. Johnston checked into a motel as Jackson Hollman. Alone."

"The man is unimaginative with names," Crane said. "We can assume he isn't very bright."

I focused on the word 'alone'. I'd been picturing the people in the balloon as a family party. Now, it seemed, that party had broken up.

"But where are the children?" I asked.

Brent shrugged. "He must have left them by the wayside. Dead or alive."

"And Sara? Was she a confederate or victim?"

"That's anybody's guess."

"It doesn't make sense. Why kidnap two children and then leave them behind?"

Because, as Annica said, they were bratty and whiny? Because having a food fight in a restaurant was only the beginning of their aggravating behavior and Sara couldn't control them? Something must have gone wrong with Holliday's plan.

I refused to believe the children had been murdered. About Sara, I didn't know what to think. "And I take it there's no ransom note."

"Not yet," Crane said. "Unless by some chance Zoller paid it secretly. But he was warned how dangerous that would be, and he still doesn't have his grandchildren."

"Maybe they escaped from Holliday," I said. "All three of them."

But then why wouldn't Sara take the children to the nearest police station? Nothing about this case had made sense, not from the beginning. Not from the moment I'd sighted what had appeared to be a happy family group enjoying a hot air balloon ride.

We had to keep looking for an answer. That is to say, the police and Brent's man, Scott, did. My role was to keep the lowest of profiles possible and, as Brent would say, bake another loaf of banana-nut bread.

If you saw him, he saw you.

But I could wonder all I liked—wonder, for example, if Sara and the children were still in Foxglove Corners. On the day Annica had seen them, had they stopped at another restaurant for lunch or dinner? How about breakfast the next morning? Children are always hungry.

Who feeds children if they're planning to kill them?

What a morbid thought.

I sensed I was on the wrong track, but I couldn't find the right one.

If Holliday had been spotted in Traverse City, Briana, Bennett, and Sara could be anywhere between here and there, which made them practically impossible to find. They could be fine or injured. Or dead.

I drank my coffee, listened to Crane and Brent speculate about possible scenarios, and thought about woods.

Fourteen

I couldn't stop thinking about woods, those dark and silent places in Michigan where the children might be sheltering—or buried. How many woods were there in Foxglove Corners alone?

Briana and Bennett might be lost, modern-day counterparts of Hansel and Gretel with no angels to watch over them. If they were dead, their bodies might not be found until some hunter stumbled across them in a future season. This might never happen.

Dead or alive, Brent had said. No one else was talking about death.

The twins' mother, Liza Cooper, interviewed in her living room, couldn't keep tears from falling as she begged the kidnapper to bring her babies home. "They're so little. They never hurt anybody." She had a message for Sara: "You can have your own children, Sara, but not mine." And for the twins: "Be brave. Mom's waiting for you."

I wished I could do something to help find them. Then there was Eric, Brent's young friend who had lost his life, presumably at Holliday's hand. That tragedy had tended to get lost in the coverage of the twins' disappearance. But every life was precious. I thought about Sara. Victim or accomplice? Dead or alive?

Because I'd last seen the children soaring over Jonquil Lane, my thoughts turned toward the woods across the lane. I recalled my plan to take the dogs for our traditional springtime hike, which reminded me of Candy's skittish behavior on previous walks. Did she know something I didn't?

I decided to schedule the hike for Saturday, after I paid my visit to Mallowmere Kennels. That promised to be a traumatic experience for humans and canines alike. I could only hope at the end of the day, Suzette would give Mandy back to Marvel and accept Brandy into her heart.

Let something in this topsy-turvy world come out right.

"Together we can break the curse," Marvel had said when I called from my car to tell her I was on my way.

That wasn't how I would have expressed our mission.

All the way to Mallowmere Kennels, over country roads and through hushed green forests, I pondered curses and luck. Good and bad. Curses, I decided, might exist, but they had no power to destroy a life unless the cursed one believed in them. As for luck, I believe people make their own.

I reached the kennel at noon as the sun was breaking though heavy cloud cover. From the driveway, I could see Marvel and Suzette sitting in wicker rockers, placed barely close enough for easy conversation. Brandy had been brought out of the kennel for a happy reunion with her sister, leaving Marvel's stunning tricolor and her remaining puppy, Andy, alone in the well-shaded run.

Brandy was playing with a red dog toy of indeterminate shape, growling ferociously at it while Mandy watched from Suzette's lap, all the while licking her little chops.

Suzette was exactly as Annica had described her. She wore a blouse with a blue and green floral pattern and had again painted her long nails a color that could be described as frosty orchid. The broken nail was filed neatly down

Neither Suzette nor Marvel was smiling when I joined them on the porch. Suzette held Mandy in her arms tightly as if she had no intention of relinquishing her to Marvel while Marvel held fast to a sheaf of papers with the same intensity.

I saw the women as if they were part of a tableau, each frozen in her place. Neither one would step away from her position. Both, of course, were right.

Marvel introduced me to Suzette as an old friend, which was twisting the truth a little. A new friend, I would have said, who might become a good one some day.

"Jennet is a collie person too," Marvel said. "She has four dogs."

You'd think that would give us common ground, but Marvel's observation stalled in the still air. She was unusually quiet this afternoon; perhaps Suzette was always that way.

Misrepresenting a situation—okay; lying about it or withholding information—often made everything worse. If Josie hadn't misled me about Sandy… Well, we'd still be in the same place. Looking for a lost puppy. But if Marvel would only agree to tell Willa Bradstone about the mix-up, it might pave the way for a happy solution or at least a compromise.

"Mandy and Brandy are both such beautiful puppies," Marvel was saying. "They look just like their sire."

I studied Brandy and Mandy, seeking the differences an experienced breeder had seen. Mandy was slightly larger. She had more bone, a slightly darker coat, and perhaps more spirit, squirming in Suzette's arms and whining frantically as she tried to get closer to Brandy.

Suzette held onto her.

The two litter sisters did resemble each other closely, though. I could see how the mistake had occurred.

"Brandy is a pretty puppy," Suzette said, "but you can't expect me to give up Mandy, not after all this time we've been together. It's too cruel."

"It's been a week," Marvel pointed out.

"That's a long time in the life of a puppy, and it's not like I'm exchanging one lamp for another."

"You have Mandy; you chose Brandy," Marvel reminded her, unnecessarily. "It was a mistake, your taking Mandy. I blame myself entirely."

"How does that help me?" Suzette asked.

The impasse was going to continue. The sun came out again. It seemed to grow warmer every minute. A bee circled around a silver-needled vine in a hanging basket, and a tiny hummingbird dipped into a feeder and flew away. The puppies started to yip.

Marvel scooped up Brandy to cuddle her. I thought again about the power of truth. Of straight shooting.

Not that I'd always adhered strictly to truth, but I considered it a laudable goal.

"Do you know how many collies Willa Bradstone owns?" I asked.

Marvel swung Brandy back and forth. "It fluctuates. Just now, she has ten adults and two litters. That's twenty with the puppies."

Did she really need another one?

"How well do you know her?" I asked.

"Not well. We met at a show last year. I sent Jess to Ohio for the breeding."

"Let's assume she's a kind person," I said. "Why don't you explain what happened? If she loves collies, she may understand."

I didn't mention the possibility that Ms. Bradstone might be a hard-as-stone businesswoman who wouldn't be moved by Marvel's plight, who would insist that she keep her part of the bargain. Nor did I allude to Marvel's desire to keep her mistake a secret from the Ohio breeder. We both knew that.

"I'll be more than willing to pay the stud fee," Suzette said. "And whatever additional amount you want. Just name it."

That seemed fair to me. "Let Willa Bradstone decide who takes Mandy," I said. "She may surprise you."

How easy it was to tell other people what to do. But someone had to step in, or Marvel and Suzette would stay locked in their tableau. Not forever. Just until Willa broke it.

"There's no curse, Marvel," I added. "You've had a run of bad luck. It's bound to change."

"Maybe it *should* be Willa's decision," Marvel said after a long pause. "Legally she's Mandy's owner unless she decides otherwise."

Suzette held Mandy a little closer. But she said, "If that's the only way to resolve this situation, I think we should do it."

"Well, then… When do you expect your company?"

Marvel consulted her watch. "In about an hour. She has a long drive."

I got up and gave each puppy a farewell pat on the head. "I wish I could stay and meet her, but today is Saturday, and I have a full schedule."

Marvel set Brandy down on the floor, and the puppies began to run in circles, chasing their tails.

"It was nice meeting you," Suzette said formally.

At last Marvel smiled. "Thanks for stopping by, Jennet."

It'll be okay, she might have added.

~ * ~

In truth, my full Saturday schedule was a hike in the woods and a chicken to roast for tonight's dinner. As soon as I came home, I changed clothes, choosing them carefully. Wearing high boots would protect my legs. I added a long-sleeved dark pink shirt, although the air was thick with humidity and the sun was warm. With luck, the mosquitoes would ignore me.

Protection was essential for the kind of afternoon I planned. I didn't stop to think what it might entail.

Observing my preparations, the dogs knew something was different. In the vestibule Candy sniffed my boots and started barking.

"Who wants to go for a walk?" I asked, ducking as four dogs converged on me eagerly. I leashed Gemmy and Candy, slipped my key and digital camera in my pocket, and we set out.

A drowsy Saturday silence hung over the land. At the lane, Candy turned left, her eyes fixed on the yellow Victorian. Once again I thought I saw a light in an upstairs window. Then it was gone. Then I saw it again. A trick of the sunlight? It had to be, and a rather unnerving one unless…

Could a vagrant have taken up residence in the house in Camille's absence? It seemed unlikely, but when Crane came home, I'd ask him to go over with me and check for signs of habitation. We had the key and had promised to watch Camille's property.

I took one final look, didn't see a light, and said, "The other way, Candy. We're going into the woods."

What magical words!

She might have understood them. Well, of course she did.

We passed the mailbox, crossed the graveled lane, and stood at the edge of the woods for a moment. Candy and Gemmy pulled on their leads, quivering with impatience while Halley and Sky waited for me to move.

Suddenly I wasn't in a hurry.

Since the last time I'd looked this way, an ancient maple tree had fallen over. Hollow inside, it had bravely spouted new green leaves for spring but had succumbed at last, taking a 'No Trespassing' sign down with it. And there it would stay as long as the woods remained unsold.

Tiny insects filled the air, and I felt the beginning of an itch on my arm. Through my sleeve. Halley sat down and began biting ferociously at her leg. Did I really want to do this?

Yes, and not because I thought I would find Briana and Bennett huddling in some thicket. All I really wanted was to keep the tradition alive and perhaps find a few new pictures for my Foxglove Corners album.

Fifteen

Shakespeare's magical wood teemed with fairy life and enchantment. The woods across from Jonquil Lane teemed with mosquitoes and the most extensive assortment of flying insects in Michigan. To say nothing of mysterious rustlings in the brush that almost certainly indicated the presence of snakes.

Why had I wanted to come here again?

Between hikes, the discomfort of a woodland trek sank to the back of my mind. The beautiful lived on in memory. Wildflowers and fresh scents and the sense of being shut away from the real world, far from everyday cares.

Being surrounded by woods had the childhood allure of playing in a tent made from blankets.

At the first underfoot rustle, I'd found a branch that served as an adequate walking stick and makeshift weapon. This I held in my left hand, saving the right for holding on to two leashes. Halley and Sky walked placidly by my side, treading their way carefully over uneven terrain and exposed roots.

Meanwhile Candy and Gemmy stuck their noses deep in every bit of brush, leaf mound, and vine in sight. The dogs were having a grand time.

So we proceeded at a leisurely pace deep into the woods, trying to keep to a straight line.

It was impossible to get lost in these woods. Depending on my direction, I would either come to a stretch of farmland, a winding trail without a name, or Jonquil Lane, just beyond the most beautiful house in the neighborhood, a white Victorian extravaganza adorned with cupolas and turrets and enough gingerbread trim to tempt any lost child.

But I didn't want to think about lost children today.

Ahead was a shimmer of silvery blue. Walking more quickly, we soon reached the edge of the stream I'd found during a past exploration. Running from east to west in the approximate middle of the forest, it was bordered by vigorous vines that bore tiny white flowers. They shone like stars on their glossy green leaves, giving a touch of brightness to the gloomy landscape.

I noticed another flower whose petals formed a pale yellow cup ideal for a fairy or a collie to drink from. I couldn't resist the fanciful thought, and Gemmy couldn't resist burying her nose in the bloom. She sneezed and shook her head violently.

Sky lay down at the stream's edge, while Halley took an experimental drink, reminding me that I'd forgotten to take bottled water for the dogs. It was warm and humid, and growing warmer by the minute. We'd better make it a short hike.

I'd never taken a picture of the stream. What a gorgeous background it would make with four collies lying in a row. However, it was unlikely I could coax my quartet to form that row. I didn't even try. The stream and the flowers alone would make a lovely picture.

I reached for my camera and dropped the stick but held fast to the wild ones' leashes. Taking my picture, I said, "One down."

Out of nowhere, a twinge of apprehension stole over me. It came so quietly that I was hardly aware of its approach. All of a sudden my heart was beating rapidly and I was conscious of moisture forming on my chest and a passing chill. All this and a stinging bite high on my neck.

Beware.

At the other end of her leash, Candy came to a standstill. For a moment she remained in that pose, ears pricked, looking more like a collie statue than a living creature.

We're not alone.

She growled, a low, threatening sound that originated deep in her throat. With a cry that was almost human, she wrenched herself out of my grasp and streaked through the woods, dragging her leash behind her. Startled, I dropped Gemmy's lead but grabbed it in mid-air, for once quicker than a dog.

The other collies began to bark. The woods, never as quiet as poets would have us believe, exploded in a cacophony of rustlings and crashings, with Candy barking, somewhere to my left.

"Candy!" The echo bounced back to me; I could hear the panic in it. "Candy, come back!"

The noise continued.

She would never come. I had to go after her. I couldn't leave her to her own devices. Not today. There was danger here. There was somebody. Someone stalking us?

The only sound in the woods seemed to be Candy's barking.

I set out in pursuit, dragging Gemmy, vaguely aware of Halley and Sky running after me, all of us hurrying to the source of the melee.

Through the drumming of my heartbeat, other sounds penetrated. A scream. A female voice crying, "Go away. Get out of here. Get!"

Pushing aside a low-hanging branch, I spied a frightening scene.

Candy had run her prey to the earth. A young denim-clad woman lay in a spill of long black hair and a nest of broken branches, clutching her knee. Candy stood over her wagging her tail, a picture of canine innocence.

I cleared the distance between us.

"Are you hurt?"

She didn't answer, but a moan broke through her lips.

"My dog didn't bite you, did she?"

The woman pushed her hair back from her face. She was quite attractive, but her angry frown made her expression sullen.

Halley and Sky lay down, keeping a respectful distance, and Gemmy sat. With Candy still on her feet, still wagging her tail, the dogs formed a semi-circle around the fallen girl.

"Get them away from me," she shouted.

"Did my dog hurt you?" I asked again.

"She jumped up on me and knocked me down. My knee… I fell on it wrong." The girl sat up, massaging it and wincing. "It hurts."

That was all? Thank heavens.

"I'm sorry," I said. "Candy! Bad, bad dog!"

"I thought it was a wolf. If it's your dog, why did you let her run free?"

Ignoring that, I said, "Who are you and what are you doing here?"

"I'm Anne. I was just looking for something."

"Do you live on the lane?" I asked.

"Nearby."

Realizing that lingering fright over what Candy might have done sharpened my tone, I brought it down a few notches but continued the interrogation. "Didn't you see the 'No Trespassing' signs? They're all over."

She continued to rub her knee. "Yeah, but so what? I didn't see anybody around. Do you own the woods?"

"Yes," I said.

So much for truth and laudable goals. This situation called for subterfuge.

I was about to introduce myself when she said, "Well, sorry." She wasn't really; her blatant sarcasm told me that. "I didn't think anyone would mind. I lost my doll."

I stared at her. She must be in her early twenties, I judged, old enough for green eye shadow and cherry-red lipstick. Too old for dolls. Young enough to be on the verge of tears. To be fair, wouldn't anyone who'd been set upon by a large dog want to cry from shock and residual fear?

"Did you find it?" I asked.

"Yes." She looked around the immediate area. "But I don't see it now. Your dog made me lose it."

I looked, too, and saw moss, golden flowers that looked like tickweed, layers of no-color leaves left over from another season, vines with far-reaching tentacles, a large tree branch forming a fork, trees. In other words, woods.

There was no sign of a doll but many places where one could have landed when Anne fell.

Halley and Sky were panting heavily in the increasing heat, and I berated myself for forgetting their water. We could all use a nice, long drink.

Candy was still barking, intermittently, annoyingly. No doubt she hoped for a friendly word from the person whom, in her view, she had rescued.

"Be quiet!" I told her.

Supporting her weight on a nearby tree, Anne, rose and took a few tentative steps, testing her knee warily. She seemed to be all right.

"Damn dogs," she said. "How do I get out of here?"

I pointed. "Walk straight. You'll come out on Jonquil Lane."

Without another word, she turned and limped off in the direction I'd indicated, her lost doll apparently forgotten.

"Bad dog, Candy," I said again. "You could have gotten us all in big trouble, young lady."

She cast me a look that communicated her utter lack of remorse. Well, she was a dog.

I tugged on Candy's and Gemmy's leashes and walked on, intending to come out of the woods opposite the farmland. All of my enthusiasm for the venture had fled.

What was Anne doing in these woods? In my experience I'd found that trespassers were usually up to no good. Strangers were suspect until they revealed their agendas.

As if I'd believe that story about a doll.

The dogs had clearly forgotten the encounter, but it had shaken me. I could as easily have met an escaped convict on the run as a relatively harmless young woman. Candy could have caused Anne serious harm, paving the way for criminal charges or even a lawsuit.

All on a peaceful Saturday afternoon walk in the woods, but when was my life ever peaceful? Objects falling from the sky, a stranger in the woods, a non-existent doll.

It doesn't pay to arrive at conclusions too quickly. I found the doll in the moss, approximately three yards from where Anne had fallen. It was an Indian maiden with long black braids, coppery skin, and a necklace of tiny turquoise beads.

I picked it up. Its costume was damp from a sojourn on the forest floor, but it seemed otherwise intact and almost new.

It was small, the size of the vintage storybook dolls on display in the Green House of Antiques, or in any northern souvenir shop.

I remembered a similar doll I'd had so many years ago. Pocahontas. We'd bought her en route to a family vacation in Harrisville. I had no idea what had happened to her.

Candy sniffed at the little doll and licked her chops.

"Oh no, you don't," I said, tucking it into my belt.

How would I return the Indian doll to its owner when I'd probably never see her again? Should I return it?

I was highly skeptical of her story. To lose the doll in the woods she must have been here before. For what purpose? And what grown woman goes into the woods carrying a doll?

I wished I'd taken a better look at Anne. I remembered makeup, long black hair, and a mouth drawn in sullen red lines. She had been angry and upset, not at her best. But I thought I'd recognize her if I saw her again. If it became important.

As for the doll, I intended to hold on to it as I had the orange scarf and the paper napkin. It might be evidence of some as yet undisclosed crime, although I couldn't see any connection to the hot air balloon mystery, which was the only local crime I knew about at the moment.

Sixteen

The ground grew more uneven with every step I took. Pools of rotting vegetation created a slippery hazard, and exposed roots lay in wait to trip me. I looked for my walking stick and realized I must have left it back at the stream.

Well there were branches all around me. I could easily find a replacement, but we were almost at the woods' edge. We had to be. We'd been walking long enough. I kept looking for horses grazing on green meadowland but saw only endless forest.

By now Halley and Sky were lagging far behind, and even Candy and Gemmy had lost a good portion of their energy. I was overly warm and felt as if I'd been dragged through the woods, acquiring a layer of grit on the way.

I'd definitely need a hot shower before starting dinner. The dogs would have to be brushed and bathed. Not today though. I barely had time to mix a meatloaf. That served me right for exaggerating my busy Saturday schedule.

My thoughts drifted back to Mallowmere and the outcome of Willa Bradstone's visit. Had she insisted on taking Mandy back to Ohio with her, as was her right, leaving Brandy to Suzette? Poor Mandy and poor Suzette. Perhaps I shouldn't have been so free with my advice.

On the other hand, puppies have an amazing ability to adapt to their changing circumstances, as do most humans. Whatever happened, Marvel would be more careful when negotiating a puppy sale in the future. Now, if I could only see a thinning of the woods and a glimpse of green ahead.

At a stand of young spruce trees, Halley sat down and gazed up at me with a silent plea in her dark eyes. Sky took the mild rebellion a step further and lay down. On her leash, Candy cast an impatient glance at her sisters.

"Come on, girls," I said. "Up. You can't stay here."

So I said, but my sympathies were with them. I longed for a shady place to rest where flowers bloomed but bugs didn't exist.

I know a bank where the wild thyme blows...

That place wasn't in these woods.

"There's water at home," I said. "Cool, clear water and biscuits. And dinner."

At the mention of dinner, they rose with marked reluctance, and after what seemed like hours, we emerged from the woods. There were the horses, four of them, grazing in their pasture so far in the distance that they looked like toy animals on a play farm. That meant we were closer to Jonquil Lane than I'd thought. This was the road home.

From here I could see the gables and turrets of Camille's yellow Victorian, its classic lines rising up to the clear blue sky. With a yelp, Candy came to a sudden halt, almost causing me to lose my balance. She and Gemmy flew into a wild frenzy of leaping and barking. I struggled to hold on to them while Sky and Halley joined the fray.

"What now?" I demanded.

As I squinted in the sunlight, a splash of vibrant color filled the sky. A hot air balloon drifted above the treetops and dipped low across the dirt trail.

Déjà vu?

Not really. From on high, Brent Fowler waved to me and called down, "Hallo! Wanna ride?"

Assuming the invitation included her, Candy jumped up high. I pulled her back down to the ground.

"All five of us?"

"Just you."

"Some other time," I said.

His booming laugh rang out through the quiet countryside. "It's a date. See you soon!"

The balloons were flying again, and Brent looked and sounded like his old jovial self. Surely that must be a sign of something good.

~ * ~

After dinner, when there was still plenty of light left in the sky, Crane and I walked over to the yellow Victorian. I checked the container of mixed annuals for dryness and decided it could last another two or three days without water. Crane opened Camille's front door, and we stepped inside.

For the first time since I'd come to Foxglove Corners, the house was dark and silent. Uninviting. Unwelcoming. The feeling of desolation and loss I had experienced so often on glancing at the house from my own home had moved inside to lie heavily on the stuffy air.

In January Leonora and I had packed away the decorations from the holiday and wedding celebrations. The house hadn't seemed empty or desolate then. It didn't realize that its mistress wouldn't be coming home any time soon.

The fanciful thought stirred my memories.

This had always been such a happy home. Exuberant dogs running free and the aroma of something wonderful baking in the oven. Warmth and welcome, and in the summertime fresh flowers in vases.

I remembered sitting in Camille's kitchen, telling her about the handsome stranger I'd met that morning—who turned out to be Crane. I'd shared countless problems and concerns with her over tea and pie. Tea and tarts. Tea and cake. Camille always listened and lent her unique perspective to any situation.

Would those times ever come again? Would Camille be different?

I shuddered, and Crane put his arm around me. "What's the matter, honey?"

"Empty houses spook me," I said.

"Let's hope this one is empty. I found a vagrant today making himself at home in someone else's cottage. There's a lot of that going on these days. It makes me wonder about the cabin."

I thought about it too. The log cabin up north was our second home, filled with cherished possessions, among them family antiques that Aunt Becky had sent us soon after our wedding.

Earlier this month, we'd driven up north to open and clean the cabin. It was now in pristine condition, ready for immediate occupancy. Ours. I'd hate to think of an intruder making free with our sheets and towels and dishes, but it was miles from the nearest town. There'd be no one to notice suspicious goings-on, nobody to notify us.

But Camille had neighbors.

"It seems unlikely anyone would break into a house across the lane from where people are living with four dogs," I said.

"You never know."

I wasn't expecting to find any indication of habitation here. The house felt truly unlived-in to me.

I stepped into the kitchen. On the windowsill, Camille's cobalt glass collection sparkled in the ebbing daylight. A blue cloth with a bright floral border covered the table. The pretty country kitchen was bare as if it had been cleared for a house staging. I couldn't see anything amiss.

Except for a jar of jam or preserves about three-fourths full on the counter. Surely it hadn't been there when Leonora and I cleaned the kitchen after the New Year's Eve party.

"Strawberry preserves," I said, reaching for it. "From *Miss Maud's Garden*. This wasn't here before, and Camille always makes her own jams and jellies—and everything."

Crane stopped my hand in mid-reach. "Don't touch it. Just in case there are fingerprints on it." His voice telegraphed business. "Was it upstairs that you saw the light?"

"In the front. With all the rooms in this house, why would anybody choose one that faces the lane?"

"We don't know that anybody did."

Ever the voice of reason and caution. But Crane didn't want me to handle the jar.

On the second floor we opened doors left ajar and explored each room. Three were spacious guest rooms with minimal furnishings. Thick floral comforters and matching pillows covered beds that hadn't been slept in for months—or had been very carefully made. Small tables and lamps. Large country baskets. Electric clocks, all of them several hours behind, thanks to our last power outage.

The room in which I'd seen the light was the smallest one on the second floor. Camille used it as a sewing room. This one had been left in some disorder. The sewing machine open, a large, overflowing basket on the floor, fabric folded neatly on a daybed, and a dressmaker's mannequin wearing a basted pink cocktail dress.

Intended for Camille's honeymoon, no doubt, but she hadn't finished it.

There was a brass candle lamp in the window. I pressed its switch, and a stream of pale illumination spilled out on the narrow windowsill.

"The light I saw was brighter, I'm sure."

"How about the overhead?" Crane switched on a large, round bulb sheltered by a half dozen curving blue ovals.

I shook my head. "No, it wasn't that bright. I guess I must have been looking at a ghost light."

"If I wanted a place to crash, I wouldn't pick this room," Crane said.

"Me neither, with three comfortable beds down the hall."

"It doesn't look to me like anyone has been living here."

"Not up here, maybe, but there's still the jar of preserves in the kitchen. It isn't Camille's. I would swear to it."

"The next time you talk to her you could ask her about it."

"I wouldn't do that," I said. "She'd only worry, and maybe there's nothing to worry about."

Neither one of us could explain the jar.

Before going back downstairs, I checked the bathroom, which was in pristine condition. The holly-and-ivy hand towels looked as if they'd just been placed on the rack. Leonora and I had forgotten to change them.

I picked up a bar of soap in the shape of a snowman and let it fall back into the holder again. It looked fresh-from-the-wrapper new.

Crane came up behind me and turned the faucet on and off again. "Everything up here looks okay to me."

While he went down to the basement, I waited in the kitchen, contemplating the jar of strawberry preserves and searching for anything else that didn't look like something Camille would buy. I couldn't find anything, and the breadbox was empty and scrubbed clean of crumbs. Who would eat preserves without bread or toast?

"All clear downstairs," Crane said.

"The light must have been my imagination," I said. "But not those preserves. We can't be too careful these days, and we did promise Camille and Gilbert we'd look after the property."

I glanced at the preserves. A strange clue, but a clue nonetheless. "Something seems wrong to me. I can't put a name to it, but I'm going to keep watching."

With four people missing and an unknown woman prowling around in the woods, I couldn't afford not to, even though if there was any invader, it was in all likelihood a homeless person who was now far away.

As we walked through the dining room, I ran my hand along the mahogany table, as always mildly surprised to find dust gathered on an unused surface.

"Just before Camille and Gilbert come back, I'm going to come over and clean house," I said.

Crane sketched his name in the dust. "I'll come with you."

Surprised, I looked at him. Crane didn't do housework. "To help me?"

"If you like," he said. "I don't want you coming here alone."

I didn't have to ask why.

Seventeen

Back at home, Crane and I settled in for a cozy, quiet evening. I'd brewed a fresh pot of coffee and set out pineapple drop cookies on a plate. Crane had been turning the little Indian doll over and over in his hands. I had no idea what he was thinking.

Finally he set it back on the mantel out of Candy's reach. She had showed an inordinate amount of interest in the doll, no doubt regarding it as a tasty treat. Since Candy was unpredictable, I was afraid she might swallow one of the tiny turquoise beads.

"I don't think you should go wandering around in the woods anymore, honey," Crane said.

For a moment he sounded like the Crane of yore—before I broke him in. That Crane had been dictatorial and dangerous to domestic harmony. A fast learner, he now phrased his orders more diplomatically and always added a touch of honey.

I poured our coffee and thought about mosquito bites, poison ivy, and ominous rustlings on the ground, all of which were irrelevant to the present conversation. He wasn't referring to natural discomforts or dangers.

"Anne was frightened and angry, but not a threat." I added my usual mantra. "Anyway, I had four large dogs with me."

"And your cell phone?"

"Well, no."

"Bottled water? Compass? Snake bite kit?"

Snake bite kit? "You're joking, right?"

"Not at all. There are snakes all around us, and a killer may have passed this way. Have you forgotten the strawberry preserves in Camille's kitchen?"

"No, but I thought you had."

That wasn't true. Crane never forgot anything important, which certainly described that mysterious jar.

I took a long sip of coffee, relaxing as its warmth spread through me. Warmth and reason. Even though I had no desire to repeat the hiking experience any time soon, should I let the matter go in the interest of keeping the peace? Should I give Crane an inch?

No. Inches can turn into miles. "Those woods are practically part of our property. I don't want to live in fear, imagining Johnston Holliday's slinking through the bushes."

"Didn't Fowler say he'd left the area?"

"So he did. I was talking about men like him."

"Did you read about the women attacked by pit bulls last week? One was peacefully jogging on a country road. The other was carrying groceries into the house. Both were mauled to death."

There had been two separate incidents, miles apart and involving different dogs. "That happened downstate," I said.

It seemed that I was always reading about such attacks. Pit bulls, German shepherds, Rottweilers. Were the dogs hungry and frustrated like so many of their owners? Or had they been trained to kill? I knew that a running figure arouses a canine's instinct to chase prey, and groceries meant food. Raw hamburger, lunch meat. Bread and doughnuts.

I let my hand rest on Halley's silky head. She opened her eyes and wagged her tail. My gentle collies might belong to a different species, but all four of them were well fed, cared for, and cherished. That made a difference.

God help the wild dogs and their victims.

I remembered when a stray retriever had jumped into the front seat of my car and stolen my take-out order. Fortunately he had left me intact, preferring the taste of stuffed cabbages.

Was Crane warning me about wild dogs in packs now?

I glanced at the locked cabinet that contained his gun collection, along with the gun he carried every day as he patrolled the roads and by-roads of Foxglove Corners. At one time, over Crane's strong objections, I'd been determined to buy a weapon of my own for protection.

Then I found myself in a life-and-death encounter and knew I could never kill another human being. So I'd let the gun idea die, electing to rely on my wits and good luck—and the dogs if they happened to be on hand.

"I can't be with you every minute," Crane pointed out.

"Of course not. I wouldn't want you to."

He frowned, frosty gray eyes conveying sheer astonishment. "You wouldn't?

"Occasional short separations are good for a marriage," I said.

He was still frowning when the collies sprang into their usual visitor-at-the-door routine, barking and dashing to the vestibule. Even my shrinking violet Sky was one of the warning or welcome committee. When had she grown so assertive?

"It's Brent," I said, glancing out the window at the blue Mustang. "He must have left his hot air balloon at home."

Crane was already on his feet, on his way to the door, telling the dogs to Sit and Stay. They sank back against the wall like a single entity, but Candy continued to bark. Crane had forgotten the Quiet command.

As he often did, Brent had come bearing a gift. This evening it was a bottle of blackberry wine.

"It was a very good year," he said with a wink. "I was thinking Jennet could bake one of her banana breads to go with it, but I see there are cookies. We could open it now."

Blackberries and pineapple? Well, why not? I read the label. "Mmm. Last year. The best."

Crane said, "All right" quietly, and the dogs rushed at Brent for attention, which he gave generously.

"I have coffee," I said. "Which will it be? Coffee or wine?"

"Wine now and coffee later."

Crane opened the bottle, and I moved the cookies to the coffee table. Brent scooped up three.

"Sit down," I said, "and tell us why you were flying over Foxglove Corners in a balloon."

"I was just doing a little private investigating of my own."

"In the air?"

"Sure in the air. You get a whole new perspective from above."

"What did you see?" Crane asked.

"Treetops and water," he said. "And Jennet with her entourage."

"Nothing else?"

"One or two anomalies. I need to think about them."

It was unlike Brent to be secretive. I sat forward in my chair. "Was this in our woods that you saw these anomalies?"

"A little farther. Close to Elderberry Road."

That was near the site of the Sky Princess crash. About twenty minutes to Clovers where Sara, Johnston, and the twins had gone for breakfast.

"Can't you be more specific, Brent?" I asked. "Did you see one of those weird crop circles? What?"

"Not exactly. You'll be the first to know when I'm ready to talk about it." Deftly he changed the subject. "Are you serious about accepting my invitation?"

"What invitation is this?" Crane asked.

"To go for a ride in one of my balloons."

In the brief pause before I answered, visions of the multi-colored Sky Princess floated through my mind. Clouds and birds and bodies slamming into the ground. The Grim Reaper emerging from the woods merrily swinging his scythe.

"Are you sure your balloons are safe now?" I asked.

"Would I be riding in one if I had any doubts?"

"Probably not."

"As long as we have plenty of propane gas and a good wind and the chase car does its job, nothing will happen."

"Jennet and I were talking about taking a color tour in the fall," Crane said. "From the sky this time."

"I'll reserve you a day. When the leaves first begin to turn? When they're at their peak?"

"October fifteenth," I said, pulling the date out of the air. "I take it business is picking up at Skyway Tours."

"Slowly," he said. "People don't forget, but they get over being nervous. I may hold on to the company after all. I brought Horace Larkin and two of his nephews in to help."

I knew Horace. A genial old gentleman, he'd sold Christmas trees at the antique shop, Past Perfect, and the following year drove an old-fashioned sleigh on the annual Holly Daze tour of decorated homes.

Brent sipped the wine. "This *is* good. I like blackberries in anything. Especially pies."

"Bring me a couple of quarts and I'll bake you one," I said. "If you promise to tell me what you saw in the Elderberry woods."

"Deal," he said. "Did you two hear about old man Zoller and the ransom?"

"I didn't," I said.

Neither had Crane. "Tell us."

"On his own, he left fifty grand in the designated place. No one ever picked it up."

"So there was a ransom note, but if Holliday didn't take the money, what was the point of kidnapping the twins?" I asked.

"Something happened between the ransom demand and the pick-up," Crane said.

Maybe many things.

"Yeah," Brent said, "and by the time Zoller decided to pay the ransom, Holliday was miles away."

"How is your P. I. doing with the search?" I asked.

Brent's frown gave me my answer. "Scott traced him to Standish and lost him again. He's still traveling alone."

Without Sara. Without the twins. Without the ransom money for which he had risked his freedom. What a strange abduction.

"Scott is always a few steps too late."

"That's why I've taken to the air," Brent said. "You can see so much more clearly when you're way up high."

~ * ~

For me, at this moment, way up high was our second-story bedroom window. Wrapped in a lacy green robe, I stood in a wave of warm air and gazed out into the night. With wisps of fog hugging the ground, I couldn't see much.

Crane had taken the dogs for their last walk of the day while I washed glasses and cups and set out dishes for breakfast.

The blackberry wine had made me sleepy, which was the reason I avoided alcoholic drinks. I liked to be alert at all times. You never knew when you'd need every one of your senses.

I couldn't see Crane and the dogs, who were due back any time now, but there seemed to be something out there moving in the shadows. A nocturnal creature that had better take cover before four collies invaded its space, perhaps? Something that didn't want to be seen.

Across the lane, Camille's house was dark. Without conscious thought, I sought out the sewing room window, a vague outline in the darkness framed by floating shreds of fog.

What had I expected? To see the ghost light shining?

We'd investigated thoroughly and concluded that the house was empty. That was then. What about now?

I had the feeling something was going on in the silent rooms of the yellow Victorian. The prowlings of a restless spirit that predated Camille's occupancy of the old house, one she'd never mentioned? Some surreptitious activity that didn't need light?

Like strawberry preserves being spread on bread. Milk in a pint from a party store. A midnight snack in the dark.

Pure imagination, Crane would tell me, and he'd be right.

But what if it wasn't?

I didn't move from the window until I heard the side door slam and the collies barking for their bedtime biscuit. Crane had come home, and I'd never seen him approach.

Eighteen

The next morning I awoke to find the house surrounded by a heavy white fog. For all I could see through the bedroom window, the yellow Victorian might have disappeared during the night, taking Jonquil Lane with it.

Fortunately it was Sunday, which meant I didn't have to brave the freeway. Last night's blackberry wine had left me with a slight headache, and resting at home seemed to be the best plan for the day.

Unfortunately Crane wasn't coming home tonight. Fortified by a breakfast of pancakes and bacon, he had taken the dogs for their morning walk before leaving for a trip up north. It was Sheriff's business and therefore confidential, but he would have a chance to stop at the cabin on his way home. He'd promised to call me later.

So having nothing pressing to do, I made a pot of tea and a list of the annuals I wanted to plant as soon as we passed the frost warning date.

Unused to so much free time, I soon grew restless. I couldn't let go of the notion that all was not well at Camille's house. That I couldn't see it reinforced the feeling. The jar of strawberry preserves nagged at me, growing in stature, until it took on the colors of a clue.

But a clue to what, exactly?

As the morning wore on and the fog failed to lift by nine as promised, I toyed with the idea of searching Camille's house more thoroughly to see if the daylight hours would reveal something I'd missed last night.

Or calling Leonora, who might remember seeing the jar on the counter. That proved to be a good idea. She confirmed my suspicion that something was wrong.

"I'm positive it wasn't there," she said. "I remember wiping the counter down just before we left. Camille's cookbooks were set out, same as always, with the canisters. That's all. Besides, Camille doesn't buy preserves in the store."

"Then someone *did* break into the house. But when?"

"Anytime between January second and now. Do you think he's still there?"

I glanced out the kitchen window. The fog was as thick as ever. I still couldn't see the lane. Wherever Crane was, I hoped he had visibility.

"He wasn't last night," I said. "Crane and I looked all over, and nothing was out of place. Just those preserves. There's more. A few times I saw a light in the window. At least I'm pretty sure I did."

"Mmm. Mysterious. Did you check the wastebaskets in the kitchen and both baths? Because they were empty."

I hadn't. What a rookie mistake.

"I'm sure Crane did," I said, "but he isn't here to ask."

"Look again, Jen. I'd love to help, but I have a lunch date."

"Since when does romance take precedence over mystery?" I asked, unable to resist teasing her. "You've changed, Leonora."

"It's with Jake," she said.

Now I understood. But I didn't like it. Leonora had apparently forgiven Jake for attempting to juggle both her and my sister, Julia, last Christmas. Or she didn't care. Jake was lucky with women in that respect. In all respects.

"Enough said. Enjoy your lunch."

I would have liked to see Leonora today. At one time we used to look for clues together and share adventures. With the yellow Victorian house still shrouded in fog, its image burned in my mind. A light in the window, a once-clear kitchen counter, as yet unexamined wastebaskets. Why not do something to liven up this boring day?

After all, I hadn't promised Crane that I wouldn't go back to Camille's house alone. He'd merely made me aware of his preference. I could take one of the dogs with me and be perfectly safe.

I can talk myself into anything; it's a gift.

On the other hand, why go searching for a mystery on a foggy morning when my imaginative powers would be in full swing?

In the end, I resisted temptation—for the moment—and settled on a different and innocuous activity: talking on the phone. Since Marvel McLogan hadn't yet called to tell me the outcome of Willa Bradstone's visit, I suspected it might be unfavorable. She'd have wanted to broadcast good news immediately.

Marvel answered on the fourth ring, sounding sleepy. I glanced at the clock. It was nine-thirty. Certainly not too early an hour for someone who raised collies.

"Oh, Jennet," she said. "I was going to call you later. I wanted to thank you for coming to my rescue. You'll never know how much it helped."

"What happened after I left?" I asked.

"Willa was late; she got lost. Suzette kept threatening to leave with Mandy, but it all worked out. I took your advice and told her about the mix-up. Would you believe that Willa made the same kind of mistake when she bought her first puppy?"

"Then she understands."

"She was seventeen at the time."

"Anyone can make a mistake at any age," I said.

"Willa took Mandy back to Ohio with her. She needs time to think about whether she wants to give up the puppy."

And she could think better with Mandy in her own kennel. That sounded natural enough and ominous.

"What about Suzette?" I asked.

"Suzette took Brandy home. Brandy's such a sweetheart. I think Suzette will warm up to her in time."

I couldn't imagine anyone not warming up to a fluffy golden collie puppy immediately, but I saw a possible problem with the arrangement. "What happens if Willa decides to let Suzette have Mandy?"

"Then Suzette will have two puppies. Litter sisters"

"Will that be all right with her?"

"I guess so. She didn't say. What I think is that it won't happen. Willa didn't want to refuse Suzette outright. She'll give me the bad news over the phone."

Possession, I remembered thinking, was nine-tenths of the law. Now Willa had her pick-of-the-litter puppy. Suzette had Brandy and the money she had offered to pay for the stud fee. On the surface, it seemed like a logical rearrangement, if one discounted the heartache of separation.

"So the situation is unresolved," I said.

"Officially, yes."

"Are you still worried that the mix-up will tarnish your reputation?"

"Well, it isn't going to help. I didn't swear Willa to secrecy, and dog people will gossip." Marvel sighed. "Willa promised to make her decision in a week."

Another week to wait, I thought as I snapped the phone shut.

Now with the Brandy-and-Mandy mix-up in another phase, I'd better redouble my efforts to find Sandy, which was easier said than done.

~ * ~

By ten the last of the fog dissipated. Weak rays of sun stole through the clouds, and the day promised to be warm. I took the dogs for another walk, baked a batch of blueberry muffins, and contemplated the rest of the day as I sampled them.

How empty the house seemed without Crane. How hard it was to remember a time when he hadn't been a beloved, powerful presence within its walls.

With Crane gone, I'd be happy with a sandwich for dinner. School work didn't interest me, nor did resting. At four o'clock I succumbed to temptation and walked across the lane to Camille's house. Her key felt like a twenty-pound weight in my hand.

Halley and Sky padded along happily at my side. Back in the house Candy and Gemmy were barking their protest at the injustice of their lives. I'd make it up to them later with still another walk and extra biscuits.

The mixed annuals I'd planted for Camille looked lonely and thirsty. Since Memorial Day was fast approaching, I decided to buy geraniums in smaller containers for the porch and give each one its own miniature flag—and to remember to keep the plants watered. That wouldn't fool anyone who had already been in the house, but he might think the homeowner's return was imminent and find another place to stay.

I unlocked the front door and stood on the threshold, listening. All was quiet inside except for the ticking of the living room clock. Sky and Halley slipped inside like shadows, neither one of them sounding an alarm. The house was undeniably empty. I should be all right.

I went straight to the half-bath on the first floor. To my surprise I found a collection of throwaways in the wastebasket. Dumping them on the small table Camille had set up for her guests' convenience, I examined them. An empty candy wrapper, a plastic water bottle, and a crumpled tissue with a red lipstick print.

The intruder was female then. She carried her own water and a snack and took time to apply lipstick. Also, she wasn't very bright to leave evidence of home invasion behind.

Except how could these items identify her? And how did she get inside Camille's house? Most important of all, when had she been here? Possibly after we'd left or early this morning, if I believed that Crane had checked the basket in the half bath.

My first thought was Anne. My second was Sara, but the easiest answer is seldom the right one. There must be more to find.

In the kitchen the jar was in the same place on the counter. On the living room area rug, I noticed a fall of green glitter where the Christmas tree had stood. Something Leonora had missed when she'd vacuumed. How unlike her to miss anything, but leftover glitter wasn't anything out of the ordinary.

Now, how had the intruder entered the house and what had she been doing in Camille's sewing room?

Every question led to another one. For me, the most puzzling was the strawberry preserves. Surely she didn't eat them out of the jar without bread or toast; and why hadn't she taken the jar with her?

Because she planned to come back again. And again. Anytime.

Apprehension returned, bringing with it a sense of oppressive silence. The house was too quiet, my breathing too loud. At the least I should be hearing the clicking of nails on the hardwood floor as the dogs explored the house.

Where were those collies?

"Halley!" I called. "Sky?"

They didn't answer and didn't come.

Quickly I peered into the other rooms on the first floor and climbed to the second level.

They were waiting for me at the top of the staircase, both wagging their tails. Sky gave an excited little yip. Holly's blue plush spaniel lay in the hallway at her feet. She picked it up with her mouth and tossed it at me.

This, too, hadn't been here last night, but there was nothing mysterious about that. On previous visits, Holly had allowed Sky to play with the toy.

"Good dogs," I said absently and relocated the spaniel to Camille's bedroom.

There was no one else in the yellow Victorian. I would swear to it. Still, I walked down the hall to the sewing room where I'd seen the light. Everything in here was exactly as I'd last seen it. Except for the window.

It was open.

Nineteen

This must be the way the intruder had entered the house. The careless female intruder who left her trash behind for the homeowner to find and forgot to close a window. But how? This was a second-story window.

I set the candle lamp on the sewing machine and lowered the window. As I attempted to lock it, I discovered that the latch was broken. Apparently it had been forced. By the secret visitor, no doubt, and recently because Camille would never compromise the security of her beloved Victorian by neglecting to secure all of the entrances.

She would have known about a broken latch as she spent hours in her sewing room and opened windows as soon as the weather grew warm. Even the ones in her bedroom. Even during the night.

"Aren't you afraid of burglars getting in?" I'd once asked her.

"How would they get up this high? There's no way." She added, "I'd never leave the first-floor windows open though."

This one had been closed last evening. That was certain. I sighed. Or was it?

I'd noticed the sewing machine, the fabric on the daybed, and the dressmaker's mannequin in her pink dress, but not the windows.

Still I remembered that the room, like the entire house, had been stuffy. An open window would have let the night air in.

But darn. I couldn't be sure.

Start with the assumption this was the way the intruder entered, I told myself. Either yesterday after we left, or early this morning under the cover of fog. Now, how could anyone reach the window without climbing a ladder?

By using the roof of the porch as a stepping stone? Not unless he was ten feet tall, and I'd been picturing a woman of average height or smaller. An Anne or a Sara. Not only that. Who would attempt to break into a house in plain view of Jonquil Lane?

How much more sensible to go around to the back and try to get inside that way. There Camille's perennial gardens swept down to an unnamed and mostly untraveled road, running parallel to acres of pastureland. That was a perfect setting for surreptitious activities. But then I'd already decided that the intruder wasn't very bright.

I replaced the lamp on the windowsill and took one more look as the postcard picture vista unfolded before me. My own house—that is, our house—sat across the lane in a surround of spring growth, with its pale green color shining in the sunlight.

Of all the rooms, I found myself in the kitchen most often. During the day, that is. The window above the sink gave me a clear view of the yellow Victorian, of Camille's comings and goings when she was in residence, and of her company.

I felt a soft velvet brush against my ankle. It was Halley no doubt wondering when I was going to move away from the window. Sky had retrieved the blue spaniel and stood in the doorway wagging her tail.

"That's Holly's toy," I told Sky, taking it gently from her. She followed its progress wistfully as I set it on the daybed behind Camille's fabric.

Not that all of my collies didn't have toys of their own at home.

Suddenly I felt like an intruder, I and my dogs. Still, I knew Camille would want me to make a thorough search, would never consider my actions intrusive. She'd surely want to know who had been prowling through her house and usurping her possessions, but I didn't want to tell her just yet, not when there was a chance we could discover what was going on and end it.

"Let's move on," I said.

To the master bedroom. Then to the full bath. Finally to the guest rooms where the doors were ajar, just the way Crane and I had left them.

That reminded me. I would have to tell Crane about the broken latch. He'd be able to fix it and maybe come up with an explanation for how the intruder had managed to scale a three-story Victorian house without a ladder.

He wouldn't be happy I'd disregarded his wishes.

Oh, well. Finding this additional concrete evidence of home invasion was worth taking a risk. He'd have to agree.

Now what else could I find?

Everything in Camille's bedroom looked the way I remembered it, except for the tops of her dresser and lingerie chest. She'd taken her antique dresser set and jewelry case with her, along with cherished mementoes like the picture of her first collie, Snowdrop.

In the guest rooms I examined the comforters and pillows again, looking for the indentation of a body. There was none. No one had taken a nap on a borrowed bed, and the bathroom that had been left in pristine condition was still that way.

Back in the kitchen I opened drawers and cabinets, knowing they'd be neat. Even Camille's junk drawer was organized, but on the shelf where she kept decorative potholders and linens, the towel on top of the stack was damp. Somebody had used it recently, refolded it neatly, and put it back in place.

Used it to…? Dry a knife used to spread preserves on the bread I'd never found? To dry her hands? Or wipe up a spill?

As usual, every unanswered question led to another. For me the most important of them were who had broken into the yellow Victorian and for what purpose.

As far as I could tell, nothing of value had been taken from the house, nor had anything been left behind except for the trash in the wastebasket and the jar of strawberry preserves.

My best chance of discovering the identity of this unknown person was to watch Camille's house from my kitchen window. Not a non-stop surveillance, of course; that was impossible. But I'd make it a point to look this way several times a day, especially in the early morning and late evening. From now on, I'd pay attention when the dogs started barking and not assume they were alerting me to visiting deer or hungry rabbits.

With a sense of incompleteness weighing me down, I called the dogs to heel. There was nothing else I could learn here.

This alien presence in the yellow Victorian was one more development in a month of extraordinary happenings. All I could do was add it to the list.

~ * ~

The next day in my classroom at Marston, I guided my class through the confusion and convolutions of *A Midsummer Night's Dream* and thought of my hike in the Jonquil Lane woods. Even with mosquitoes and snakes, plowing through the woods had been infinitely easier.

After reading each speech I translated it into simple language and dealt with a host of questions. Names proved to be a problem. Helena and Hermia. Why did they both start with 'H'? Who had weird names like the actors? Bottom, Flute, Snout? Hyppolyta, the Amazon queen, fascinated them.

"That's Wonder Woman's mother," Jimmy informed us. "Does that mean the Duke of Athens is her father and she's a duchess?"

I hadn't expected anyone to make this connection. In truth, I'd never thought a comic character would find her way into our study of Shakespeare's comedy.

Since I prided myself on my teaching skills, I couldn't dismiss this inquiry as irrelevant, although I suspected it was Jimmy's attempt to leave me floundering for an answer.

"I suppose so," I said. "But Wonder Woman—her real name is Diana, right?—won't make her appearance for years yet."

Jimmy smirked, but no one argued with me. Commentary delayed the even flow of the play, not to mention the end. Everybody, including me, was eager to reach the grand finale so that the groups could begin rehearsing the scenes they were going to put on for Leonora's class. I'd been setting aside time out of every class period for preparation. This group work had rapidly become the high point of the hour.

The hottest topic was costuming. Bits and pieces of old Halloween costumes and masks were being recycled, and one enterprising young man was fashioning an ass's head for Bottom out of *papier-mâché*.

Every day I congratulated myself on my innovative idea.

We reached the end of the assigned reading early. As the students moved their desks into cozy groups, I scanned the next day's work. *In another part of the wood...* Attention always increased briefly when we came to a new scene.

In another part of the class, conversation had veered away from preparation to the Band's coming field trip to Cedar Point in Ohio. I sauntered over to the circle of desks and asked to see their plans, which they swore were completed. To my surprise, they were well on their way.

"Wonderful," I said. "This group can go first."

That didn't please them, but it brought an end to the Cedar Point talk.

In still another part of the class, Suzy pulled a long purple gown out of a backpack to a chorus of oh's and ah's.

"It's my sister's old prom dress," she announced. "Does it look like something Titania would wear?"

With a little imagination. "Definitely," I said. "It's lovely."

"I don't know how I'm going to make wings, though. Does she need wings, Mrs. Ferguson?"

"Well… Every fairy I've ever seen has them."

This set the would-be thespians into gales of laughter, which hadn't been my intention. I'd been thinking of fairy pictures.

In the front of the room, near the door, Andrea and Nancy were arguing about Titania's crown. Was it called a diadem or tiara or coronet? What was the difference? And wouldn't a garland of fresh flowers, not those plastic ones, be better than cardboard painted gold?

"You decide, Mrs. Ferguson," Andrea said.

"Flowers would be charming for a fairy queen."

And great oversized wings made of... Gauze and paper painted in soft shades of mauve and aqua and yellow?

Another part of the wood, I thought. Forest dwellers don't have costume problems.

~ * ~

With so much happening in my life, it was only natural that I let Sandy's disappearance fall to a lower rung on my priority list. The little collie puppy had been missing for quite a while now. No one had responded to my posted notices, and Brent's reward hadn't even netted an inquiry.

I thought the puppy was gone forever, possibly picked up by a compassionate motorist and taken to another area. Or dead.

Josie hadn't lost faith in my ability to bring her puppy back. She called me that afternoon after school, apologizing for bothering me but… Had I found Sandy yet?

I cringed at the fragile hope in her voice.

"Not yet," I said. "Maybe you'd better prepare yourself. We may never find her."

As if she hadn't heard me Josie said, "My mom says maybe I can keep her. She has a whole long list of conditions, but that's something, isn't it?"

I agreed, while wondering if Josie's mother felt it was safe to make a concession at this point when the pup's return was doubtful. I never used to be so cynical.

"Sandy is going to be so big when we get her back," Josie said.

"Puppies usually grow fast."

"Do you think she'll remember me?"

"Well…" Sandy had spent one afternoon and one night in Josie's home before running away. How many images and emotions stayed in a little puppy's mind? Should I encourage Sandy to keep hoping for her 'Lassie-come-home' reunion?

"I don't know what she'll remember," I said, "but you two can start making new memories."

As soon as Sandy comes home. If that ever happened.

I didn't think it would.

Twenty

'Kidnap Suspect Spotted on Island'

A beef stew bubbled merrily on the burner and biscuits waited for their turn in the oven while the pie finished baking. The dogs kept their vigil as close to the stove as I'd allow them. With dinner mostly done, I seized my chance to read the *Banner* story that had caught my attention when I first opened the paper.

Johnston Holliday, a suspect in the kidnapping of Briana and Bennett Cooper, had been sighted on Mackinac Island sitting on the porch of a hotel by three elderly women on the first day of their vacation. He wasn't registered at the hotel, nor had he remained on the porch for long.

"But it was him," their spokeswoman said. "Sitting and reading the paper as clear as day. No question about it. Then, poof! He was gone."

Where he'd gone she couldn't say, but she implied there was something uncanny about his disappearance. I was tempted to believe her. No one but the vacationing ladies had seen him. It isn't easy to go unnoticed on an island.

A photograph of Holliday accompanied the article, along with an update on the case and another plea from the distraught mother for the return of her children.

I studied the picture carefully. I hadn't seen this one before. Johnston Holliday was quite attractive with his mustache, which gave him a dapper, sophisticated look. He looked relatively harmless—which had no doubt been an asset in a career of crime.

Apparently Sara Hall wasn't traveling with Holliday, and there was no mention of the ransom money.

Holliday appeared to be moving steadily in one direction: north. He might be planning to go all the way to the Upper Peninsula. What made him think he could hide? In the remotest of areas, there might be someone who'd recognize him.

To my knowledge, this was the first time he had allowed himself to be seen in a public place.

I suppose he thought that being on an island removed him from the threat of being recognized. Not true when the island was a popular tourist destination. Especially not true when fellow vacationers were observant.

Crane joined me at the table, still in uniform, still wearing his gun belt. Candy padded over to lie beside him and earned a pat on the head.

"Did you read the Holliday story?" I asked.

"I heard about it," he said.

"You'd think the man had a cloak to make himself invisible."

"Sooner or later he'll slip up and forget to put it on."

I folded the paper neatly and noticed that Candy's move had brought her closer to the stove. I'd have to watch her. Last Sunday, while I was clearing the table, she'd snatched a chicken breast from the roaster and wolfed it down before I realized what she'd done. The stew was boiling hot.

I wondered if Brent's man, Scott, had billed him for a vacation to Mackinac Island. But what I said was, "I wonder where the twins have been all this time."

"I hope they're okay," he said.

"You'd think someone would remember seeing them."

"Unless they're tucked away someplace. It's been a long time since they were snatched."

I suspected that he was referring to their bodies.

"You don't think they're dead, do you?"

"I deal with facts, Jennet. Nobody's reported seeing them since that breakfast at Clovers on the day you saw the balloon. Little kids need someone to take care of them. They need to be fed and have a safe place to sleep at night."

Like a little lost puppy.

"They may be with Sara," I said.

Which was what I wanted to think. From a hot air balloon to a restaurant for a pancake breakfast to the grave? That was untenable. No one had seen Sara either. She might well have shared the children's fate, but I preferred to think that she'd spirited them away from Holliday. Perhaps someone had responded to another plea for help.

Crane covered my hand with his own. "It's possible they're still alive somewhere, honey." He rose and picked up his toolbox from beside the kitchen door. "I'm going over to Camille's. You stay here."

"With my stew? Sure. I can't leave it cooking on the stove. It should be done, though."

"I won't be long," he said quickly.

He was going in his capacity as a deputy sheriff with a gun belt strapped to his waist and, incidentally, as a handyman. My job was to see to that he had a hot dinner when he returned.

I got up and swirled a wooden spoon through the stew. Whenever I made a beef stew, I thought about a similar dinner Camille had cooked for her former husband, an abusive and vile man. She'd added poisonous mushrooms to the mix, intending to free herself from his tyranny once and for all.

Fate had stepped in, however, and saved her from committing a crime, but that was a story from the past.

Always, before he took a bite of my stew, Crane pretended to search for mushrooms, although we both agreed that attempted murder was no laughing matter.

I scooped the bottom of the Dutch oven and brought up diced carrots, potatoes, and a chunk of tender meat swimming in gravy. A verse from *Macbeth* slid through my mind.

> *Double, double, toil and trouble;*
> *Fire burn and cauldron bubble.*

This is your dinner, not a witch's brew, I thought.

Why couldn't I stop thinking about ghastly things tonight? Woods and gingerbread houses; evil women in peaked hats, and children lured to their doom.

One day, I thought, *I'll open the* Banner *and read a story about children found and kidnappers apprehended. And, for good measure, on that same day I'll find Sandy.*

~ * ~

A half hour later, I was still waiting for Crane.

I turned the stew to 'warm', fed the dogs their dinner, and set the dining room table. The apple pie was cooling, and I'd left the biscuits, unbaked, on the counter. Every now and then I glanced across the lane at the yellow Victorian. There was a light in the sewing room tonight, and the entire first floor was lit up.

He'd had time to fix the latch and walk through the house at least four times. What could he be doing there so long? What could he have found that I overlooked?

When I saw the last light extinguished, I slid the biscuits into the oven and began mixing the salad. Crane would want to take a quick shower before dinner; with luck he'd be ready when the biscuits were.

The dogs were already barking at the side door, anticipating his return. He let himself in and told them to Sit.

"What did you find?" I asked.

"For one, the way in. The side door was unlocked."

"But how can that be? We locked it." Remembering back over the months, I realized that Leonora had locked it. It never occurred to me to double check.

Camille's side door wasn't visible from our house, unless I walked to the edge of the porch. I'd always focused on the front of the house.

Here was one more facet of the puzzle. "What was the point of turning on a lamp in the sewing room then?"

"I don't know, but the latch is fixed now; and I checked all the others."

"What else did you find?" I asked.

"Three things. A crumpled-up napkin, a white Delicious Do-nut bag, and a coffee-stained paper cup with lipstick stain on it.

My, he was thorough. "What color lipstick?" I asked.

He paused for just a moment, frowning. "Red. Dark red."

"She was over there this morning," I said.

"When you were."

"It must have been sometime after I left." I'd hoped Crane had forgotten my little confession. I should have known he didn't forget.

Quickly I said, "I had Halley and Sky with me."

"Sky! She's our quietest collie."

I didn't think he meant quietest. Maybe least aggressive or shyest.

"She has a nice set of teeth," I said, and to change the subject added, "You're sure that woman isn't there now, hiding somewhere."

He cast me one of those incredulous deputy sheriff glares. "I'm sure."

"Then I don't understand—unless she's looking for something. But in Camille's house? I can't imagine what it would be."

"Camille has a lot of valuable stuff. As far as I can tell, it's all there. But this woman might be planning a heist. Checking the place out."

Biding her time. Admiring the silver and crystal. Making lists.

"That's possible," I said. "Maybe that's it!"

"You're not to go over there again," Crane said. "Even with the dogs."

He had dropped the diplomatic phrasing and left out the touch of honey. I bristled at his official tone. I could have sworn we'd moved beyond that point in our relationship, but he was talking to me as if I were the intruder.

"I'm speaking as your local law enforcer," he added.

"Well, then, I guess I'll have to keep my distance. But shouldn't you wrap yellow tape around the house?"

The slightest glint of amusement flashed in his frosty gray eyes. "I might just do that," he said.

~ * ~

Later that evening, while skimming the *Banner* to make sure I hadn't missed anything important, I came across an enticing sidebar. *'Who is Sara Hall?'*

Below the article were pictures of Briana and Bennett and two other young kidnapping victims from past years whose disappearances had never been solved.

Who is the female suspect in the abduction of Briana and Bennett Cooper? Is she a woman pining for a child of her own as the twins' mother claims? Or did she make the age-old mistake of trusting the wrong man?

Not much was known about Sara Hall before she whisked the Cooper twins away on a water park excursion. The reporter referred to her as the mystery woman. Sara had grown up in Wyoming and come to Michigan as a teenager to live with her aunt. She was still young, in her mid-twenties, and apparently her only work history was a job with Lambs and Ducks Day Care Center in Oakpoint, Michigan.

Her ambition was to teach kindergarten, but she hadn't attended college and didn't have plans to do so. Her fellow employees didn't know her well but agreed that she was wonderful with young children. They described her as wholesome, enthusiastic about life, and conscientious about her duties.

Apparently the impeccable references with which she'd obtained the position of babysitter to Briana and Bennett had been forged. Her former employers were imaginary. Mrs. Cooper had been duped. She believed that Sara, knowing the children's grandfather was wealthy, had planned the kidnapping even before approaching her.

I seemed to see Sara again, flying in the hot air balloon laughing down at the entranced collies, then letting her orange scarf with the hidden SOS float to the ground.

She seemed too nice to be anything but a victim.

Twenty-one

I told Leonora about the unlocked door the next morning as we made our way to Oakpoint through heavy white fog. In some respects her memory of the day we'd taken apart Camille's holiday decorations was a little hazy. Other details stayed in her mind.

"You were carrying the tree outside and making popcorn strings for the birds," she said. "I was taking out trash bags. Why do you always have the glamorous jobs?"

I gave her a sly smile. "Because I was in charge of the clean-up. That reminds me. When you vacuumed in the living room you left green glitter on the rug. For the next wedding we'll change duties."

"I should say. The next wedding will be mine."

"Are you thinking of Jake in the role of groom?"

"Maybe," she said. "A girl can dream."

Neither of us mentioned Jake's other favorite blonde, my sister, Julia. Making a mental note to call Julia, who had been suspiciously quiet lately, I said, "Let's go back to that day. You were working in the kitchen. Tell me everything you did. Every little detail."

"I emptied the sugar and flour canisters and cleaned the counter. There was no jar of preserves anywhere. I checked the refrigerator and threw out the perishables. Then I swept the floor. All the trash bags were at the side door. I took them out together."

"Then you made sure the door was locked?"

She squinted into the distance. "Is the lane closed ahead? I thought I saw a flashing light."

"I can't tell with all the fog. Just slow down. Be ready for anything. About the door..."

"I closed it. Didn't it automatically lock?"

"You have to push it way in."

"Oh no! Then it's my fault. All those priceless heirlooms Camille had... Everything…"

"Relax," I said. "She still has them. Nothing seems to be missing."

"I feel terrible," Leonora said. "I have to call Camille and apologize."

"No, you don't. She doesn't know."

"But she has to."

"Right now, everything is under control. I'll tell her when she and Gilbert get back."

Our lane *was* closed ahead. Leonora frowned into the rear view mirror and turned on her signal. "Let's hope whoever is behind me sees it."

The fog was thicker now. Folds of condensation moved with the car as if they had a life of their own. Eerie pinpoints of light tried to make a dent in the dense white wall. Visibility was close to zero, but there was no turning back.

Even carpooling with Leonora, the long commute to Marston High School was my least favorite part of the day, especially in inclement weather. I'd never get used to it and once again fantasized about teaching in a school closer to home, no more than twenty minutes away. I could put all that saved time to good use.

Someday I'd do it.

~ * ~

The injustice of it. The ignominy. Miles and miles through treacherous fog. Over an hour of driving into danger only to hear a wail from a girl who was, one would think, beyond wailing age. Meg held half of a broken pencil in her hand; the other half was on the floor. Her pretty face was contorted with rage.

"Ray broke my pencil, Mrs. Ferguson. What are you going to do about it?"

Nothing.

I went back to my desk and opened the top drawer. Inside I had a supply of pens, along with everything I'd need in the course of a typical day.

"Here," I said, handing her a pen. "English papers have to be written in ink. You know that."

With a triumphant smirk at Ray, Meg slammed the pen on top of her textbook.

"What are you going to do to him?" she demanded.

Turn him over to the pencil police?

"You should apologize to her, Ray."

"She's lying," he said under his breath.

"Am not!"

The noise level in class dropped and disappeared. We all waited.

"Sorry," he mumbled at last.

"And one of you, pick up that pencil piece."

This was my one freshman class, my least favorite because on the whole, the group was immature and surprisingly loud for the first hour of the day. They hated to stay in their assigned seats and loved to play juvenile pranks on one another and, occasionally, on me.

With a smaller group of eleventh graders, the second period was easier, and by the time World Literature class streamed into the room, I was ready to meet the challenge of Shakespeare from a sophomore's point of view. We read the day's assignment together. It went well in spite of what seemed like endless plot complications to keep track of.

In another part of the wood, I thought. Tomorrow all sorts of exciting things were going to happen. In the play, that is. Now it was time for group work.

The mechanics of the project were simple. In actuality, the students were putting on fragments of scenes. For the sake of brevity, they were allowed to trim the speeches, although they couldn't tamper with the language. I'd offered extra credit A's to those who memorized their parts. The others were allowed to use index cards. Cards versus memorization was the object of a current complaint.

"Reading from cards is going to look phony," Andrea said.

She had the part of Helena, and several in her group had already committed to memorizing their lines.

Ken, who was playing Lysander, chimed in with a complaint of his own.

> *O Helen, goddess, nymph, perfect, divine!*
> *To what, my love, shall I compare thine eyen?*

"I can't say that with a straight face. Heck, I can't even say it."

"You just did," Celia pointed out. "But you mispronounced eyes."

Every now and then I second-guessed my brilliant idea, but as with a foggy morning commute, there was no turning back.

"Trade you parts?" Alec said.

"It's too late." Andrea, who was naturally bossy, had appointed herself the group leader. "We're going first, remember?"

Apparently she was the only one who did.

"I have an idea, Mrs. Ferguson," Alec said. "Why don't we flip a coin for first up?"

"I don't want to wait around," Gail said. "Get it over with."

It was time for the teacher to step in. "Somebody has to start. I thought you people were ready."

Since the only response was a collective memory loss, I moved onto the next group where the purple prom dress had been joined by a wide leather belt with a flashy, turquoise-studded buckle.

"Who's going to wear this?" I asked.

"It's for the Duke," Bert said. "Isn't it neat?"

Fine, I thought. *He'll look like a Halloween cowboy.*

~ * ~

The long school day dwindled down to minutes. Again Leonora and I were on the freeway heading north, this time without fog. Long ago I'd learned to leave the cares and frustration of the day behind in Oakpoint. My after-school hours were already crammed with a generous helping of both.

Sandy, Brandy and Mandy, and, even though they weren't technically my concern, Briana and Bennett Cooper. Sometimes I felt that I should be doing something to help bring the twins home. In unguarded moments an idea shimmered for a sliver of a second in my mind, then disappeared. Was I overlooking something important, a stray detail no one else would be likely to know?

If so, I couldn't hold onto the shimmer long enough to understand what it meant.

At home, I disregarded Crane's wishes yet once again—sort of. Trailed by all four collies, who anticipated a riotous romp through the stately rooms of the yellow Victorian, I walked around the side of the house and made sure the side door was locked.

Unless she threw a rock through a window the mysterious girl or woman couldn't let herself into the house. Camille's possessions were safe.

Now we would never know the intruder's identity or her reason for prowling through another person's home.

I'd continue to keep watch over Camille's property though, just in case this particular episode wasn't over.

~ * ~

The next day, home after a longer than usual staff meeting, I looked at the kitchen clock, investigated the contents of the refrigerator, and set out again for take-out dinners.

Clovers was the only restaurant I knew where the food tasted like home cooking and sometimes surpassed it. Inside I found Brent Fowler being served a plate of steaming meatloaf and mashed potatoes. He had both soup and salad, together with a breadbasket.

"Jennet!" he said. "Join me?"

"In a minute."

I ordered two stuffed cabbage dinners and a whole cherry pie, then a cup of coffee to drink while waiting for them. As I slid into Brent's window booth, I noticed the map of Michigan pushed to one side to make way for his dishes.

"I was going to drop over later," he said. "My man, Scott, is hot on the trail of Holliday. He turned up in Bear Lake."

"Where's that?" I asked.

Brent pointed to a large red X on the map. "Still on the east coast of the state. Not far from Standish."

"Then he's not going farther north," I said. "I had visions of him hiding out in the Upper Peninsula."

"It looks like he's heading south again. Coming back home maybe."

"If this area is his home. He's acting like he's been on vacation rather than on the run."

Brent paused to scoop up a piece of meatloaf. It looked good, thick and topped with mushroom gravy. Maybe I should order another two dinners for tomorrow.

"It's hard to tell what he's up to," Brent said.

"In all this time, he must have seen a paper." He had, I remembered. He'd been observed reading a newspaper on the porch of his hotel, if indeed he'd been there. "Holliday must know the police are looking for him."

"He's not acting like it."

"Your private investigator is good at losing him," I said. "I'll bet I could do a better job."

He winked at me. "I'll bet you could too. Unfortunately you're busy with school and Crane."

"And lost dogs and dogs with the wrong owners," I added.

"I feel like we're moving backwards in slow motion. I promised Eric's family that his killer would rot in jail. It isn't happening."

"It will. But I know what you mean. It's high time something happened."

As soon as I'd said that, I wished I could take it back. Or be more specific. I wanted something good to happen. Not just anything.

Twenty-two

When two days passed and nothing earthshaking happened, I breathed a sigh of relief. It appeared no one up there had heard me, that life was going to go on without a ripple, a succession of cookie cutter days, all the same.

For the present, that was good.

Josie, having grown impatient with the status quo, called again. "Mom says I'm bothering you, Mrs. Ferguson, but is there any news yet?"

"I'm afraid not," I said. "And you're no bother, Josie. Call me anytime."

I realized I might regret issuing that invitation. In truth, I hadn't looked for Sandy lately. By now her trail, never red hot, was cold. My search had turned passive as I waited for somebody to contact me.

I had to change that. But how?

"I've called all the animal hospitals within a thirty-mile radius," Josie said. "No one brought a collie puppy in, and I keep calling all the shelters."

"That's good."

Assuming someone had picked Sandy up, this told me the person wasn't conscientious about having a vet examine her. Or she'd been taken far away from Lapeer County. Or, of course, the little pup was dead.

"We're not going to find her, are we?" Josie said quietly.

The air of resignation in her voice tugged at my heart. "Nobody knows the future, Josie."

She sighed. "Gosh, that's like what Mom says. 'We don't know what tomorrow will bring.'"

I thought of all the lost-dog-found stories I'd read or heard in my life. Dogs left behind on vacation turning up at home sometimes years later. Pets being reunited with their owners after natural disasters. I could tell a few happy ending tales of my own involving my collies and those of my friends.

The problem was Sandy hadn't been with Josie long enough to think of Josie's house as her home.

"We'll keep looking for her and hope for the best," I said.

I closed the cell phone gently, adding to myself, "But where?"

~ * ~

One person in Foxglove Corners who did know what was going to happen in the future—sometimes—was my friend, Lucy Hazen. A celebrated author of horror novels for young people, Lucy was a multi-talented lady.

Along with reading tea leaves, she knew when a disaster was imminent. When a tornado was forming or some other dark force was making its way into our lives, Lucy often had prior knowledge of the event. I wished I'd been able to consult her earlier.

Lucy had been away, visiting her sister in Texas. She'd timed her vacation to escape the hottest of the southwestern weather, but she should be home now. With the cell phone still in my hand, I punched in her number.

"Come over anytime, Jennet," Lucy said. "The sooner the better. I'm missing a month's worth of news."

"A lot's been happening. As usual I'm involved in some of it."

"I wouldn't expect anything less," she said, and we settled a time: the next day after school.

Lucy lived in an atmospheric country house she'd christened Dark Gables. It sat far back from Spruce Road in a surround of private woods. Well protected by towering evergreens and hardwoods, it provided Lucy with the solitude she craved for her writing.

Visits to Lucy always included cups of tea and fortunes and sometimes a hint of future happenings. Could Lucy possibly shed any light on the whereabouts of the kidnapped twins? Having just returned from Texas, did she even know about the abduction?

I soon found out. When I stopped by the next day, I saw that Lucy had a stack of newspapers on her desk in the sunroom at the back of the house, the one bright oasis at Dark Gables. Easily, a month's worth, I estimated.

In spite of a month under the Texas sun, Lucy had retained her fair complexion, and she looked rested and even radiant. Whether she was working alone or entertaining company, Lucy was always impeccably attired in black. Her jewelry was always gold. Today a bright sun brooch shone on the deep V neckline of her dress.

Everybody needs a month-long vacation, I thought.

She had the water boiling for tea. Cups and saucers were set out on a wicker coffee table with a plate of sugar cookies. Lucy's elegant blue merle, Sky, not so long ago a puppy, lay on the wicker sofa, with her front paws crossed.

She never took her eyes off the cookies. Sky liked sweets as well as any dog, but she was quite different from Candy. Gentle and genteel, I thought. Polite. Like my own Sky. Knowing Lucy would offer her a tasty tidbit in time, she wasn't going to help herself.

Although Lucy and I were engrossed in our conversation, there were still a dozen cookies on the plate ten minutes later.

"Good dog," I said. "What a good, good dog!"

Sky flattened her ears against her head and wagged her tail. She knew that, but it was nice to hear.

The teakettle whistled and Lucy poured boiling water over measures of Queen Mary. "I've missed the leaves," she said. "My sister, Lorinda, is a non-believer. We drank that strong Louisiana coffee all the time I was in Texas."

Lucy had a collection of teacups adorned with flowery patterns, but the plain white ones were best for telling fortunes. An important symbol might easily get lost in a spray of painted forget-me-nots.

"How did Sky like Texas?" I asked.

"Not much. It's too hot. We're both glad to be home. Everything is so cool and green here." She gave the leaves a brisk stir. "Tell me what you've been up to."

Between sips of tea, I went through the list: hot air balloons, an SOS from the sky, collies in peril, a stranger in Camille's house, and the missing twins.

"All in one month," she said. "Amazing. I've been reading news stories about the Cooper twins, and Brent brought me up to date. He was so happy he bought Skyway Tours. Like a kid with a new toy."

"Brent?"

"We had dinner together last night," she said.

"Well..." While I was wondering what to say, Lucy added, "You're not mixed up in the case, are you?"

"Not any more. I just saw the people fly by in the balloon."

"And the woman with the auburn hair asked you to help her."

"Indirectly. And I didn't."

"Well, what could you have done?

Lucy wasn't the first to ask me that question. The answer was always the same. Not a thing. Still, both question and answer haunted me.

"Do you have any premonitions about the twins?" I asked.

She reached for one of the old newspapers. It was turned to the second page where the article on Sara Hall was located. For a long while she stared at the print.

"No," she said. "Not at this time. Let's see what the tea leaves say."

After many fortune-telling sessions, I knew what to do: Turn the cup toward myself three times, drain the excess liquid, let the leaves form into patterns. Make a wish. *The charm's wound up.*

It all seemed highly theatrical, if I stopped to think what I was doing. Of course I didn't. I just turned, drained, and wished. I had a superstitious streak and in the past had ample proof of Lucy's powers.

Lucy took the cup from me and peered into it. "All's peaceful in your home," she said. "There are no upheavals, no threats. Wait!" She was frowning.

I held my breath; Lucy continued to scrutinize the formations inside the cup.

"What?"

"I see something near your home. It's dark and misshapen. I can't make out what it is."

"Animal? Vegetable? Mineral?"

"I can't tell. Are you positive you're not involved in anything dangerous?"

"Not that I know of."

Nonetheless, I stopped to consider. The kidnapping case was in Mac's capable hands. Camille's doors were locked against all future intruders. Searching for a lost puppy couldn't possibly have anything to do with a sinister shape closing in on my home.

"Tell me more about this misshapen object," I said.

"I see Evil. And Danger."

"Don't stop there."

Lucy turned the cup around and around. Her bracelets jangled. Sky tilted her head and gave a little whimper. While I waited for Lucy to speak, time seemed to leap ahead. The world turned at an impossible speed. Seasons changed.

I reined in my runaway thoughts. At this moment I wanted nothing more than to be in my own house, far from portents in a china cup. But I'd agreed to have my tea leaves read. I'd looked forward to Lucy assuring me that my wish would come true. All of a sudden, without warning, fun had turned on me.

"At least tell me what to do about it."

"I don't think you can stop it," Lucy said. "But you can meet it head-on. Whatever it is."

~ * ~

Evil. Danger.

On a fragrant spring afternoon when the daffodils on the lane were sheer golden perfection, thoughts of an evil, misshapen force dissolved in the fresh air.

I allowed myself one practical thought. How could Lucy tell the encroaching object was misshapen if she didn't know its shape?

In my experience, Lucy's premonitions had always been reliable. The tea leaves, less so. Besides, where would this dark shape come from?

Out of the woods.

I glanced across the lane where shadows were already dancing amid the trees. Snakes, coyotes, deer, rabbits and small game—yes. Danger possibly. Evil? No.

I looked away from the woods, found solace in the graceful lines of my green Victorian farmhouse, and went inside.

The dogs were eager for biscuits, fresh water and their walk, not in that order. I leashed the wild ones, and we set out for Squill Road.

Camille's perennials seemed to have grown a foot since I'd walked over to lock the side door. When I'd first seen the yellow Victorian two years ago, walking this same way with Halley, I imagined that they were trying, incidentally or subconsciously, to hide the house. From the beginning, I'd thought of Camille's giant plants as sentient beings.

At the time Camille was tending her gardens diligently. She had now been gone since January. If she stayed away much longer, she'd come home to a virtual jungle.

The red geraniums I'd placed around the porch with their miniature flags gave the old Victorian a lived-in look, but people who buy spring plants and keep their lawns mowed don't usually let their gardens grow wild.

The house was still vulnerable, I felt, still broadcasting its vacancy to whoever chanced to wander this far up the lane.

I glanced at the sewing room window. I could see the lamp on the sill, but there was no light.

Still, something didn't seem right. Something strange appeared to be off. Not exactly something dark and misshapen, but the feeling was strong. It would be worthy of Lucy herself.

Plague take my wild imagination.

On an impulse, I backtracked to the side door, taking four surprised collies with me. Sidestepping vines that had begun to grow over the walkway, I turned the doorknob and pulled it forward. It didn't budge. The door was definitely locked.

Twenty-three

As we continued our stroll up Jonquil Lane, I realized Candy had been acting perfectly normal. Normal for Candy, that is. She insisted on investigating every scent in our path, but so did the other dogs.

She didn't come to a sudden stop and freeze, giving the impression she sensed something just beyond my ken. So, freed from apprehension, I focused on the bright springtime scenery. If a misshapen object was within sniffing distance, surely one of the four collies would alert me to the danger.

The air was warm and muggy, and the wind had picked up, tossing leaves and twigs in our path. It whipped my hair around my face, as wind is wont to do; I brushed it back with my free hand. Thunder rumbled across the sky. How much time did we have before the rain?

Enough for a decent walk, I decided.

The route to Squill Lane meandered past a quartet of mansions built in French chateau style. I still thought of them as the new construction, even though the mini development had been abandoned several months ago before all the houses were finished. The overgrown landscaping suggested that everyone had lost interest in the project.

Small, untrimmed junipers had been overrun with weeds and tall grasses. A tree felled by last summer's tornado lay across one of the circular driveways. That alone told me the properties had been practically written off.

They might serve as shelter for a vagrant, except these houses were different. Never inhabited, they lacked comfortable beds and well stocked larders. Already they looked a little sinister, like well-preserved structures in a ghost town, unwanted and superfluous.

Who could afford to buy a fancy country mansion in these hard economic times?

Beyond the new development was a shortcut to Squill Lane, an inhospitable curving stretch that was best avoided.

It was a mere trail fashioned by some unknown person through dark woods. Strange shadows and wild vegetation inspired fancies of an alien planet, perhaps one in Ray Bradbury's galaxy. The shortcut exited on acres of rolling pastureland. The only house in this direction was the charming storybook cottage at Lane's End. Once a rental, as far as I knew, nobody lived there now.

The cottage and the shortcut itself held fearful memories for me. We never went that way. I'd be surprised if anyone did.

On this day for some unfathomable reason, Halley turned onto the shortcut. Sky, ever her shadow, followed. Both collies wandered happily down the trail, heads low to the ground.

So much for normal canine behavior. How complicated my life would be if my two docile collies launched a rebellion. Candy and Gemmy, held prisoner at the end of their leashes, set up a loud clamor. They wanted to veer towards the shortcut too. I didn't.

"Sky! Halley! I called. "Come!"

They padded back to my side, albeit reluctantly, Sky carrying a long branch that she dropped at my feet as a propitiatory offering.

"How pretty," I said. "Thank you, Sky."

A sharp cry cut through the stillness. Its echo, carried on the wind, drifted out of the woods. A bird call, maybe, but what kind of bird made a sound that resembled a human cry?

Perhaps a struggle to the death between forest predator and prey was in progress at this moment. I couldn't do anything to help. At any rate, I didn't want to be a part of it; nor did I want my dogs involved. Candy cast me a desperate, pleading look and tugged on her leash. Gemmy started barking.

"No!" I said sharply.

I'd been down that path before two summers ago and imagined all sorts of fearful beings treading behind me. Not for anything would I step on the shortcut again, not even to investigate the sound.

Tugging back on leads, I soon had all my collies walking sedately up Jonquil Lane again. Nothing except distant thunder disturbed the tranquility, but the air was thick with foreboding. Perhaps the misshapen object was getting closer.

You're getting paranoid, Jennet, I told myself. *The only thing getting closer is the rain.*

~ * ~

The first drops of rain landed on my hand as we approached our house. What perfect timing! Sky flinched as a lightning bolt slashed across the heavens. I hurried the collies along and reached the door minutes before the downpour.

Safe inside, I filled the dogs' water bowls and passed out biscuits before turning the teakettle on. Sky took refuge under the table with her share of the loot. As I settled back with a treat of my own from the cookie jar, I noticed I'd missed two calls on the cell phone I'd once again forgotten to take with me. But there were no messages. Strange. Well, some people didn't like to talk to machines. I was one of them.

Putting the matter out of my mind, I turned my thoughts to dinner. Crane was working late tonight, so I needed something that wouldn't lose its appeal by the time he came home. A casserole from last night's beef roast, maybe? A salad. A pie.

A measure of tinkling notes rippled through the air. I picked up the cell phone again

"Hello, Jennet," Camille said. "How are things in Foxglove Corners?"

I leaned back in the oak chair. Hearing Camille's voice was almost as good as sharing tea and cookies with her as the day wound down.

"They're quiet," I said. "It's raining."

Perhaps I'd hesitated a second too long.

"It's raining here too. Is something wrong?"

"Nothing I can't handle."

"I don't like the sound of that."

"It's nothing, really. Mostly collie rescue stuff."

"I'm calling to let you know we decided to come home a week early," she said. "I've been worrying about my abandoned garden."

"They're fine," I said. "The foxgloves will be taller than you are. You'll just have to do a lot of weeding. I bought potted red geraniums and little flags for your porch. There's a large container too with a pretty mix. I know you love spring plants."

Sometimes I give myself away by trying too hard to be chatty.

"Something *is* the matter," Camille said.

I hadn't wanted to tell her about the break-in, but now we were talking, it seemed wrong to keep it from her.

"We've been watching your house, but someone broke in," I said. "I'm not sure when it happened. It was a woman, we think."

I told her about the light in the sewing room window and our subsequent discoveries, including the lipstick blot. "Somehow the side door was left unlocked. That's probably how she got in. But don't worry. Crane and I both checked, and it doesn't look like anything's missing. In fact, she left a jar of strawberry preserves on your kitchen counter. I'm assuming it isn't yours."

"Not if it's store-bought," she said. "Are you sure the door is locked now?"

"Yes. I just checked it again today."

"Jennet, would you do me a favor?" she asked.

"You know I will."

"Look in my dresser drawer, the top right one. There's a box wrapped in silver foil. It's a little smaller than a shoe box. Would you see if it's still there, and call me back?"

"Did you want me to look inside?" I asked.

"No. Just check to see that the seals are unbroken."

"I can do that," I said.

And I'd have to stifle my curiosity. Camille had never mentioned the box before, but why should she? Obviously it was personal, containing mementoes from the past, perhaps, or an emergency fund. Maybe both. It must be something special for her to ask about only that one possession.

"I'll go over as soon as the rain stops." I glanced at the key that hung from a peg.

There was no need to tell Camille that Crane didn't want me to be in the house alone. Then she'd be sure to worry. By the time it stopped raining, Crane would be home, and he could accompany me.

But darn! I hated to have to wait for him. I stole another glance at the key. It was so close. It would be so easy…

"We'll be home for Memorial Day," Camille said. "Gilbert wants to beat the holiday traffic."

"Then I think we'll have a barbecue. We'll make it a welcome home party. I've missed you," I added.

"And I've missed you. There are many lovely people in Tennessee, but old friends are the best. I think our living plan is inspired. Winters in the south, summers in Michigan. Neither one of the dogs like the heat."

"I'll see you soon," I said. "Have a safe trip home."

I closed the phone and realized that I'd better start making plans of my own. If Crane and I were going to host a barbecue, I'd have to go grocery shopping. One day soon Leonora and I had to clean the house and air it out. We'd stock Camille's kitchen with fresh staples and buy a bouquet of spring flowers for the dining room table. I'd bake a coffeecake.

It was going to be like old times.

~ * ~

The hot air balloon dipped under the clouds and glided toward the woods. From my lofty vantage point I could see the shortcut. It snaked its way from Jonquil Lane to Squill Lane. The long, sinuous body filled me with alarm.

Bad things happened on that shortcut. Bad things waited in the woods to spring out at the hapless traveler. There were reptiles and coyotes and ravening deer sheltering amidst the twisted trees. Small animals running for their lives. A cry that sounded as if it originated in a human throat, but it was something else.

I should have investigated that cry.

Danger and Evil, Lucy had said.

But I was safe from both, above the treetops, far from the ground. I saw my house with its graceful green gables and stained glass windows, saw Camille's yellow Victorian and the daffodils that bloomed on the lane. And the dark woods across the lane.

We soared over the woods, and time slipped backwards. One year... Two years...

I was going to be happy in Foxglove Corners. Things were going to be different here. I'd see the handsome deputy sheriff again soon. He had invited me to a Fourth of July festival up in Bereton.

Brent Fowler put his arm around my shoulder. "Didn't I tell you, Jennet? You can see so much more clearly when you're way up high."

~ * ~

I woke to a roll of thunder so loud it must have split the heavens open.

Where was Crane? What was Brent Fowler doing in my dream, and why was I smiling up at him? Whence came that rush of exhilaration?

Reality raced to catch up with me. It was nighttime. It was still raining. I was in bed with the top sheet twisted under my arms.

Crane slept on beside me, undisturbed by the storm. As for Brent, I'd left him behind in the hot air balloon. In the dream.

I turned around and punched my pillow. Why would I dream about Bent Fowler? Like an echo of thunder, that heady exhilaration and excitement had followed me into wakefulness. That feeling belonged to Crane.

But Brent owned Skyway Tours. He was riding over Foxglove Corners looking for clues on the ground. It was as simple as that. And besides, how futile was it to try to find sense in a dream?

Brent had said something to me. I tried to remember what, but it slipped away.

Letting it go, I eased myself out of bed and glanced at the clock and padded over to the window. All I could see was rain pounding against the panes.

Then lightning flashed overhead, illuminating the yellow Victorian. For a fragment of a second, I saw a light shining in the sewing room window. Then rain drowned the scene in unrelenting darkness.

Twenty-four

I turned to look at Crane. Should I wake him up? He had been so tired last night when he'd come home. I didn't want him to go out in the rain until he had to.

There couldn't possibly be anybody in Camille's house. I'd just tried the side door this afternoon. Both doors were locked; all the windows were latched.

So what had I seen? Who had turned on the candle lamp?

Let him sleep, I decided and went back to bed. My thoughts slid over to Camille's box. What treasure did it contain?

A dresser or nightstand was the worst place to stash money or valuable jewelry. I'd read that burglars always look in bedrooms first, then in freezers or kitchen canisters, those supposedly clever hiding places.

Camille had no need to find a secret cache for her valuables. Before marrying Gilbert, she rarely left her house. Besides she had two large dogs. Then when she did leave, she took Twister and Holly with her and stayed away for five months. During that time, anyone could have figured out nobody was home. But how could anyone know about the box? She'd never mentioned it to me, and we were friends.

Quit thinking. Go back to sleep.

I closed my eyes and ordered a dream of Crane. I then told Brent Fowler to stay in his hot air balloon. Married only a year, I still thought of myself as a newlywed. Crane was the only man in my life. Brent had long since given up flirting with me, and I'd never encouraged him. Oh, except once when I was trying to get him to incriminate himself in a murder. That was a long time ago.

That box... What was in it? Would I find it untouched in the dresser drawer? It stayed in my mind, shining like a silver nugget, as I felt myself drifting off to sleep.

~ * ~

In the morning, I glanced through the gray drizzle at Camille's house. There was no light in the sewing room, no light anywhere I could see. Washed clean in last night's storm, the old Victorian's soft yellow surface glowed, but all the windows were dark.

Still I knew I'd seen a lamp shining in that brief moment when lightning sizzled across the sky.

Impossible though it seemed, somehow the woman had managed to get inside Camille's house. She must walk through the house in the night hours and go elsewhere by day.

But where? It wasn't as if there was a mall or a park nearby. Just the new development and the woods. The other houses on Jonquil Lane were occupied. All of the surrounding land was deeply forested.

It occurred to me that she could well return to the house during the day when neither of us was at home. The dogs could bark non-stop. There'd be no one to hear them except the intruder.

Crane believed I'd seen a light. My handsome gray-eyed husband with his gun belt and his shiny badge pinned on his uniform always believed me. Crane's gun gave me an illusion of safety even when I didn't have any particular reason to feel threatened. Sitting at the breakfast table in my own home, for instance.

Why, why on earth would I dream of another man's arm around me? My thoughts were running in wild circles this morning.

I set two slices of whole-wheat toast next to Crane's plate of scrambled eggs.

"We can check the light out before I take off for the day," he said.

"Good, and we'll try both locks."

"If somebody is still getting in, we'd better have the locks changed," he said.

"I'll take care of it."

I thought about the silver box again. Crane didn't find it mysterious, only important, since it was important to Camille.

"It's probably old love letters or diaries," he said. "Remember, Camille used to keep a journal."

That had disappeared a long time ago, and whose letters would she keep? Those from her abusive first husband, the man she'd plotted to kill?

"I don't think so," I said. "Why would she be worried someone would steal old writing?"

"You'll have to ask her." He smiled at me. "You have another mystery, Jennet. A nice safe one."

"It's going to be a busy week," I said.

I wouldn't have much time to solve the dual mysteries of the silver box and the nighttime intruder. Or to plan the menu for our barbecue or clean Camille's house. Fortunately we had a half day of classes on Friday in honor of the Memorial Day holiday. As usual, every minute of the intervening time was planned.

~ * ~

I stared at the counter where the jar of strawberry preserves had been. It was gone. The entire expanse was empty, wiped clean, as Leonora had said she'd left it.

"That woman was here," I said. "To pick up the jar or put it away?"

Crane opened the refrigerator and shook his head. "It's not in here. She must have taken it with her."

That seemed unlikely to me. The entire scenario seemed unlikely. "In a thunderstorm?"

"She must have another reason for breaking in. Don't forget to call a locksmith today."

"I'll call from school this morning. I wish I hadn't told Camille everything was all right."

"As far as you knew, it was. Let's have a look upstairs."

At the top of the stairway, Crane strode down the hall to the sewing room while I slipped into Camille's bedroom and switched on the light. The silver box was where Camille had said it would be, stored with winter gloves, cashmere scarves, and a collection of bejeweled evening bags, items Camille didn't need in a southern winter.

No one had tampered with the box's silver wrapping or the snowflake seals. Could this be a never-opened Christmas present?

Unable to resist temptation, I picked it up and shook it. There were papers or cards inside, nothing heavy. Maybe Crane was right. Old cards kept out of sentiment. Letters. Invitations to long ago parties. But why was Camille concerned about them? And if there were old cards and the like inside, why had she bothered to wrap the box? I didn't have an answer.

Crane's footsteps echoed down the hall. "Did you find the box?" he asked.

"It's still here. What did you find?"

"Nothing out of place."

I gave the box one last look and closed the dresser door.

Downstairs, while Crane checked the rest of the floor, I opened kitchen cupboards. The raspberry and blackberry jams that Camille had put up last year were neatly lined up on a shelf next to the syrup. The store-bought jar of preserves was nowhere in sight.

Without warning, an uncomfortable feeling wrapped itself around me, a sudden chill without an apparent source.

Camille was in Tennessee, packing for the return trip to Michigan, but it seemed to me she was also in the kitchen. At the cupboard, cutting slices of freshly baked cake, sitting at the table in her favorite chair, listening to whatever problem I'd brought her, or just chatting about the weather or flowers or the dogs' antics. As friends do.

Or hovering just outside the kitchen in the hallway. Her presence was practically tangible. And was that the clink of a dog's tag against her chain?

Don't be silly, I scolded myself. *Camille can't be here in spirit unless she's dead. Unless she was in an accident...*

What a horrible thought!

I rushed to fill it with another one, the first time I'd seen Camille's charming blue and white country kitchen. I was new in Foxglove Corners and a little curious about her as I felt both the house and its mistress were keeping secrets. We drank tea together, ate freshly baked coffeecake, and talked about Crane, the man who had captured my attention at our first meeting.

The musty air was thick with memories; it bristled with tension. If I stayed in this room much longer, I might see something I didn't want to see.

I strolled into the first floor half-bath where we'd left the wastebasket. There were no additional throwaways to give us even a blurry picture of the woman who came and went through locked entrances.

After what seemed like an hour, Crane joined me in the kitchen. "Everything's clear as far as I can see. The hatches are battened down."

"Then I saw a ghost light," I said. "Turned on by a ghost girl."

He smiled. "Not this time, honey. I don't think ghosts need light to see, and I'm sure they don't eat preserves." He pulled me into his arms and kissed me quite thoroughly. "The lamp didn't turn itself on. A real person was prowling around the house last night. I still don't want you to come over here alone. Not until we find out what's going on."

There was that dictatorial tone again, the one that had forced me to curb my curiosity and wait until Crane could accompany me on the long, perilous journey across Jonquil Lane.

"But the house needs to be cleaned," I said. "It needs airing out. Hours and hours of fresh air."

He frowned and reconsidered. "Leonora is going to help you, right? Two of you and four dogs should be safe. But wait till the locks are changed."

With one last look at the empty counter, I followed Crane to the door.

A ghost light shining in the rain. A ghost girl moving like mist through the darkened halls. Secrets and swirling clouds of Gothic atmosphere. Suddenly I had no desire to dust and vacuum in Camille's house alone.

"I'll give you this one," I said. "But don't ask for any other concessions."

~ * ~

We left the house through the side door. The weeds and vines had almost taken over the walkway, and the plants in Camille's backyard garden appeared to have grown a foot since yesterday. Another impossibility, except for my belief the seeds Camille sowed had magical powers.

As he strode through the untamed vegetation, Crane had his eyes trained on the ground.

"What are you looking for?" I asked.

"Footprints in the mud," he said. "Anything that looks like it doesn't belong here. Evidence."

"Flowers trampled down by somebody walking on them?"

"Anything."

"Nobody could approach the house without leaving footprints," I said.

But it appeared somebody had. And that person, who could only be the intruding woman, hadn't brought a single grain of dirt in with her. Either that or she'd swept the floor clean.

She could have used a broom to obliterate her prints. Camille had a broom closet in her kitchen.

A faint throbbing appeared behind my left eye, a clear warning of pain to come.

"This situation is giving me a headache," I said. "And I have a long day at work today."

"Then don't think about it. There's an answer. I just have to find it."

He grabbed my hand a second before I stepped on a large forked branch obscured by a thriving patch of noxious weeds.

"Stay home if you're not feeling well," he said.

"I'd love to, but I have to be in school today."

We were winding up our study of *A Midsummer Night's Dream*, and the rest of the week would be devoted to last-minute rehearsals and preparations. Then there was the upcoming sale of the last school paper of the year in Journalism. No, I needed to be with my students. A sub couldn't handle that.

"Mac is keeping an eye on the place," Crane added.

We parted company, then, Crane to patrol the quiet lanes and by-roads of Foxglove Corners, I to settle the dogs for their day and take a pain pill. That done, I loaded the car and headed for Leonora's house. A lot could happen before Crane and I met again.

I wondered if the woman came back when the coast was clear and, for what must be the hundredth time, why she had chosen the yellow Victorian for her daytime haunt.

Twenty-five

My amateur thespians were almost ready to perform their scenes for Leonora's class. Costumes and props were stored in the closet for safekeeping, along with the June edition of the school paper, fresh from the printer. Having completed the reading of the play, we were devoting the week to review and final rehearsal for the first groups.

Leonora's class was also ready with their interpretations of Julius Caesar. We compared notes during our twenty-minute lunch break in Leonora's classroom.

"Grimsly will be out of the building for three days," Leonora announced. "He left for up north with an evaluating team."

"I wonder if he timed it to miss our plays," I said, not at all disappointed at the prospect his absence.

"I doubt it." She sprinkled a package of Parmesan cheese on her lasagna. I unwrapped my tuna salad sandwich. Taking the first bite of my starvation fare lunch, I gazed at the richness out the window.

The spectacle of spring unfolding managed to soothe me even when a class spun out of control. Leaves seemed greener and fuller every day. Weeds and wildflowers grew in sweet harmony. Would that they could inspire our students.

"I've been thinking about the trouble at Camille's house," Leonora said. "You're convinced some woman has been breaking in, but did you ever wonder if the twins were hiding there?"

"I don't see how," I said. "Or where or why. I never saw a sign of them. Briana is too young to wear lipstick, and growing children need more to eat than an occasional spoonful of preserves."

"The hot air balloon went down nearby. Think about it."

I did. It still didn't add up. The last time the twins had been seen, they were at Clovers, a fair distance from Foxglove Corners.

"Both Crane and I have been inside the house," I said. "Where were the twins then?"

"In the basement? Hiding in a closet or maybe the attic?" Warming to her theory, she added, "Kids love to rummage around in old attics."

"And why were they hiding?"

"They were afraid of you?"

"One time Halley and Sky were with me. The dogs would have known if anyone was in the house, and there's still the problem of their food.'

"Well, the next time you're in the house, look in all the unlikely places."

"I can't see myself climbing up to Camille's attic," I said. "The house is spooky enough. Without Camille there, I mean."

"How so?

Deciding to give her an edited answer, I said, "It's easy to imagine sounds. I thought I heard a dog tag clink against a chain."

"Anything else?"

I shrugged. "Shadows. They always freak me out."

"Those are harmless, but the sooner we go over and clean, the better. Can you do it after school tomorrow?"

I did a few quick calculations. "Sure. I'm free."

"With two of us working, we'll have the place ship shape in no time, just the way it was when Camille left it."

"It always amazes me how dust accumulates in an empty house," I said.

What if the house wasn't empty, though? Leonora thought I'd dismissed her idea, but it had taken root. I couldn't wait to explore the old Victorian again. With the locksmith at work possibly this minute, it was bound to be safe.

~ * ~

Marvel McLogan called that afternoon as I was eying the new keys on the kitchen counter. 'All done', Crane's note informed me. My man of few words.

Marvel's voice bubbled over with enthusiasm. "Hi, Jennet. I have good news, finally."

I could guess what it was.

"Willa Bradstone brought the puppy back. Mandy is already in her new home with Brandy."

"That *is* good. How did it come about?"

"There's a little string," she said. "A condition."

There always was.

"Willa is leasing Mandy to Suzette for two years. Suzette will return Mandy to Willa when Mandy comes in season. After she's been bred to a stud dog of Willa's choosing, Willa will whelp the litter. Then Suzette can purchase Mandy formally."

"That sounds fair to both ladies," I said, "but it'll be hard for Suzette to be without Mandy again."

"It isn't an ideal solution, but it's better than I hoped for. Suzette is overjoyed. So is Mandy. You should have seen how happy that puppy was when she saw Suzette."

I wished I could have been present at the reunion since I'd played a small part in making it happen.

"Now if you could just find Sandy, the curse would be broken," Marvel said.

I sighed. Surely Marvel didn't still believe in the curse. If the situation had a happy ending, it was the result of hard work, luck, and compromise.

Instead of pointing that out, I said, "Sandy may never be found. It's especially sad because Josie's mother appears to be changing her mind about letting Josie keep the puppy."

"Poor little Sandy. Where could she be?"

Marvel wasn't asking the right question. She should wonder what could have happened to her. But maybe with leftover luck, Sandy's story would have a happy ending too. There was no point in anticipating the worst.

"Thanks again for all your help, and keep in touch," Marvel said. "I'd like you to see Andy. My little black duckling is turning into a swan. I think I'm going to keep him."

I promised to visit Mallowmere Kennels when my life slowed down a little and said goodbye. Then I crossed Mandy and Brandy off my mental list. That left Sandy.

~ * ~

My renewed contemplation of keys to the yellow Victorian reminded me that I'd promised to tell Camille the results of my latest search. I punched in her number, and she answered on the second ring.

"Your box is still in the drawer, safe and sound," I said. "The seals are unbroken."

Camille's sigh of relief was audible. "Oh, thank goodness."

Now she'll tell me what's inside, I thought.

But she only thanked me for the small favor. "I can't understand the light in the sewing room. Why there, of all places? I keep an emergency money envelope in that room," she added. "I'm the only one who knows about it, and it's in a place where no one would ever think to look. So I'm not concerned."

"Did you want me to check on it?"

"No, dear. Nobody will ever find it. Not in a million years."

She'd probably folded it in a length of fabric.

"There's something else," I said. "Those strawberry preserves disappeared. Somebody got in again, so Crane and I had the locks changed. I hope that's all right."

"It's fine. I'm so grateful for friends like you and Crane."

"We're family now, Camille. Don't forget."

I could imagine her blush. "I didn't… Oh, I guess I did. These break-ins have me flustered."

"The new locks should put an end to whatever's going on, and we're still watching for strangers loitering around when we're here."

I decided not to mention Leonora's theory about the twins hiding, or being hidden, in the house. It was about as far in left field as she could go, even though I still planned to look for them.

"We started packing," Camille said. "I can't wait to get home. But when we're living in Michigan, how do we know what's happening in Gilbert's house in Tennessee? Maybe maintaining two households isn't the best idea."

My heart sank. Suppose Camille and Gilbert decided to make their permanent home in Tennessee? I'd hardly ever see her then.

"Lots of people do it," I said.

"I know. We're called snowbirds."

"Whatever's going on up here may never happen again, especially now that you have new locks. How could it?"

Her pause suggested that she wasn't convinced.

"I hope you won't stay in Tennessee year around," I said. "You and the yellow Victorian belong together." Inspiration struck and I added, "Your garden is beginning to look like a jungle. I'd do some weeding, but I might yank up valuable plants by mistake. Those giant foxgloves should be staked, and the ferns are choking out the lilies."

My rambling had the desired effect.

"I love my gardens," Camille said. "I could never duplicate them in another place. Especially in the spring, they need their mistress."

I had a suspicion the danger of losing Camille as my nearest neighbor had passed. Unless Gilbert disagreed with her.

~ * ~

That night I had the balloon dream again. I woke with a start and lay still under crumpled sheets until my heartbeat slowed. Fragments danced in front of my eyes, constantly rearranging themselves like chips of colored glass in a kaleidoscope.

Brent was with me, again. His arm rested heavily on my shoulder. His dark red hair shone in a too-bright sun, and I felt happy to be flying over the magical land of Foxglove Corners. Happy to be with Brent.

How was it possible for people to have the same dream on different nights?

We were gliding over the woods, over Jonquil Lane. The clouds were high above us. The daffodils below had petals of pure gold, and all the springtime greens shone as if they'd been sprinkled with emerald dust.

"In order to see everything clearly, you have to view it from the air," Brent said. "Otherwise, you can be right close to something and still miss it."

I was about to ask him what there was to see or miss when I heard the hiss of escaping gas. When we began to fall.

Twenty-six

Five minutes passed; then ten. Even in a waking state, the dream stayed with me, still vivid and terrible. I felt as if I were plummeting toward the earth with the hot air balloon dissolving around me. In seconds I would be a splatter on the ground.

I couldn't help wondering what the dream meant. Did it mirror my subconscious fear of crashing? Could the explanation possibly be that simple?

There were other factors to consider. Brent owned Skyway Tours. He'd offered to take us on a color tour of Foxglove Corners in one of his balloons this fall. At present, Brent was searching for signs of the Cooper twins from the air while his private investigator tailed Johnston Holliday across Michigan.

All legitimate reasons to dream about Brent and his balloon.

A glance at the alarm clock told me that I had another hour to sleep or continue dissecting my dream, whichever activity I preferred. The dream won. After coming so close to death, I was wide awake.

I felt calmer now. The dream had ended before we hit the ground. That's often the way with dreams. They stop at odd times, like a DVD movie freezing in mid-scene when a defective disk refuses to move forward.

Surprisingly it wasn't the knowledge that we were about to crash that troubled me. It was the presence of Brent Fowler at my side and the happiness I'd felt in his company.

That burst of joy was foreign to the reality of my life. I'd never been attracted to Brent. I might have enjoyed his admiration, his attention, and the flattery that came so easily to him. What woman wouldn't? But Crane was my only love.

No matter what my deluded subconscious was implying.

You're taking this way too seriously, I scolded myself. It was only a dream, for heavens' sake.

One that repeated itself and took on nightmare proportions. Surely that meant something.

At my side, Crane slept on. Usually I could talk to him about anything, but how could I tell him I was dreaming about Bent Fowler?

Don't even think about telling him.

I closed my eyes and let my body relax. If I went back to sleep, by the time I awoke, the dream would have slipped away into oblivion. There was only one problem. What if it kept coming back?

~ * ~

The French toast was hot with golden brown edges, the bacon crisp, and the coffee steaming. I prided myself on cooking a big breakfast for Crane every morning. Placing the syrup pitcher beside his plate, I sat down and sipped my orange juice, which was all I wanted at this early hour.

Crane looked especially bright today, freshly shaven and, as always, handsome. He looked especially right. The overhead light played on the silver strands in his blond hair, and his frosty gray eyes had a beguiling gleam as he contemplated the stack of French toast.

"Leonora and I are going to clean Camille's house today," I said. "It shouldn't interfere with dinner, but how would you like something from Clovers tonight?"

"Whatever you want, honey."

"I'll get something good and a pie for dessert."

He cut a large piece of French toast and poured more syrup on it. "Take one of the dogs over to the house with you. Gemmy would be best. She's the most aggressive of the four. And be careful."

Even with new locks on the doors, even though there would be two of us, Crane was still concerned about our safety. I hadn't told him about Leonora's theory. Not that a pair of children could be dangerous. Unless, of course, Sara Hall or Johnston Holiday had stashed them there and were stationed somewhere nearby.

"And don't work too hard," he added.

"We're just going to dust and vacuum," I said. "The day before Camille and Gilbert come home, I'm going to buy a bouquet for their table."

"It'll be good to have the place occupied again," Crane said.

I nodded. "We can relax our vigilance."

Not entirely though. The woman who had breached the security of the yellow Victorian might still be in the neighborhood, but when Twister and Holly returned to their territory there would be two barking dogs to chase her away. Twister alone was a formidable guard.

"I almost forgot," Crane said. "Fowler's dropping over tonight. He thinks he made a discovery on one of his balloon jaunts."

I felt a wave of warmth spread over my face and, hoping to hide it, drained my juice glass. There was no reason for that blush. Thankfully Crane hadn't noticed it.

"Why doesn't he tell the police?" I asked.

"He thinks he's doing that."

"I'll order an extra dinner then."

Crane laughed. "He does seem to know when we're eating, even if the time changes."

"I wonder what he discovered," I said.

Could the mystery of the missing twins finally be moving toward a solution?

~ * ~

I pulled a handful of dust cloths out of Camille's rag basket and gave half of them to Leonora. "Do you want to start upstairs or down?"

"Aren't we going to search the house?" she asked.

"We could, but there's no one here. Can't you tell?"

"It *is* quiet."

Gemmy, who had accompanied us, lay down in the doorway waiting to see what we would do. Leonora moved into the dining room and stood still, looking into the kitchen.

"It's too quiet," she said. "I can understand why you described it as spooky, but I don't hear ghostly dog tags clinking or a howling in the attic. Just one collie panting."

"Let's start looking then," I said. "I still have to drive over to Clovers to pick up dinner."

"And Jake called. We're going out tonight. Just for a burger at the Lakeside Inn."

Leonora was even better at packing her days with activities than I was. At the moment, evidence to the contrary, she was determined to find some indication the twins were hiding in the house. A doomed endeavor if ever I saw one. Gemmy was my barometer. She was telling me all was well.

Leonora led the search. I followed, and in a half hour we'd checked out all the unlikely places, which were mostly closets and basement corners. Gemmy followed us like a vigilant shadow but didn't suggest in any canine manner anything was amiss.

At the top of the narrow wooden staircase that led to the attic, we paused.

"Do you think we should?" I asked.

I'd never like attics, convinced they harbored bats and other night creatures, real or imaginary.

"We don't want an incomplete search," Leonora said. "I'll go back downstairs and get the flashlights. I know where Camille keeps them."

Left alone with Gemmy, I thought of my own neat attic filled with never-opened boxes from my move to Foxglove Corners and with possessions Crane wished to keep but had no immediate use for. We hadn't lived in our house that long, and it was relatively new, but Camille had resided in the old Victorian for decades. I suspected her attic would be quite different from ours.

It was. On the other side of the door we found paintings, vases, and bric-a-brac stored in no particular order. There were the requisite trunks and boxes with curling tape and loose string. Like most attics it was dim and cold. Faint light barely penetrated the small windows, and dust motes floated lazily through the thick air.

Gemmy finally came to life. Presented with a whole new world of things to sniff, she took off down a makeshift aisle.

I shone the flashlight on a painting of a garden scene far too colorful to end its life in a shadowy attic space. There were lamps on every available surface; some with crystal bases fairly cried out for a place in the sun. Tall floor lamps. A pair of dresser lamps with cupids sitting on clouds. Lamps whose dusty Tiffany shades once had jewel-bright colors. All these luminaries and not an electrical outlet in sight.

Camille had once mentioned her lamp collection. Presumably it had grown too unwieldy to be displayed downstairs.

I took a few careful steps forward, surveying Camille's castaway treasures. She could easily have furnished a small antique shop. But under one of the small windows, placed where it would receive the meager light, was something different. A small maple table, plain and well-worn, with two chairs.

Instead of being squeezed together, the three items looked as if someone had actually used them to sit on during a quick meal and, on finishing, pushed them back and left them there. Off to the side, two matching chairs were stacked one on top of the other.

I ran my hand over the table's top. There were no crumbs but no dust either. Someone had sat at this table recently—and left a white candle with a blackened wick behind.

"This is the candlestick from Camille's buffet. She has two of them."

"I was right," Leonora said. "Somebody was here, but why would they come all the way up to the attic with this whole rambling house?"

"Probably what you thought," I said. "To hide from us?"

"Do you think it was the Cooper twins?"

I remembered all my arguments from our last conversations, especially the problem with the food. I didn't see any discarded paper cartons or plates. Just this table that had been wiped clean of dust.

With what? I didn't see a cloth or rag nearby.

"They might have been here," I said. "But I can't see two little kids lighting a candle. Every child is cautioned not to touch matches. Besides, kids that age wouldn't leave a house in order."

"A grown-up then? The woman?"

"Looking at the chairs, I'd say two people. The lipstick woman and a companion. They must have been in the attic when we were in the house before. Crane probably didn't look up here."

"Then they were afraid of you."

"More likely they were afraid of being caught."

At this point, my imagination was clamoring to announce its theories.

When I'd seen the ghost light, could it have been the candle burning? This part of the attic was located directly above the sewing room. Two of the small windows looked out on Jonquil Lane.

I backed up and nearly lost my balance on the uneven attic floor. Looking down, I saw a plastic bottle.

"Here's more evidence," I said. " Exhibit Two."

Great Lakes Pure Spring Water with a few drops left at the bottom. It was probably the youngest object in the room.

Elsewhere in the attic, Gemmy sneezed. She sneezed again and again. Four times.

Leonora shivered. "Is anyone there?" she called.

"Of course not," I said. "Come, Gemmy."

"We did what we came to do," Leonora said. "Let's get out of here."

She was the first one through the door.

Twenty-seven

I grabbed the water bottle and candlestick and followed Leonora down the stairs, feeling like the heroine of a Gothic novel descending from a haunted attic. Gemmy trailed reluctantly in our wake. She'd forgotten her sneezing fit and wanted to continue exploring.

After the cold attic air, the rush of warmth on my arms felt comforting as did the sunlight streaming through the windows on the landing.

On the way down to the first floor, I checked Camille's sewing room and bedroom and opened the dresser drawer. There was the mysterious silver box, still undisturbed.

In the living room, I found the candlestick that matched the one I carried. Its white taper had never been burned. The intruder had moved it to the right of Camille's mantel clock, no doubt in the hope nobody would notice the other one was missing.

Following my gaze, Leonora said, "You probably obliterated the fingerprints."

"True." I took a detour into the kitchen. "I'm going to leave them on the counter—right where the jar was."

"Why?"

"For Camille to see."

"All right, but why?"

"I want her to see the evidence,"

I didn't know what that would accomplish, except with new locks, we wouldn't be likely to find proof of unlawful entry again.

Unless the woman broke a window. Could she be that desperate?

Desperate for what, I wondered. For shelter? Or a place to hide? Or, perhaps, to continue a search for some unknown object?

In only a few days Camille and Gilbert would return to Foxglove Corners. In the meantime, we'd made her house presentable. With fresh flowers as a welcome home touch, our long period of surveillance would be over. We'd literally hand over the keys.

Gemmy dashed to the front door and stood patiently, her noise pointing to the doorknob.

"Well this was fun," Leonora said with a wry smile. "Now I have to wash away the dust and dress for my date with Jake." She glanced at her watch. "I only have an hour to make myself irresistible."

"You'll manage. And I'm off to Clovers."

I locked the door behind us and pocketed the key. One more errand and I could relax and review everything I'd learned about… Everything.

What had begun as a hot air balloon sighting on a spring morning had turned and twisted in several directions. It was time to sit back and gather all the dangling strands into a single coherent bow.

Good luck, I thought.

~ * ~

Annica tossed her head. She had espoused the safari look this evening, all khaki with white accents and a chunky necklace of wood beads. Her earrings, unique as usual, were enamel tigers. The tiny beasts had emerald chips for eyes. Small as they were, they blazed green fire. More or less like the eyes of their owner.

"Nice tigers," I said.

"Thanks."

"What's good tonight?"

"Short ribs with roasted vegetables and pork chops with rice," she said in clipped tones.

Her jaunty mood was noticeably missing.

"Is anything the matter?" I asked.

"Not a thing."

"That's good. The status quo is always best."

When she didn't comment, I realized that she was obviously miffed about something.

Giving me a withering look, she said, "I thought we were going to work together to solve the case. I haven't heard a word from you in ages."

"I haven't had a word to give," I said.

But I wondered if that was the truth. Since our last encounter, I'd collected bits and pieces of information. Nothing cohesive, nothing to share.

She thawed quickly and completely. "As it happens, *I* do. I may be stuck behind this counter, but it gives me access to the hungry fringe of the town. I saw a person of interest earlier today."

"Who's that?"

"The Holliday man. He was here for lunch. He ordered the pork chop special and apple pie. Two pieces."

"Are you sure it was Johnston Holliday?"

"Positive. We taped his picture by the cash register in case he came in again. He didn't have his family with him this time."

"Brent was right," I said.

"About what?"

"He said Holliday was coming back to this area. That could be significant. Did you call the police?"

"Not yet. It's been crazy around here today. Our pork chop special always brings in a crowd."

I couldn't believe Annica's lackadaisical approach to mystery solving. She had two fifteen minutes breaks a day and one for lunch if her shift covered the noon hour. That was plenty of time to notify the authorities.

"Did you forget about the reward?" I asked.

"Isn't that for getting the kids back?"

"Sure, and Johnston Holliday took the kids. If your information leads to his capture, you'll have extra money and that publicity you wanted."

Annica leaned on the counter, order pad forgotten. "I tried to get him to talk, but he just ate and ran."

Ran where? I wondered. Was Holliday still traveling or had he returned to the scene of the crime? That scene was dangerously close to my home. Well, if he stayed in Foxglove Corners, he'd be easier to capture.

"He's a cute guy, but he looks mean," Annica said. "He only left me two quarters for a tip. I'll bet he killed the others."

"Don't look on the dark side. No one's found any bodies."

"Sure they have. How about Eric?"

"Oh, gosh, yes. Eric." The first victim, Brent's young friend, the man for whose death Brent felt responsible. I was ashamed to admit I'd forgotten him.

"And I remember the way Holliday yelled at those kids," she said.

"For throwing food. Well, I can't blame him for that."

"So are we working together?" Annica asked. "If Holliday comes again, I have a plan…"

Clovers' co-owner, Mary Jeanne, stepped out of the kitchen and surveyed her domain. Her gaze came to rest on Annica, who quickly picked up her order pad.

"So you'll have…?"

"Three short rib dinners and a lemon meringue pie to go," I said. "About that plan…"

Mary Jeanne hadn't moved. Annica was busy writing. She lowered her voice. "Tell you later. If that individual comes in again, I'll give you a call."

I had to be satisfied with that.

~ * ~

I thought I might feel uncomfortable around Brent Fowler that evening.

Uncomfortable because of a fleeting emotion in a dream? That was ludicrous. So I told myself as I set the table for three.

Both Brent and Crane were perceptive. If I acted self conscious or even slightly flustered, they would be suspicious. And, for the last time, I didn't have anything to feel guilty about. As it turned out, I didn't have to worry because nothing untoward happened.

Brent was his old self, congenial and convivial. He was paying more attention to the four collies than to me.

Sky lay quietly at Brent's feet. She was still shy around company, but Brent was one of her favorites. There was something about him…

"What's this discovery?" Crane asked when we were all comfortably seated around the fireplace.

"I saw a white shirt or sweater tied to a tree house," Brent said. "Or maybe it was caught on it. I couldn't tell."

"Where?"

"In the woods between Jonquil and Squill Lanes."

"White is for surrender," I said. "Why do you think it's significant?"

Brent stared at me. "Have your detecting powers gotten rusty, Jennet? I flew over those woods a dozen times before, and this is the first time I noticed it."

"The tree house or the shirt?" Crane asked.

"The shirt. I thought it was an SOS."

"I saw that tree house a few years ago," I said. "I don't know who built it or if any kids still play in those woods."

I sat back and thought about the tree house.

Kids at play. Or in flight. Had either Briana or Bennett owned a white shirt or sweater? They could reach the house easily by climbing the old ladder I remembered seeing.

"It's worth investigating." Brent was proud of his discovery. "I thought we could all go together."

"I'm surprised you didn't already check it out," I said. "Couldn't you have just steered the balloon down to the ground?"

"Not with all those trees, and you don't just steer the balloon. Besides, I wanted to wait for the Sheriff and the girl detective." He winked at me. "Just in case there's trouble."

"It's too late to go tonight," Crane said. "We can't all be together until Jennet comes home from school. But I'm with you. I think we'd better investigate. How about if you and I go first thing in the morning?"

He was talking to Brent. One man to another.

"Okay by me," Brent said.

"I don't like those woods anyway," I said. "I never ever take that shortcut."

A memory of past trauma raised its head. And something else. Halley and Sky had turned happily that way on our last walk. They hadn't wanted to come back.

Always, always listen to your dogs, I thought. Then there was the cry I'd attributed to a predator and its prey.

"I'd thought all along the twins might be in the woods," I said.

I could easily see Foxglove Corners as one vast forest with various scenarios being acted out in different parts of the woods. Like the make-believe Athens wood in *A Midsummer Night's Dream.* No one could be certain of what anybody else was up to.

The image blended into one of lost children coming across a candy-studded gingerbread house in the wilderness. No. That was a tree house.

I'd been concerned about meals. Children lost in the woods would soon discover the wild berries were edible. Dewberries, Camille had called them.

"It's settled," Crane said. "We'll go tomorrow morning."

"Without me? I'm the mystery maven." I wouldn't be afraid of the woods with two stalwart companions.

"We'll give you a full report," Brent said.

Apparently it was decided.

I left Brent and Crane talking about rumors of a cougar sighted near Lost Lake and took my Clovers dinners out of the oven. I had roasted extra potatoes and baked Crane's favorite biscuits, putting my own stamp on the chef's cooking; when Brent complimented me on the five-star meal, I didn't enlighten him.

Twenty-eight

We took our coffee and pie into the living room. As if on cue, the collie pack moved with us. Sky resettled herself at Brent's feet. He rewarded her with a pat on the head.

"Now that dinner is over, I can tell you the latest news," I said.

Brent raised an eyebrow. "What does dinner have to do with your news?"

"We have a rule," I said. "No serious conversation at the table. Nothing distressing."

"What happened?" Crane asked.

"Johnston Holliday is back in town. Annica saw him at Clovers today."

"Damn!" Brent said. "Why didn't I know? What am I paying Scott for?"

It was a rhetorical question, but I felt like elaborating on the subject. "Criminals always return to the scene of the crime, so I've heard. I wonder why? You'd think the opposite would be true."

"They have unfinished business, Jennet," Brent said. "Just like one of your ghosts."

My ghosts?

"I don't have any ghosts this time around."

"Glory be!" Brent stuffed a chunk of pie into his mouth. "This is good. You're a champion pie maker."

He was right—about the pie. The meringue was a culinary masterpiece, light and fluffy, and the custard filling was just sweet enough. In other words, Clovers' dessert was perfection.

"Thank you," I said. "All in a day's work."

Crane cast me a conspirator's smile. It was Crane and I together now; Brent sat on the sidelines.

"All we need are Sara and the twins to make the balloon family complete," I said.

"You're not still hoping to find them, are you?" Without waiting for an answer, Brent added, "I'm afraid Johnston bumped them off before he went up north."

"Don't look on the dark side." Hadn't I already said that today? "Remember the sweater or whatever it was in the tree house."

Apparently unable to think of a response, Brent gobbled the rest of his pie.

Crane looked grim. He must be thinking of Holliday's proximity to Jonquil Lane. As I was. Why had he come back this way, and what might his return mean for me?

He'd seen me from the hot air balloon, had probably noted the location of our house and the two collies who had been so fascinated by the multi-colored flying object.

He could find us again.

Suppose Holliday had killed Sara and the twins. He might think I could identify him.

And what of Annica and Marcy, who had waited on them? Holliday couldn't hope to track down the other diners at Clovers, but he might target the waitress who had dealt with him. Until he was apprehended, we were all in danger. I hoped Annica had contacted the police.

"I have a feeling something bad is going to happen," I said.

"We'll be ready for it," Crane assured us.

But a shadow had stolen quietly into our house. It threw a darkness on our cozy gathering. Several days had passed since the twins' abduction and the crash of the Sky Princess. Was I the only one who held out hope Briana and Bennett were still alive?

~ * ~

At Marston the next day, the rehearsals were done, the props and costumes assembled, and the troop of actors, otherwise known as my World Literature class, was ready for opening day.

Because all the scenes in *A Midsummer Night's Dream* were to be acted out in a forest, the students in charge of scenery had fashioned large cardboard trees colored with poster paint and festooned with paper leaves.

They were grouped together in the front of the blackboard that was covered with chalk drawings of trees. Leonora and I had opened the divider, turning our classrooms into a makeshift auditorium. In addition to the trees, we had paper fairies pasted on branches and a luminous yellow moon suspended from the ceiling. On the floor, potted pansies filled in for woodland wildflowers.

Behold the enchanted forest filled with lovers and actors and a mischievous sprite named Puck.

"They did a fantastic job with the props," Leonora whispered as she turned off the lights.

"We'll have to find a place to store the trees," I said. "I can almost believe we're in a wood near Athens."

"That's known as the willing suspension of disbelief."

I nodded. "Showtime!"

The first group was waiting in the hall, attired in their homemade costumes. The others, ready for their entrances, were in their assigned seats, an entire classroom serving as backstage. We'd decided—or I should say I'd decided—to present the scenes in chronological order with a narrator to fill in the connecting action.

As Lacey Fredericks read a short summery of the opening action, my thoughts wandered over the miles to our own enchanted forest, the woods between Jonquil and Squill Lanes where Brent and Crane were investigating a white sweater tied to a tree house.

It was definitely a sweater, I'd decided. A white spring sweater worn by a little girl.

The woods in Foxglove Corners had seen strange sights in the past. Bodies buried in the earth, old structures like the tree house, ghost dogs, and assailants with murder on their minds. I'd met all of them at one time or another and, for the most part, emerged from the encounters unscathed.

I hoped my intrepid explorers would be careful and safe and that they'd find the kidnapped twins or perhaps Camille's intruder.

Lacey read: "When Hermia's wicked father tries to force her to marry Demetrius, Hermia and her true love, Lysander, decide to elope. They run away to the woods to take refuge with Lysander's aunt…"

I turned my attention back to a double classroom in Marston High School, where the real magic was that I'd finally come up with an innovative idea to bring Shakespeare to life for a group of formerly indifferent tenth graders.

The play was in full swing. In trooped Demetrius with a besotted Helena in hot pursuit. "The wildest hath not such a heart as you!" Helena cried.

I had to smile. I'd heard Andrea, who played Helena, say that line to her real life boyfriend in the hall yesterday.

What my students liked best about the play was the love potion that tore the pairs of lovers apart and matched them with different partners. And, of course, they loved Puck.

In another part of the forest, Puck, wearing green wings, peered around a faux tree to watch the unfolding drama while Titania, the fairy queen, lay under a tree asleep.

My amateur thespians were good, even the ones who read their lines from index cards. And the audience, Leonora's students who would be presenting scenes from *Julius Caesar* next, was watching attentively. Perversely I wished the principal were in town to see our play. He'd never been one of my fans, and Leonora had fared only slightly better. It was time he appreciated his English teachers.

~ * ~

Once again Crane and I were entertaining Brent Fowler, this time at our kitchen table with cold drinks and potato chips. The two adventurers were giving me a detailed account of their morning foray into the woods. They had taken the sinister shortcut and, half way to Squill Lane, had found the tree house exactly where Brent said it would be.

"It was a child's sweater," Brent said. "The kind a little girl would wear. It had ruffly edges."

I knew it.

Once again I called back my memory of the twins as I'd glimpsed them in the hot air balloon. They'd both worn shirts with comic book characters on the front. If Briana had brought a sweater with her, it hadn't been visible from the ground. Besides, fancy white sweaters were for Sundays and birthday parties.

But wasn't the trip to the water park supposed to be a birthday excursion?

"Did you bring it back with you?" I asked.

"We left it there tied to the tree house," Crane said. "We're going to keep an eye on that spot."

"I still think it was an SOS," Brent said. "Some kid is lost in the woods, a little girl, probably; but we sure didn't see anybody. We both called out. No one answered."

"And nobody reported children missing," Crane added. "Not since the twins."

I leaned forward. "Then who left the sweater there and when?"

"Like I said, I haven't seen it before, and I've been flying over that area every day."

That must have been the clue he'd been so secretive about before, the one he wasn't ready to talk about.

"I'm thinking it means surrender," I said. "You know. Like in *The Wizard of Oz.* Surrender, Dorothy. A kid's game."

My reasoning broke down with the ruffly sweater. What child would wear such a garment for rough-and-tumble play?

"I hope no kids hang out in that house," Crane said. "It's old and rotting. Someone should tear it down."

"Now that I think of it, the only child I've seen in the neighborhood is Will Ross' little girl, Cindy. She's too young to go in the woods alone."

"We don't know every family," Crane pointed out.

"There must be more kids around," Brent said. "You just haven't seen them. Woods make a great place to play."

Still, dark, mysterious, and dangerous. How easily a person could get lost in a forest. To one who didn't know the way out, one acre would be the same as eighty. A small child would feel like a dwarf under those tall trees.

Now, with Johnston Holliday back in town, any place in Foxglove Corners could be dangerous. The woods especially so.

"You see a lot from the air, but hiking is good too," Brent said.

"I agree. Like that Indian doll I found when I took the dogs walking in the woods across the lane. I'd never have seen it from a balloon."

Brent didn't know about the doll. I told him now and mentioned the black-haired woman, Anne, who had been looking for it, allegedly.

"That's a strange story," he said. "Did you ever see her again?"

"No, and I don't believe she lives in the area. For a while I wondered if she was the one who broke into Camille's house."

That was another story Brent didn't know. After I told him about the light in the window and the strawberry preserves, he said, "You're surrounded by mysteries, Jennet. Shouldn't you be solving them?"

"I will. All in good time."

But not soon enough. Camille and Gilbert were coming home this weekend. All we'd accomplished was to have the locks changed and send a key by Priority Mail to Camille.

"I'm taking the Sky Princess up tomorrow afternoon," Brent said. "How about joining me, Jennet?"

"In the air?"

"Well, yes. In the air. Balloons fly."

An image of the Sky Princess in pieces formed in my mind, followed by others equally disturbing. Myself a splatter of red on the ground. A coffin draped in spring flowers. A black collie to mourn me. Crane…

The dream crash was so vivid and powerful that there was no room for a misplaced feeling. No reason for a self-conscious blush.

"I'd rather wait for the leaves to turn color, like we planned," I said.

Coward. The voice was in my head. It fairly dripped with derision. There was no reason for me not to accompany Brent in his balloon. Not a single one.

Leave well enough alone, I thought and brought three more root beers out of the refrigerator.

By the time Crane and I took our color tour in the fall, all of these mysteries would be in the past, and my dream of Brent would be so long forgotten that I wouldn't even remember it.

Or so I hoped.

Twenty-nine

Then something happened. Not what I'd been expecting, but welcome nonetheless. Brent had seen a small sable and white collie strolling down Squill Lane. On sighting the low-flying hot air balloon, it dashed into the woods.

"At first I thought it was a coyote," Brent said, "but that little mite could be the puppy you're looking for, Jennet. Too bad I lost her."

"Sandy!" I said. "Just when I'd almost given up hope of finding her. She's been living in the wild."

"Some of the time, anyway."

Again Brent sat in our kitchen. Again Crane was home. This time Brent had come to invite us to have dinner with him at the Hunt Club Inn. We were both happy to accept as the Inn was Foxglove Corners' premier restaurant. A favorite haunt of Brent's, it was memorable for subdued hunt décor and a deplorable fox head wreath.

"I wish we could know for certain it's Sandy," I said.

"Are there any other missing collie puppies in Foxglove Corners?" Brent asked.

"None that I know of."

"Well then. What's that you said to me last night? Don't look on the dark side?"

I smiled at him. "I'm glad you're listening. I guess I'd better not tell Josie yet."

I was tempted to dial her number right away. Josie would be overjoyed to have her precious puppy back and, with luck, she would be able to keep her. And Marvel could stop worrying about her little lost one. 'The curse is broken,' she'd say.

But these happy scenarios were premature.

"Wait a while," Brent said. "We know the little dog is alive, but catching her will be a problem."

"Not for Jennet," Crane said, as always demonstrating his faith in my capabilities. I who had no such faith started to protest, but he said, "Is the sweater still there, Fowler?"

"Still there."

I fell silent, thinking about all the times I'd taken the dogs walking up and down the lanes. Usually I turned right on Squill Lane, hoping to see the horses grazing at the Brittons' stables. But at some point, I or one of the dogs should have been aware of a collie puppy living in the woods.

Now that I stopped to think about it, Candy had sent me her own unique signals that something was amiss in our surroundings. Then there was the cry in the woods, which, incidentally, were a long way from Lakeville.

Could four small legs have carried Sandy this far? What had she been eating? And had she tangled with any wild creatures?

Only last week I'd read an article in the *Banner* about an English setter bitten by an Eastern Massasauga rattler, the only poisonous snake living in Michigan. Presumably the setter had stuck her head in vegetation or under a log and surprised the viper. She was going to be all right, after receiving prompt veterinarian care because her owner was nearby to rush her to an animal hospital.

What if something similar happened to Sandy? She had no one.

I reminded myself that, as of this morning, Josie's puppy was able to stroll down Squill Lane. Stroll, Brent had said. Not run or limp, but stroll as if she traveled on a familiar path.

I said, "We have to find her."

"How?" Brent asked. "We can't just wait for her to reappear. It might never happen. She might move on."

"We'll just do it," I said. "It's wonderful news about the puppy, but what about the Cooper twins?"

Brent feigned exasperation. "Please. One discovery at a time."

"Now I have news," Crane said. "I didn't have a chance to tell Jennet yet. Mac described the sweater to Mrs. Cooper, and Briana had one just like it—white with three-quarter-length sleeves and ruffled edges. It's missing from her closet."

I was elated. "That means the twins are near!"

He nodded. "If it's the same sweater, it proves that the kids were in the woods. Maybe they're still there."

Brent pounded the table with his fist. "I'm right! It's an SOS. They need help."

He was right. "We'll concentrate on that part of the woods.

With the shortcut path, I thought, the path I'd sworn never to traverse again.

"Mac already sent a man out to search," Crane said. "They didn't find anything."

A connection tugged at me. It was a faint glimmer, too faint to withstand Brent's blustery voice.

"They will," he boomed. "Or I will. Let's celebrate with steak and ale."

I felt it was too soon for celebration. "What if Johnston Holliday is looking for them too?"

"Then we'll get him," Crane said.

With this bombardment of male confidence, how could we not succeed in any undertaking?

Crane and Brent were both standing, ready for meat and potatoes—and ale. It was later than our usual dinner hour, and I was hungry too; but if it hadn't been so dark out, I would have begun my own search immediately.

"We're getting closer," I said.

And I had a feeling every minute counted.

~ * ~

As always, my other life and commitments intervened. The next day after school, Leonora and I made plans on the way home. "We should get an early start on grocery shopping for the barbecue," I said.

I entered the freeway and watched for my chance to merge into northbound traffic.

Leonora had another idea. "I'd rather go for a walk in the woods. Who knows what we'll find?"

"We have the rest of the weekend,"

Tomorrow Principal Grimsly was dismissing school two hours early for the Memorial Day recess, a good decision as a majority of the senior class had already left for spring break.

"I'm not used to hosting large gatherings," I said. "I want to be prepared."

Leonora had volunteered to help me assemble side dishes and make desserts. Crane and Brent were going to man the grill. They planned on barbecuing chicken, which I had to buy. Ever since I'd thought of the idea, the guest list had been growing. By now it was going to be a gala outdoors affair.

"I want to stop at Clovers, too," I said.

I hoped Annica would be working. I wanted to give her the news about Sandy and the white sweater in person. Fortunately she was rearranging cakes and pies in the dessert carousel. The restaurant wasn't particularly busy, and Mary Jeanne was on her dinner break.

Annica, like her desserts, was decorated in red, white, and blue. Tiny flags sparkled on her ears and a bracelet loaded with patriotic charms jingled as she rearranged the plates. She also thought of Johnston Holliday.

"It makes sense now," she said. "He came back to Foxglove Corners for the kids. I wonder how he lost them in the first place?"

"He must be an amateur kidnapper," Leonora said. "One of those stupid crooks you read about."

"Or the kids were super smart," I added.

"I think he was inept," Annica said. "He demands a ransom, then doesn't bother to pick it up. How dumb is that?"

The untouched ransom was still a mystery, but I considered it a minor one.

"Who gets the reward for finding the puppy?" Annica asked in a dizzying change of focus.

"Probably Brent Fowler," I said.

Brent must be worth millions and would most likely donate the reward money to an animal charity. But wait! Part of the money for Sandy's return had come from his own pocket.

"I could use some extra cash," Annica said. "What do we do now, Jennet? Form a search party? Arm ourselves with dog treats and rope?"

I thought it best to distract her. "If you don't have plans for the weekend, you're invited to our barbecue," I said. "It's on Saturday around four. You can bring a date if you like."

"I accept!" Her eyes lit up. "Will Brent Fowler be there?"

"Yes, but he's too old for you."

Annica had met Brent at our wedding. I doubt if she'd seen him since, although he did occasionally frequent Clovers.

Annica's brilliant red lips formed into a childish pout. "Says who?"

Leonora said, "Isn't he a notorious playboy?"

"And an avid fox hunter," I added. "You don't look like the kind of girl who condones hunting down poor little creatures."

"Jeez," Annica said. "I just asked a question."

"We'd better hurry if we have to go to the grocers," Leonora pointed out.

"Let's buy dessert here," I said.

We settled on a dozen small cupcakes topped with flags in coconut nests that Leonora pronounced too cute to leave in the carousel. She planned to copy the decoration on a sheet cake.

Annica arranged the cupcakes in a white box, a sly secretive smile on her face.

"See you soon," she said as I handed her the correct change.

The prospect of a celebration to welcome summer had an euphoric effect on me. Although I loved solving mysteries, for once it was a pleasure to anticipate pure fun.

~ * ~

The hot air balloon glided lazily over the shortcut woods. Its colors mirrored those of nature. Blue sky, green treetops, yellow sun, and red.

What was red?

Below us, the narrow shortcut meandered through the woods, turning and twisting its way from Jonquil Lane to Squill Lane.

"The best way to see the countryside is from the sky," Brent said. "Look how clear everything is."

I looked. I saw endless woods and the shortcut path and the dilapidated tree house with a child's white sweater tied to its porch post. But not the puppy. We were looking for Sandy whose name rhymed with Mandy, Brandy, and Andy.

Like a flag, the sweater waved languidly in the breeze, a sure indication that the twins were near. Johnston Holliday was stalking them. And in another part of the forest, something was stalking him. I couldn't see Holliday's pursuer, but I knew he was there, one of Lucy Hazen's menacing shadow people, dark and dangerous, closing in on him.

The wind carried us along, across Squill Lane, across meadowland where horses grazed peacefully in the afternoon light. Peacefully, quietly.

Why was the wind so strong?

"I thought of a snappy new slogan for Skyway Tours," Brent said. "It's 'Come fly with me.' What do you think?"

"I think it's nice."

Skyway's original owner, Cameron Lodge, had said that once to Camille and me.

Brent slipped his arm around my shoulders, and pulled me close. Too close, and I didn't object.

All of a sudden the winds picked up. Monstrous gusts tossed the balloon to and fro. And down! We were falling. Going to crash. Almost one with the ground.

Time disappeared.

And I knew what was red.

Blood.

Thirty

I opened my eyes. The bedroom furnishings seemed to have a red cast. I lay still, letting the nightmare dissolve around me and the color drain from the darkness.

This was the third time I'd had the dream of sailing in a hot air balloon with Brent Fowler. The third time I'd seen a preview of my death while Brent kept his arm around my shoulders and I offered no objection.

In a dream, Jennet. In a dream. A dream.

But surely the nightmare crash was a premonition of disaster to come. Or, perhaps inspired by the crash of the Sky Princess which hadn't involved me? That would be less worrisome. I'd promised myself not to obsess about Brent's intentions, not even to think about them.

But for my peace of mind, I needed to squeeze in a visit to Lucy Hazen sometime today. In the meantime, what interpretations could I come up with?

My subconscious was warning me of danger. *Don't go on that autumn color tour in Brent's balloon. Say you're afraid.*

And stay away from Brent, which would be difficult to do when he considered himself a family friend. When he *was* our good friend.

Oblivious of my unease, Crane stirred, turned, and went back to sleep. As I had better do. Tomorrow would be another busy day. The inside of the house was clean and neat, but an outside gathering would involve tending the flowerbeds and putting away the dogs' toys. Crane had already mowed the lawn. Later, Leonora and I were going to get a head start on salads and desserts.

I began making mental lists.

As usually happens when the brain winds itself up, sleep evaded me. The normal sounds of the house at night seemed unnaturally loud and, now that the red cast had gone, the moonlight pouring into the room was too bright. I realized I was hungry and began to think of grabbing a quick snack in the kitchen.

But that would mean disturbing the dogs, who would then want snacks of their own, followed by another outing. I'd never go back to sleep.

Just water then. A quick drink of ice water from the pitcher in the refrigerator. In the kitchen, out of the kitchen. Or, better still, tap water from the bathroom.

I slipped out of bed, and as I often did, glanced out the window. Across the lane, the yellow Victorian was ablaze with light. Bright, blinding ghost light.

I gripped the windowsill and stared into the night. It looked as if every single lamp in the front rooms had been turned on, as well as the porch light.

Then I saw Camille's Chevy parked in the driveway. It was all right. Better than all right. Camille and her husband were home. Their presence would banish at least some of the strangeness.

~ * ~

After breakfast when Crane and I were ready to begin our respective days, the yellow Victorian was dark and still. I would have thought the midnight light festival was another dream except for the reality of the Chevy, looking tired and dusty from the long journey back to Michigan.

When I pulled into my own driveway at the end of the shortened school day, Camille and Gilbert were both in the garden wading through high grasses as they whacked weeds out of existence.

Holly, now grown to full collie size, dashed across the lane and ran in dizzying circles around my car. Even Twister, the black Belgian shepherd, making a more sedate approach, padded over to say hello. They hadn't forgotten me.

As I opened the car door, Holly jumped up on me, throwing me back into the seat. Camille and Gilbert, who had followed the dogs across the lane, finally caught up to them.

"Holly, Down!" Camille called.

Holly sank into a graceful Sit but kept her eyes on Camille, waiting for permission to continue her welcome. Collie faces filled the kitchen window, and the barking of six excited dogs fractured the country stillness.

"Welcome home," I said, finally managing an awkward exit from the car.

Camille enveloped me in a tearful hug.

She and her groom looked years younger, tanned and glowing, their happiness a magical cloak that embraced me in radiance.

Love should always be a magical cloak.

"The last time I saw Foxglove Corners it was buried in snow and ice," Camille said. "Now everything is green, and it's so cool. I'd almost forgotten."

"Tennessee is green too," Gilbert reminded her.

"But not cool."

"You're right. It's been downright hot. In the South we live in a small town," Gilbert said. "I'm looking forward to summer in the country."

"We're not even unpacked yet," Camille said. "We just got our old clothes out of the suitcase and came out to work in the garden. We already unearthed the prettiest forget-me-nots."

I remembered them because last year Camille had given me several plants that had reseeded themselves. Little pink and blue flowers shining like stars, they were among the first flowers of spring.

"Is everything okay in the house?" I asked.

"All the important things," she assured me. "It doesn't seem possible somebody broke in, but I saw the telltale trash in the wastebasket. I'm so glad you had our locks changed."

Darn. Wasn't she going to mention the box? Maybe she meant to keep it a secret from Gilbert.

"Everything's all right in the sewing room too," she said, knowing that I'd remember her mention of a secret stash of money. "Why anyone would venture up there is beyond me."

"I was beginning to think your house was haunted when I saw the light in the window," I said.

She laughed softly. "It's a mystery, but there's no ghost, I'm sure. There never has been. And if one took up residence in our absence, we'll send it on its way."

"With bell, book, and candle," Gilbert added.

"What can we bring to the barbecue?" Camille asked.

"Nothing. Just walk across the lane. Everyone we know will be here."

"Before then let's get together over tea and cake."

"It's a date," I said, wondering if I could still find time to visit Lucy.

"As soon as you take care of your dogs, I want to hear everything I missed," Camille said.

"There's been a lot going on."

Where should I begin? Kidnapped children, a lost puppy, and stalkers in the woods, not to mention the body of a young man and a missing private investigator.

I gave her the highlights. "Brent found Briana's sweater on a tree house in the woods. The kidnapper came back to town, but the police haven't caught him yet. Oh, and Brent spied the lost puppy. Apparently she's living in the wild."

"Brent's been busy." Camille reached for her husband's hand, and Holly, seeing her mistress was distracted, sprang up. She and Candy might have been cut from the same cloth.

"We came back just in time for the excitement," Camille said.

I glanced at the old yellow Victorian so mellow in the afternoon light. So infinitely peaceful. "Your house looks happy again," I said. "It's been grieving."

Gilbert followed my gaze, a puzzled expression on his face. Camille understood.

"You're in Foxglove Corners, Gilbert," she said. "Even our houses have emotions."

~ * ~

Lucy lifted my teacup, a motion that set the gold Zodiac charms on her bracelet jingling. She peered inside and pointed to a tiny black blob. "It's still here," she said. "The shapeless shadow. I think it's a little closer to your home."

This was an ideal time to remind myself that I didn't believe Lucy's predictions would necessarily come true. As for Brent's behavior in my dreams, I hadn't mentioned it. Along with my determination to dismiss it, I suspected that Lucy and Brent might be closer than I'd thought. He was escorting her to the barbecue tomorrow. So I focused on the crash.

Pointing to my own symbol, I said, "Could this blob be a balloon?"

"No. I don't see any hot air balloons in your cup. They're all in your dreams."

"Then I guess I won't die in one."

She smiled. "Not likely. Unless a balloon falls out of the sky and flattens you."

I ran my hand along Sky's ribcage. She responded by wagging her tail slowly. With a dog's affection, even the horrible lost its sting.

"Then why did I have three dreams about crashing?" I asked.

"Who can say?" Lucy set the cup down on the coffee table. "Dreams are just dreams. Only rarely are they previews of coming events. The crash is probably weighing on your mind. But nobody died when the Sky Princess went down, did they?"

"So far as we know, no. Brent's young employee, Eric, was shot earlier, presumably by Johnston Holliday."

"I'd be more afraid of an airplane crash," Lucy said. "And you have a choice, Jennet. You don't have to go up in a hot air balloon. Ever."

"I won't."

Even though you can see more clearly from the air. Brent had said that, both in the dream and in reality.

A faint glimmer slipped into Lucy's sunroom, hardly noticed amidst the brightness of the late afternoon sun. Again something tugged at me. It was a nebulous something. An important something that was growing desperate to be noticed.

Then it was gone, a candle flame winking out. We were alone, Lucy, Sky, and I, with an empty teapot on the coffee table and a plate filled with cookie crumbs.

Lucy frowned and picked up my cup again. "There's something I forgot to mention. Ah! Here it is. I see a tunnel."

She passed the cup to me. “Right next to the blob. Do you see it?”

She was referring to a long leaf that could possibly symbolize a tunnel—to one who had a talent for telling fortunes by reading tea leaves. Not having that gift, all I saw was the long leaf.

“I wish there was a light,” I said.

At Lucy’s startled expression, I added, “The proverbial light at the end of the tunnel.”

“Oh. For a moment I thought you meant the light you’re supposed to see as you cross over to the other side.”

Good grief! That wasn’t what I meant.

“I was thinking of clarification. Logical answers to all the mysteries. Happy endings for everyone and for little Sandy too.”

But Lucy, albeit unwittingly, had left me with a frightening image. Down the dark tunnel. Follow the light out of this world and into the next.

One of these days I had to stop participating in this fortune telling business.

Thirty-one

Camille poured the tea and cut thick slices of cranberry orange bread. Three other loaves were cooling on the counter, along with pecan pies for tomorrow's barbecue. Camille always found time for the activities she loved most and for her friends, even after a long road trip and a day of weed whacking.

Her blue and white country kitchen looked lived-in now with the counters in a state of cheerful clutter and sweet spices scenting the room. The time when a jar of strawberry preserves, origin unknown, had been the only item in sight seemed part of the distant past.

Our reunion was truly like old times except that now Gilbert was visiting with Crane in our house and a diamond wedding ring sparkled on Camille's left hand. But the kitchen was still a place of peace and solutions. I'd never brought Camille a concern too great to be reduced to manageable size.

"I've been wondering," I said. "Now you're happily married, do you ever think you could dream about another man? Not pine for him. Just interact with him in a dream?"

"That's an odd question. Would you like to tell me what inspired it?"

"I was just curious."

"I never dream much," she said. "When I do, I don't remember my dreams."

She had sidestepped my question. I tried again. "Hypothetically, do you think it's significant that a married woman, who's a hundred percent satisfied with her husband, would dream about another man?"

"Romantically, you mean?"

"Yes, but not graphically. He's just there. His arm is around her. In the dream, that is. She enjoys it."

"Without even a passionate kiss? That's a pretty low-key dream."

"Still it bothers me."

Darn it. Double darn. I'd given myself away.

"Ah!" she said. "So this question isn't hypothetical."

I sighed, feeling like a fool. But I didn't add the man in my dreams was Brent Fowler.

Camille's lips curved in a reminiscent smile. "You'll remember how miserable I was in my first marriage. After I escaped from Richard I wasn't interested in forming a relationship with another man. I had my garden and my ambition to write cookbooks. I honestly thought that was sufficient until Gilbert came along. Nowadays my whole life is one long wonderful dream."

How sweet, I thought. "So is mine."

I broke the cranberry bread in small chunks and wondered if Camille had actually answered my question. But had I phrased it in an intelligent way?

What I really wanted to know was simple enough. Why would I dream about Brent Fowler as if I were a single girl on a date with an eligible man? Why had I felt the burst of excitement that comes with romantic beginnings?

If I rephrased the question, perhaps Camille would be able to give me a helpful answer.

But the words eluded me. So I told her how good her cranberry bread tasted, and we agreed that dreams were too amorphous and unreliable to be analyzed.

After all, what significance could there be in dancing toast or upside down rainbows?

"As long as you're still in love with Crane, I wouldn't worry," Camille said.

"I am. Deeply. There's no doubt about that."

"Then don't be afraid to dream."

In that moment she sounded like Lucy, and in the next I had an epiphany of sorts. Brent had always been my not-so-secret admirer. Now he seemed to have fallen under the spell of my friend, Lucy. Perhaps my dream self was simply and understandably jealous.

~ * ~

On Memorial Day a tantalizing smell of barbecued chicken filled the still air. Crane and Brent had set up their headquarters near a card table where Annica, ever helpful, had volunteered to keep the waiting chicken parts safe from flies and hungry collies.

I suspected she also planned to keep Brent under surveillance.

Preferring the taste of cooked chicken to raw, the dogs ignored the card table and lay down as close to the grill as they were allowed.

Except for Holly and Gemmy. Deputy Sheriff Jake Brown was amusing them and himself with a rousing game of Frisbee in the wildflower meadow. They'd rarely had a more enthusiastic playmate, nor one who could throw a Frisbee higher. Poor Candy was torn between the progress of the barbecued chicken and her favorite pastime, chasing a flying object. She kept an eager eye on both.

At the grill, Brent told anyone who inquired, "The drumsticks have my own special sauce. Texas style."

"That means super spicy and hot," I said, passing by with a large bowl of potato salad.

"And delicious. It's an old family recipe," he added.

"I didn't know you had Texas roots."

"That is, Lucy's old family recipe. She's the transplanted Texan."

"Well, it smells wonderful," I said.

I paused for a moment, savoring the sight of my friends and family gathered together under the sparkling blue sky. Everyone I'd invited had come. Most of them were friends I'd made after moving to Foxglove Corners. All except Gilbert, they were people with whom I'd shared mystery and adventure.

Crane, of course, and my sister, Julia, whom I hadn't seen in weeks. Then Camille and Gilbert; Lila and Letty Woodville from the animal shelter with Henry McCullough; Miss Eidt and her young library assistant, Debby; and Annica who'd bought two chocolate meringue pies from Clovers' kitchen. The celebration had the ambience of Thanksgiving in spring. The very air carried a blessing.

Leonora set a buffet table with paper plates and real silverware wrapped in linen napkins while Julia followed her, placing bottles filled with wildflower sprays and tiny flags at intervals. In the *Who-Ends-Up-With-Jake?* race, Leonora was clearly in the lead. Julia appeared not to mind. She had one goal these days: to earn her Masters of Arts Degree in English Literature a semester early.

"It truly doesn't matter," she'd said to me in a whispered aside. "I'm plowing my way through Victorian novels. Who has time for frivolous romance?"

A most uncharacteristic sentiment from my glamorous, romance-minded sister. But I could only take her at her word. I noted she had arranged her golden-blonde hair in a becoming French twist and was wearing glasses.

Jake, that dark and handsome man, the prize, had arrived at the barbecue alone, but he had taken Leonora to an art fair last week. He and Julia were quite cordial to each other. Everyone mingled freely and happily together with the camaraderie essential for a successful party.

Making a snap decision, Gemmy dashed over to join the Frisbee game, leaving Sky and Twister to guard the grill. I watched the bright pink disk fly through the air, watched Gemmy leap up, jaws open. She caught it and ran back to Jake, who tossed it up to the sky again.

The game continued, the Frisbee flew, and I thought of the day I'd seen the hot air balloon over Jonquil Lane and of everything that happened afterward. Murder, abduction, home invasion and strange clues that appeared like ghost lights and led nowhere. We were deep in another mystery; this day was only a pleasant interlude.

"Everything's ready," Leonora said, surveying the picnic tables. "I have thirteen chairs. I took some out to the porch."

"Thirteen," Lucy echoed.

"Oh my gosh. That's an unlucky number, isn't it?"

I did my own calculations; I certainly didn't want to host a bad luck barbecue. "But you didn't count Crane and me. We make fifteen."

"That's all right then," Lucy said, and Leonora nodded.

When had we all grown so superstitious?

Crane ladled sizzling chicken pieces onto a large platter. Brent, aided by Annica, filled a tray with the hot and spicy Texas drumsticks. His booming voice stilled the buzz of conversation. "I say let's eat!"

~ * ~

"Hey," Brent shouted. "Who the h—heck! Who's the comedian?"

He and Lucy had stepped away from their corner of the picnic table to scoop up a helping of the pasta salad. I stood, pie server in hand, beholding his irate form. All eyes, except those of the people on the porch, turned to see what had caused the outburst.

"Come on!" he said. "Give me my dinner back."

Candy!

But Candy was on the porch. I'd taken the precaution of feeding the dogs before the rest of us sat down to eat. Presumably they were too full to beg for handouts. All but one.

Hearing her name, Candy ran up to me, a picture of falsely accused innocence.

I walked over to the bench. "What's wrong Brent?"

"Somebody stole my plate. It isn't funny."

"Brent." Lucy laid a hand on his arm. "We're all friends here. Who would steal your dinner? My plate's here. But… I thought I had another drumstick. I *did*."

As she spoke, I saw a trail of spilled food leading from the bench into the meadow that backed up to the woods. Beans, corn relish, potato salad, sliced tomatoes—a colorful mess. I couldn't see the paper plate.

"Calm down, Brent," I said. "The culprit is an animal." I pointed to the food in the grass. "The smell of your good cooking lured the woodland creatures out of the woods. There's probably a coyote now gnawing on a chicken bone. I hope he doesn't choke. Anyway, we have plenty of food." I paused to take a breath.

Quietly Crane set another plate heaped with food in Brent's empty place. "Here you go, Fowler. Eat it up."

Brent glared at his tablemates: the gentle Woodville sisters and genial Henry McCullough. Annica, sitting on the end, was having trouble containing her mirth.

In truth, Brent's wrath over his missing plate bordered on the comical. I was tempted to laugh myself if I dared. A hostess doesn't laugh at her guest.

"Didn't the rest of you see anything?" I asked.

"We were talking about all the pretty collies," Lila said.

Annica leaped up. "I see one now! Jennet! Look!"

A small, scrawny canine watched us from a safe distance, its white ruff splattered with barbecue sauce. It licked its chops and held its ground. The little thief definitely wasn't a coyote. It was…

"Sandy!"

"After her," Annica cried.

The puppy turned tail and melted into tall grasses, bound for the woods.

"Annica! Come back."

Didn't she know that no one catches a dog who wants to run away? A canine has four legs and speed. A human has two and inferior stamina.

Still, this Sandy sighting was too good an opportunity to bypass. Forgetting my duties as hostess, I took off after Annica, dimly aware of Crane calling my name and of Candy and Gemmy running behind me.

The chase was on.

Thirty-two

Breathing heavily, Annica flopped down on the trunk of a fallen tree. I joined her, surprised to find it made a comfortable bench. Gemmy lay down at my feet, panting, but Candy sniffed her surroundings intently, satisfied with other woodland scents.

"That little demon got away," Annica said, checking to see that her turquoise earrings were still attached.

Ahead of us the new construction loomed, silent and eerie. 'A French chateau in a charming country setting', the ads had proclaimed. Now unfinished houses were abandoned, and expensive lumber lay rotting in the damp weeds. Walls without windows trembled when the wind blew.

Beyond the development rose a tangle of close-growing trees and deadwood. With Sandy nowhere in sight, there was no point in continuing the chase.

"She's taken cover in the woods," I said. "That's what any sensible dog would do. She may have a well-appointed lair somewhere."

"Can't we set a trap for her?" Annica asked. "We could come back with chicken, if you have leftovers."

"We could," I said. "I'm not prepared to keep watch all day and night though. Maybe she'll come back to the food source if we go away quietly."

"You mean to the party?"

I nodded. "Or the house."

"Sandy!" Annica called. "Here, Sandy. Good puppy. Chicken!"

Candy tilted her head and came running back to us. A bird began to sing, its happy trilling incongruous in the dark silence of the encroaching forest.

"Do you think Sandy remembers her name?" Annica asked.

"I doubt it. She wasn't with anyone long enough."

I thought I could safely call Josie now that I knew Sandy was alive. Maybe Josie's sister or mother could join in the search, and Brent would help. He loved dogs and by now would have already forgiven the little thief who had absconded with his expertly barbecued chicken.

Annica said, "Can we come back again and look for her with some kind of tasty bait? I can bring something from Clovers. Maybe meatballs."

"I don't think we'll accomplish anything by tramping aimlessly in the wilderness," I said.

"Isn't there a path up a little farther? We could follow that."

"Yes."

The shortcut. Even after all this time, the mere thought of it sent a shiver coursing through my bloodstream. Footsteps and shadows and strange cries. They were all magnified on that twisting trail, and I couldn't rid myself of the notion at its end something malignant waited to strike.

But Annica wanted so desperately to be a part of my search. For the puppy, for the twins. To her, I suspected it didn't matter which.

"When are you free?" I asked.

"Next Wednesday. I don't have a class and I don't have to work."

"Wednesday it is then, after school. Unless I find Sandy by then." I brushed aside a long strand of prickly green vine that had attached itself to my leg. The fallen tree trunk was growing more comfortable with each passing minute. "We'd better go back."

"I hate to return without Sandy," Annica said.

"So do I, but she outran us."

Annica got up and stretched. Her red-gold hair found a patch of sunlight, acquiring an instant fiery cast. "I wonder if Josie will be able to tame her after she's lived in the woods?"

"Dogs crave human companionship, and Sandy is still young. She's going to be all right."

Good crunchy meals, fresh water, toys, loving pats, treats. What dog wouldn't trade the freedom of the wild for a real home?

With the dogs in the lead, we made our way out to Jonquil Lane, where the walking was easier.

Like a kaleidoscope, Annica's focus shifted. "I haven't had any dessert yet. I hope they left us something."

"We haven't been gone that long."

About twenty minutes, I'd guess. I had never meant to desert my guests. As co-hostess, Leonora would cover for me, and Crane would understand. They all would. But like Annica, I'd rather be returning with the runaway puppy in my arms, a tangible prize to justify the disruption.

I'll catch her soon, I thought.

~ * ~

In our absence, Brent had enlightened the others about Sandy's convoluted history and, in the process, stoked the fires of curiosity. Everyone wanted an accounting of our adventure in the woods. I let

Annica spin the narrative, which she did with high drama and the requisite embellishments.

"Running after a puppy isn't the best way to catch her," Crane informed us.

"We felt like a little exercise after dinner," Annica said.

"Did you forget about snakes in the woods?" he asked

She had. Cleverly hiding her dismay, Annica tossed her head. "We didn't see anything dangerous."

To her delight, a whole pecan pie remained on the buffet. Brent was still eating and, as I'd imagined, his jovial mood had returned. Lucy sat quietly at his side, drinking iced tea brewed in the sun and nibbling on one of the patriotic cupcakes from Clovers.

Apparently Brent had also mentioned the white sweater because Miss Eidt asked about the twins.

"I guess you didn't see any signs of those poor little children or their babysitter? What was her name again? Sara?"

In the heat of the chase, I hadn't thought about them, but I didn't say that. "We were running, and we didn't go very far. Just up to those new houses that never sold."

"And never will," Brent said. "That development will never even be finished."

"The builder declared bankruptcy," Letty Woodville added. "I read about it in the paper."

"What will happen to them now?" Miss Eidt asked. "They were going to be so beautiful. Surely they won't tear them down."

Nobody knew. The conversation veered toward greedy, unscrupulous developers and the despoiling of our precious state. Destruction of the wetlands, wild creatures driven out of their habitats, elegant ruins left where woods had once risen proudly to the sky. It was criminal. Sinful.

Abducted children and a little lost puppy drowned in a tidal wave of relevant issues. But they were relevant too.

~ * ~

The white sweater was gone.

On Sunday morning Brent had sailed over the shortcut woods in the Sky Princess. No sweater flapped in the breeze. He'd trekked back to the site and found no trace of it.

We were together again, this time sitting on the porch while steaks sizzled on the grill. One of them was for Brent.

"Gone. Vanished. Without a trace. How do you explain that?" he demanded.

"A bird made off with it," I said.

That was a handy explanation for anything that went missing in the woods.

He was unconvinced. "Wouldn't it be too heavy for a beak?"

"Not a Foxglove Corners bird," Crane said with a teasing glint in his eyes. "Could our thief be a hawk?"

"Why would a hawk want a little girl's sweater?" Brent asked.

"For a man of the woods, you're being unusually obtuse tonight, Brent," I said. "To build a nest."

"There's a possibility that someone came to help the twins," Brent said, holding on to his SOS theory. "Briana could be wearing that sweater right now on her way home."

"In that case I'd know about it," Crane pointed out. "The case is still open."

Speculation was futile but a diversion of sorts. We eased into a familiar debate. If Briana's sweater had been snagged on the tree house, it couldn't be an SOS. A true symbol of help would be anchored in some other way, its sleeve tied to a post perhaps.

Brent remembered thinking that the sweater had been both snagged and tied.

I said, "How about this? Briana and Bennett climb up to the tree house, she loses her sweater on the way down, and for some reason they leave it there?"

"That's all conjecture," Crane said. "I'm going to go with your nest theory, honey."

I could tease too. "Also conjecture."

Brent said, "I have another mystery. Scott doesn't answer my calls. He missed our last meeting. He missed payday."

"Scott must be in trouble," I said.

"That's what I'm afraid of."

"Did you report him missing?" Crane asked.

"He's an adult, and I can't say for sure when he fell off the radar. My radar, that is. Scott never missed a payday before."

"Maybe he met up with Johnston Holliday," I said.

"I hope so. That was his mission."

Brent wasn't following me.

"I'm thinking of a fatal confrontation."

A gun, another body laid at Holliday's doorstep. Eric, Sara and Scott (maybe), the twins.

No, please not the children.

Brent's eyes blazed with fury. "If he killed Scott too, I'll…"

I regretted bringing up the possibility. "We don't know that."

Crane left us briefly to check on the steaks. My contributions to the dinner were salad and biscuits, one chilled, the other hot. Brent had brought a pineapple cheesecake from the Home Town Bakery.

"When were you and Scott supposed to get together?" I asked.

"Yesterday."

"That was Memorial Day."

"A private investigator doesn't stop what he's doing to celebrate a holiday," Brent said.

"Well, he's only a day late. Don't give up on him."

"Steaks are done," Crane announced.

We were going to eat outside on the picnic table tonight. As I brought the salad and biscuits out, I glanced across the wildflower meadow. No bright eyes watched us from a comfortable distance. No small collie puppy waited for the humans to set the steaks on plates, hoping for a moment's inattention.

But she was close by. I sensed it. If anything could lure a hungry puppy out into the open it had to be the smell of Crane's famous charcoal-broiled Porterhouse steaks. He'd cooked an extra one, planning to make sandwiches tomorrow.

So we'd eat our dinner, and when we were finished, I'd suggest we leave the table and keep our own watch from inside. It was as good a plan as any.

"We're ready," I said.

Thirty-three

Sometimes when one event occurs, whether it's momentous or seemingly insignificant, a chain reaction starts. For so long the mysteries that had begun with a hot air balloon flying overhead remained static. Then Brent saw and subsequently lost track of the white sweater. Scott trailed Johnston Holliday across Michigan back to Foxglove Corners only to join the ranks of the missing.

Then two boys playing space pirates in the new construction, a forbidden zone, therefore a fascinating zone, discovered a man asleep in what would have been an elegant chateau. His pockets were empty. There was a band of pale skin where a watch might have been.

Only he wasn't sleeping. He was dead, shot once in the back of the head. The police identified him as Johnston Holliday, also known as Johnny Holliday, wanted for questioning in the murder of Eric Morrow and the abduction of Bennett and Briana Cooper. In a heartbeat, our villain disappeared from the canvas.

Curiously a white sweater with ruffled edges lay close to the body, giving rise to new speculation. Had Holliday removed the sweater from the tree house? Had he also been searching for the twins?

Unbidden, a ghastly scene took form in my mind: Briana falling out of her sweater and dissolving on the forest floor. Bennett? He wasn't with her.

Reality was ghastly enough. Brent's private investigator and the Cooper twins were still missing. So was Sara. How would we find them now? One more mystery joined the queue: Who had killed the killer? Johnny, I decided to call him. It made him seem a little less dangerous.

There must be somebody else skulking in the shadows, a person of whose existence we were unaware. An unknown entity? I sighed. How was that possible? Perhaps Holliday had been shot for his wallet and watch, which didn't explain Briana's sweater.

In another development, Brent's private investigator surfaced, claiming he'd had the flu. Since Holliday was dead, Brent paid him and they parted company. That was one happy outcome.

Meanwhile the warm June air bristled with inaudible whisperings and forebodings. It felt as if a thunderstorm were about to roll in, although the sky was blue and clear. A psychic storm, Lucy would say. Electric, I thought.

Here on the porch with four collies in various stages of rest, I was enjoying a rare respite from activity. School was over for the day. Crane wouldn't be home until later; his dinner was in the refrigerator. For once no one had dropped over unannounced for a visit.

With no enticing cooking aromas to waft across the wildflower meadow into the woods, the puppy amused herself elsewhere. She hadn't emerged from her woodland lair yesterday to sample leftover steak. I didn't expect her to come today. I was alone with nothing urgent to tend to.

The calm before the storm?

Not quite. The collies were restless, especially Candy, who kept her eyes trained on the sky, who held her ears in alert mode to catch every passing sound. Who waited.

Dogs know what we never can. But why did Candy watch the sky? Was she still looking for a glorious flying object with people inside to break the monotony of her day?

Dogs keep their own counsel.

I folded the *Banner* and set it on the wicker side table. The discovery of Johnny Holliday's body claimed the headline and most of the front page. Related stories dealt with updates and pictures of the Cooper twins and their alleged kidnapper, along with a sidebar devoted to the mystery of Briana's sweater and a new statement from the twins' mother.

"If Briana's sweater was in those woods, then so are my children," she'd said. "Why don't they keep looking?"

I imagined they were. They just weren't finding anything significant.

In any event, Mrs. Cooper was coming to Foxglove Corners to conduct a search of her own. I wondered what had taken her so long and if she planned to bring a companion with her. The twins' father was out of the country, traveling somewhere in South America. There was no quote from him.

My cell phone rang its measure of rippling notes, overly loud in the afternoon stillness.

"Hey, Jennet," Annica said. "My class got cancelled, and I'm off work. How about if we go today instead of tomorrow?"

"Go?" I'd conveniently pushed Annica's puppy search plan to the back of my mind.

"Looking for Sandy. Unless you're busy."

I wasn't. Why not take our walk in the woods today? Then tomorrow would be free. There was also Crane. We hadn't had an opportunity to discuss the shooting of Holliday yet. With a murder so near our house, he might take exception to the search. Yes, going into the woods today would be best.

We wouldn't find Sandy, of course. It couldn't possibly be easy, but Annica would be happy; she'd feel as if she were helping a detective.

"Let's do it then," I said. "Only for about an hour though. It looks like rain."

Now where did that come from? White clouds, deep blue sky, sunshine, a hint of wind—but wind was a given in Foxglove Corners.

"We'll take that shortcut through the woods," Annica said. "Unless the police cordoned off the whole forest."

"They wouldn't do that. The kids found the body in the new construction."

"I'll be right over then. Give me twenty minutes."

She would tear up the quiet country roads, unmindful of hidden patrol cars. With her luck, she'd escape notice. I'd have time to change to a sweater, jeans, and tall boots. Woods clothes.

"Be sure to dress for a hike," I said.

"I'm calling from work. If I go home, we'll lose time."

I had to smile as I closed the cell phone. If Annica was coming straight from Clovers, she'd be wearing a brightly colored dress certain to snag on wayward branches, fancy earrings, and perfume to attract an army of mosquitoes.

It should be quite an adventure.

~ * ~

Barking indignantly, hoping to call attention to themselves, three collies clustered around the front door. They knew I was going somewhere without them. I'd already shepherded Candy out to the porch. Unhappy with myself for disappointing the others, I squeezed through a people-sized opening.

I only wanted to take one dog with me. The lucky winner was Candy, who for once didn't seem to mind being on a leash. My reasoning was simple. She was the one who seemed most attuned to changes in the environment.

Annica sat on a wicker chair waiting for me. She wore a green knit dress with white running shoes and no earrings. She'd blend right in with the foliage and brush. On her lap she balanced a large white bag.

"Meatballs," she said. "Mary Jeanne's best. Want one?"

Candy licked her chops.

"No, Candy," I told her. "These are for the puppy. If we don't find her, they're yours to share with your sisters."

"Do you think she understood that?" Annica asked.

"Oh, sure she did. Except for the part about sharing."

We set off up Jonquil Lane. Candy pulled ahead, wagging her tail happily. Past the unfinished houses, one of them enclosed in yellow tape, hereafter to be associated with a violent death. Past the place where the woods grew thicker. Past bursts of wildflowers that added their blues and yellows and pinks to the green.

As we turned onto the shortcut, I felt only the slightest twinge of apprehension. Annica's constant chatter and frequent cries of 'Sandy' left little room for fearful thoughts.

Still I recalled the last time I'd gone this way. That day had been filled with unnerving sounds, cavorting shadows, and long stretches of darkness where branches on either side of the road touched one another, obliterating the light.

The shortcut was narrower than I remembered. High grasses and vines grew along the edges, encroaching on the path. At present we could walk two abreast, but there was the first of several sharp turns ahead. Who knew what lay beyond them? We were still a long way from Squill Lane.

Once a killer had waited for me in the woods, aware of my approach, biding his time. He'd sprung out at me and caught me neatly in his trap. At the memory of all that followed, I suppressed a shudder.

But this was a different time, a different walk, and I wasn't alone.

"Sandy!" Annica called. "What bad little puppy wants a meatball?"

As always, Candy looked over her shoulder hopefully.

Belatedly it occurred to me that this wilderness trek might not be the brightest idea I'd ever had. Suppose Holliday's shooter hadn't left the area as any sane criminal would do? Suppose it happened again? The dangerous villain, the trap, the nightmare time?

To take my mind off dire developments, I started to tell Annica about my last walk on the shortcut path. Without warning the fuzzy idea that had been tugging at me, the one I had never been able to catch, burst into form.

The cottage at Lane's End!

The charming little house had been built decades ago beside a cornfield that seemed to go on forever. This was the direction I never took on walks with the dogs, telling myself the horse farm lay the other way and the dogs loved to see horses.

Look for the children there!

How could I have forgotten about the cottage?

In Foxglove Corners, the house was unique, a historic treasure that had once been a stop on the Underground Railroad. Owned by a wealthy woman who lived elsewhere, it had been crammed with period furniture and vintage clothing, enough to stock an antique shop. It even had a tunnel in a closet.

The tunnel in my teacup?

"Sandy!" Annica called. "Here, girl!"

There had been a fire in the cottage, fortunately confined to the kitchen and easily repaired. Fresh new paint covered the walls, and most of the antiques had been sold to collectors. It was a pretty place, cleaned and refurbished and ready for new occupants.

Unfortunately the property often stood vacant for long periods of time as few people cared to live quite literally at the edge of nowhere. They'd move in and stay for a while, then leave. Since the cottage was in an out-of-the way location, those of us who lived on Jonquil Lane would be unlikely to notice.

All of this I knew from Camille, who kept abreast of local happenings.

If the house was presently untenanted, who knew what we might find there? The children? The puppy? Perhaps someone unwelcome like Camille's intruder, locked out of the yellow Victorian, her first choice.

We'd almost reached Squill Lane, and so far nothing terrible had happened. Even the sounds were innocuous and pleasant. We'd broken the spell by walking the shortcut trail together, Annica and I. I'd never be afraid of it again.

"There's a little cottage on Squill Lane where it ends," I said. "Let's go check it out."

Thirty-four

The last time I'd seen the cornfield, a scarecrow had been flapping his dark arms in the wind. He was still there, ragged and weary, a veteran of many a snow and rainstorm. There was wind today, too, tossing the leaves, pushing us forward.

The cottage at Lane's End had acquired a look of desolation that spoke of neglect. Thick weeds covered the broken concrete driveway. With its unmowed lawn and scraggly flowerbeds, it seemed as if the cottage had been set down in the middle of a wilderness field and promptly forsaken. Adding to the illusion, its outer walls backed up to woods that appeared to be advancing on the house.

Candy tugged on her leash, the object of her desire a rock shaped vaguely like a soup bone. We made our way through tangled weeds to the porch. As we approached the cottage, she pulled me up the stairs, whining plaintively.

"Nobody lives here," Annica said. "No wonder, with only a scarecrow for a neighbor."

"I'm afraid you're right," I said, noticing a No Soliciting sign on the door. As if that had ever been a problem.

"In a different location, it'd be a nice country retreat."

For a recluse, I thought.

"Well, it was a good idea." I said.

I wasn't ready to abandon it. I could easily see two little lost children trudging up the dusty lane or emerging from the woods to find this fairy tale cottage waiting to welcome them. Like Hansel and Gretel, I thought, stumbling on a wondrous little house where they could rest and feast on frosted gingerbread and gumdrops…

"What now?" Annica said. "Do we go back? Call it a day?"

"I wonder if we could get inside."

"Jeez, Jennet. Isn't that a crime?"

I nodded. "It's home invasion, but there's obviously nobody living here, and it's for a good cause."

"A lost puppy?"

"I'm thinking of the twins."

"The twins! I thought we were looking for Sandy."

"They might be together."

I peered in through the front window. Beside me, Candy placed her paws on the sill. Pressing her nose to the glass, she took a look of her own.

"What do you see?" Annica asked.

"Not much. Furniture covered with white sheets. The curtains are in the way."

"Not the twins?"

"Well, not in the living room."

The last time I had entered the cottage through a broken window, but I'd had an excuse for trespassing. Smoke and fire.

"Well it's obvious nobody's renting the place now," I said. "I'm going in. We've come this far. We might as well go all the way."

"But how?"

I tried the window. It didn't budge. "I'm not sure yet."

"Aren't you afraid of anything?" Annica asked.

"No," I said.

Only Crane's disapproval, and he'd be sure to disapprove if he knew I was contemplating breaking the law. Of course, he'd never know unless I told him.

Try the door.

I turned the knob and pushed. To my surprise, it opened. If I had any doubts about exploring the cottage, they were gone. An open door was an invitation to go farther.

"Do you see any patrol cars?" I asked.

"Out here? You must be joking."

"Then we're home free. Are you coming?"

Candy was already four steps inside the vestibule, whining desperately.

"I guess so."

Annica followed me, closing the door but careful to leave it slightly ajar. "I wonder why they left the door unlocked?"

"That *is* odd."

We stood in the living room, our eyes adjusting to the diminished light. This was a dark house. The woods that shadowed it gobbled up most of the sunlight, and the lace curtains were drawn tightly over front windows. Consequently the room had a bleak, desolate look, the furniture draped in ghostly white, the air musty and the interior soundless.

"Like a mausoleum," Annica said. "Not that I've ever been in one."

She stood under an archway while I looked around, remembering.

He had brought me to this cottage, the nightmare man. He'd tied me to a chair and started a fire in the kitchen. I thought I'd die in this room and lose everything I loved. I *did* lose consciousness. That terrible time had lain dormant in my mind for many months. After five minutes in the cottage at Lane's End, it was alive again.

"This place creeps me out," Annica said. "Let's take a quick walk-through and get out of here."

I let the memories go. The last time I'd been here, this room had been overcrowded with furnishings that hadn't been moved or cleaned in decades, even though the cottage had a tenant. Magazines from the mid-1950s filled a mahogany antique magazine stand.

I looked for the piano. It was there, uncovered and dusty. Sheet music lay against its rack. A piece by Schubert, *Heidenroslein*, one of my favorite melodies. The nightmare man had been a concert pianist. Had the music belonged to him or to the last tenant?

At any rate, someone had drawn the curtains, draped white sheets over chairs and tables, and left sheet music at the piano—but left nothing of himself or herself behind.

A person who couldn't wait to vacate the ghostly cottage?

Candy was pulling me into the hall, wagging her tail, hot on the scent of something. A smell of food of some sort? There was a lingering aroma in this part of the cottage. It wasn't appealing to me, and I couldn't identify it.

"The kitchen is this way," I said. "There was a fire..."

This room alone had changed, brought back to life after the fire's destruction. It had new wallpaper and tile, stainless steel appliances, and on a remembered table, an autumn bouquet in a hollow pumpkin.

I touched a purple chrysanthemum. It was imitation, as was the pumpkin. And this renovated kitchen looked as if it had been the scene of a wild party. I stared at the disorder, at the unappetizing mess, in amazement.

The sink overflowed with dirty dishes. Two cereal boxes sat on the counter beside an open package of oatmeal cookies. Discards and recyclable soft drink bottles spilled out of a tall white wastebasket. Mud dried on the floor, and, strangest of all, on the floor I saw a soup bowl with a dainty pink dogwood pattern that matched the set of china in the corner cabinet.

A drinking dish for a dog. Sandy!

"I'll bet they took in Sandy," Annica said, echoing my thought.

Most telling was the jar of strawberry preserves on the counter. Could it be the same jar transported from the yellow Victorian to the Cottage at Lane's End? I picked it up. About a quarter full, it came from *Aunt Emily's Kitchen*. It wasn't the same then.

In one determined swoop, Candy grabbed the cookies and began to tear frantically at the packaging with her teeth.

"No!" I shouted, retrieving it.

"It looks like we found the person who broke into Camille's house," Annica said.

"No…" How many women would create and leave such a mess behind? Even in a borrowed house? "I think we found the place where the twins have been staying," I said.

~ * ~

Maybe we had, but they weren't here now. Before we left, we went through the cottage, opening doors. In one bedroom, twin beds were a jumble of sheets and blankets. Pillows and a patchwork quilt with chewed edges littered the floor.

Farther down the hall, I recognized the bedroom in which I'd been imprisoned. The closet had been emptied of vintage dresses and accessories. A scent of lavender, too potent to be pleasing, drifted out.

There were no sweeping skirts and long bathrobes to hide the tunnel. I tugged on the small door built close to the floor. It opened to black darkness. Chill, dead air flew out in our faces.

"Wow!" Annica said.

"I walked down that tunnel once," I said. "Never again."

"It's amazing. You'd never know it was here. I wonder what it was used for."

"In the middle of the nineteenth century, this cottage was a stop on the Underground Railroad," I told her. "My guess is it was used for escaping."

Candy sniffed at the threshold eagerly. She wanted us to go inside, to follow the strange scents, to see where this fascinating new walkway would lead regardless of whether I accompanied her. I held tight on the leash.

Annica stepped back, shivering. "Imagine getting trapped in there."

"It leads to the woods. Not far from Jonquil Lane."

"But suppose the opening at the exit is blocked. Like by a fallen tree."

"That could happen, in which case, we'd come back to this closet. But we're not going in."

"No, and we'd better leave," Annica said.

"Straight to the police," I said.

Although I'd have to confess to the crime of unlawful entering. Maybe not.

"Did you ever investigate the cottage at the end of Squill Lane?" I heard myself asking. I even saw Lieutenant Mac Dalby's face, his condescending expression. "No one's living there. It would be a perfect place for kids to hide and play. There's a cornfield next door with a scarecrow."

That would be the truth without a word of my involvement.

I could even mention the tree house not too far from cottage. What child could resist a little playhouse built in a tree?

By the time the police came, the twins might have returned. Perhaps with Sandy.

We walked through the dim rooms, back to the front door. It was half open.

"Hey, I closed it," Annica said. She paused, her head tilted to one side. "Did you hear that? It sounds like a wolf."

"It's just the wind," I said.

Thirty-five

Outside on the porch Candy slammed on her brakes. To my chagrin, she sat down and refused to take another step. I tugged on the leash. Then I tried to push on her shoulders, urging her gently forward. To no avail. She was as solid as a boulder, a collie made of stone and defiance.

"What's the matter with her?" Annica asked.

"She doesn't want to leave."

"Well you're the person. Tell her we're going."

"Candy, Up!" I said. "Heel! We're going home now. Dinner," I added in a cheerful tone. I should have thought to bring dog treats. But Annica had meatballs…

She got up reluctantly and coughed, pretending that her chain was choking her, an old trick.

Annica gasped. "You're hurting her!"

"She's all right—I'm sure."

Annica started walking. I coaxed Candy down the stairs and followed, the wind pushing us along.

Waves of dead, dried leaves blew across the overgrown field that passed for a front yard. In the cornfield, the scarecrow flapped his arms wildly. The wind had thrown nature into a frenzy, and I felt as unsettled as the weather.

Something was going to happen, something unwelcome blowing in with the wild wind.

"We'd better hurry," Annica said. "It looks like rain."

Not to me. The sky was still a deep shade of blue, and white clouds moved languidly to the north. They were headed in our direction.

But there was the great wind. In the short time we'd been inside the cottage, it had intensified. As we fought our way out to Squill Lane, Candy kept glancing back over her shoulder with an occasional whimper. I didn't like that.

Listen to your dog.

I'd learned that lesson long ago.

"I don't want to take the shortcut back," Annica shouted. "If a tree falls, we could get squashed."

"Neither do I. We'll take the lanes like ordinary people and hope the trees stay in the ground."

A cloud of grit landed on my face, sweeping my words away. I brushed my hair back, wishing I had something to tie it with. I had dressed for a hike in the woods but left essential items behind including, I realized, my cell phone. I hoped I wouldn't need it.

The wind was raving now, a predatory beast, determined to overtake its prey. It was an effort to make ourselves heard, useless to try to carry on a conversation.

As a gust slammed into her, Annica grabbed hold of a poplar that grew close to the lane. "I can hardly stand up!" And I could hardly hear her.

We were about the same weight, no match for the powerful gusts, but I had Candy at the other end of the leash. She gave me a sense of security.

"It can't be another tornado coming up," Annica shouted. Then, "Can it?"

"It's just a high wind."

I should be used to high winds after living in this part of Michigan for the past two years. And I should be able to tell the difference between a tornado and a Foxglove Corners wind.

But this wind was like a living creature wailing through the woods on our left and the vast field on our right. As Annica had observed, it sounded like a wolf howl.

Or a human cry.

I heard the sound again. Yes, a human cry.

In response, Candy spun herself around, almost dragging me off my feet.

"Jennet!" Annica reached out to steady me. We held on to each other, and I gripped the leash tightly; but I couldn't budge Candy.

For a brief, terrifying moment I was afraid we'd both be blown airborne. Only Candy seemed immune to the power of the wind. As long as I held on to her, we'd be okay. She knew where she wanted to go. Back to the cottage. And she was taking me with her.

Listen to your dog!

I grabbed Annica's arm. "We have to go back."

"What?"

"Back. To the cottage."

"Why?"

I could hardly hear her voice above the wind's keening. Before I could reply, she cried, "It *is* a tornado! Oh my God! We're going to be caught out here in the open."

"No, I think..." I gasped for breath, struggled to find my voice, to be heard. "We overlooked something."

~ * ~

Back to the cottage. Backtracking. Back...

We hadn't gone that far, not a quarter of a mile. We were moving into the wind now, though, and the going was harder. Just staying on the ground was a Herculean task.

In the cornfield, the scarecrow was dancing crazily on its pole. About three yards from the house, a young tree, slender with fresh green leaves, bent down to the ground, snapped, and fell across the lane. Undaunted, Candy leaped over the end of the trunk, taking me with her. Annica went around it and met us on the other side.

The cottage door, blown open, swung madly, banging against the frame, then against the inner wall. Withered brown leaves littered the porch that had been relatively clear a few minutes ago.

I grabbed onto a porch post and stood still, regaining my equilibrium, letting my hair fall in place, a mass of dark wind-tangled curls. Candy nudged my hand.

Annica held the door still, and we hurried inside where it was only slightly quieter. But we could hear each other's words now and Candy's heavy panting; and I heard the rising panic in Annica's voice. She still believed a tornado was about to bear down on us.

"Maybe we should stay here till the wind dies down," she said, sinking into an armchair, unmindful of its sheet cover.

"That may not be for hours."

I hadn't left a note for Crane, having planned to be home before his shift ended. He'd be worried about me. He wouldn't recognize Annica's car and would wonder why Candy wasn't with the other collies. I hated for us to be separated in any kind of natural upheaval.

"We searched the whole cottage," Annica said. "What do you think we overlooked?"

"The tunnel. That last cry didn't sound like wind to me."

"I don't know how you can tell."

I shrugged. "I just know. And look at the way Candy is acting."

Having had her way, having reached her destination, she was still intent on moving. Through the living and dining rooms, into the hall, back to the room with the tunnel entrance in the closet.

Listen to me! The plea was in her straining muscles, in her eyes, in her haste.

We followed her. "You think the twins are hiding in the tunnel," Annica said.

"They could be. I want to make sure."

"But that doesn't make sense. You'd think they'd want to be rescued."

"Yes, but..."

They didn't know us. We might be the wicked witches come to shove them into the oven.

My thoughts were in motion, as if blown to and fro by a strange wind. I hadn't analyzed the situation, had barely considered another possibility. Bennett and Briana might have been imprisoned in the cottage and found themselves marooned when Johnny Holliday didn't come back. After being once traumatized, they'd naturally be wary.

No, no. That was wrong. He'd gone on a jaunt up north, leaving the ransom money uncollected, and eventually came back to Foxglove Corners where he met his killer. Because he'd apparently found Briana's sweater, I could assume he hadn't left them anywhere.

"We don't really know what's been going on with them," I said. "It's all guesswork."

And I couldn't think clearly with the wind shrieking around the cottage and Candy pulling me toward the closet.

"I'm not going in that tunnel or through it or whatever," Annica said. "I'll wait here in case there's trouble. Consider me your back-up."

Again I thought of the time I'd followed the tunnel to its opening in the woods, traversing that malignant silent darkness with only a candle to light the way. It all came back to me as if it'd happened yesterday. Shadows coming to grotesque life, urging me onward to an unknown fate. Stagnant air. The sensation of being buried alive while still in motion. The fear of bats and other vile things.

Could I go through that again on the slight chance that I'd find those elusive children at the tunnel's end?

I didn't have to—not yet anyway.

"I'll send Candy," I said. "That's where she wants to go anyway. If there's anyone there, she'll let us know. I'll leave her leash on," I added.

The quicker to grab her with.

"But will she come back? That dog is so headstrong."

I hoped so. Correction. I knew so.

"I'll use an oatmeal cookie as a lure," I said.

"I guess that's better than going in yourself. Better still, take a meatball. What the…?"

"Good idea."

She paused. I turned to look at her. "What's the matter?"

"What did I do with the meatballs?" she said. "I had them when we started out…"

"I don't remember."

"Did I set them down someplace?"

I hadn't thought about them since Candy had licked her chops at the sight of the bag in Annica's lap. No, since Candy had refused to leave the cottage.

"We'll figure it out later," I said. "In the meantime, cookies will do."

We reached the bedroom door, closed, as we'd left it. I pushed it open and Candy pressed her nose to the old wood. Her wagging tail beat against my leg.

Inside the closet, I knelt down to pull open the tunnel entrance. I could feel Candy pressing against my side, feel her nose nudging my wrist, feel an icy blast of air as the barrier gave way.

Candy gave an impatient little yelp, easy to interpret: *Yes!*

"I'll get the cookies," Annica said as I dropped Candy's leash.

"Go Candy," I said. "Find the twins."

I reached out to pat her flank lightly and found myself patting air. Candy was gone, my gallant Lassie to an uncertain rescue.

Almost immediately I doubted the wisdom of what I'd done. Would she be all right? She wasn't a search and rescue collie, only a dog with a canine's keen perception and a one-track mind. The word 'twins' wasn't in her vocabulary.

We waited. My heart began to pound. I could hear her barking, a faraway sound. She must be halfway through the tunnel.

"She's found something!" I said. "I should go in."

But I stayed frozen to the closet floor.

"Don't go," Annica said. "Call her, Jennet."

I did. She didn't come which was no surprise. She just kept barking.

This was no time to be a coward. Candy was my collie. She might have found what she was looking for, or she might be in danger.

"I found a flashlight in the kitchen," Annica said. "It works. I just tried it."

Taking the flashlight in one hand and a cookie in the other, I crossed the threshold and gingerly stepped on the first of the remembered stairs that led to the tunnel floor.

Thirty-six

I moved cautiously through the old tunnel, following the flashlight's faint beam. Candy was still barking. She might have found the twins or spied a rodent or a bat or… I let the thought drift away. My imagination, always ready to take off at a gallop, was capable of creating a monster out of shadows, although the villain of our hometown drama was dead, neatly erased from the scene.

No matter. There was always another villain to take the place of the vanquished one.

Besides, I had Candy. She was a natural protector. Because of her, this second trek through the tunnel was less traumatic than the first one had been.

Candy's barking grew louder and shriller, so piercing that it could almost crumble the tunnel walls. She ran to meet me, dashing straight into the beam of light. A limp object vaguely resembling a small body dangled from her mouth.

Briana?

On reaching me, she dropped it and circled around me in a wild collie dance, all the while barking.

"Candy girl." As I slipped her a cookie, I saw that the object was a baby-sized rag doll with a basket of vegetables and fruits attached to a mitten-hand. Not a child's plaything but the kind of fall decoration made for setting on a bale of straw or tucking in a porch chair.

I took it from her and shone the light directly on the dusty face. Orange yarn curls, gray buttons for eyes, and a wide smile stitched with black thread. The doll wore a brown polka dot dress with short sleeves and a long back tie that had come undone. She looked like a cross between a tiny scarecrow and a harvest maid.

"*This* is what you found, Candy? *This* is why we had to come back?"

She wagged her tail. Her dark eyes sparkled. *Yes! This!*

"Well you can't have it. It belongs to someone else." I picked up her leash. "Come."

She was happy enough to go back through the tunnel entrance with me. Now that I'd gotten over my initial surprise at seeing Candy's find, my thoughts started spinning.

How did a harvest decoration end up in the tunnel?

I recalled the little Indian doll in the woods, the one the black-haired trespasser, Anne, claimed she was looking for. I remembered Mrs. Cooper saying in one of the kidnapping stories, "Briana still likes dolls but not to play with. She keeps them on shelves and looks at them."

Assuming that Briana had fled to the tunnel with Bennett, they wouldn't have stayed there, not with the two witches whispering at the entrance. Being resourceful children, they'd go all way through the tunnel and come out in the woods, free and safe for one more day. Briana must have dropped the doll in her haste to get away.

Candy dashed through the opening ahead of me, no doubt, following the scent of the oatmeal cookies in Annica's hand.

"Thank God you're back, Jennet," Annica said. "I'm getting spooked in this room." Spying the harvest doll, she added, "What's that?"

"Candy found it in the tunnel." I brushed the grit off the doll's face and laid it on the bed, as good a place for it as any. Candy had transferred her interest from the doll to the cookies.

"But where are the kids?" Annica asked.

"They weren't there." I explained my theory. "We could trail those two until doomsday, but they'd always be one step ahead of us. It's uncanny."

"We don't have any proof they were here," she reminded me.

"Sometimes you don't need proof to build a scenario. Bits and pieces will do. We have those."

A kitchen trashed as if a food fight had taken place within its walls, a china soup bowl on the floor, a harvest doll left in a secret tunnel. Oh, Briana and Bennett had been in the cottage, quite possibly at the same time we were. I didn't doubt it. And they'd had Sandy with them.

I thought with relish of Lieutenant Mac Dalby, who prided himself on being a match for anybody. Certainly he could handle two young children and a runaway puppy. The twins' little vacation in the woods was about to end.

~ * ~

Annica returned the cookies to the kitchen counter, and once again we headed out to Squill Lane with the wind behind us, pushing us along. It was a little tamer now, a little quieter. We could hear ourselves talk, and it seemed unlikely an energetic gust would blow us into the treetops.

"This is a funny wind," Annica said. "It was so terrible a little while ago. Now it's died down."

The wolf howl had become a plaintive wail. "It comes and goes," I said. "Let's hurry."

But we were tired of walking, and Candy insisted on stopping every time a new scent drifted her way. The simple act of moving our legs required a tremendous effort.

As we came to the tree that had fallen over on the lane, I saw a white bag trapped in a nest of branches.

Annica noticed it too. "That looks like my bag. It is. Look at the green clovers." She knelt down and tugged it free. "And it's empty. Blast it!"

"You must have dropped it here," I said.

"Or somewhere. I don't remember. And something ate the meatballs."

"Not Candy. She was with us."

"Well, we didn't need them after all." She crumpled the bag and stuffed it into her pocket with a comment about keeping the woods free of litter.

"I feel like we're wandering around in circles, going nowhere," I said. "Do you know Shakespeare's play, *A Midsummer Night's Dream?"*

"Sure. I saw the movie."

"Then you remember the characters are in different parts of a forest. No one knows what the others are doing. We're looking for Sandy and the twins. They're hiding from us. We let ourselves get sidetracked in the cottage. Crane…"

My scene faltered. I hadn't worn my watch, but I suspected that Crane was home by now. He could well be in another part of the forest searching for me. Brent might be with him or possibly Mac Dalby. And let's not forget the villain I'd fabricated to take the place of the late Johnny Holliday. We needed supernatural intervention to bring us all together.

Unfortunately none was forthcoming. As I'd told Brent, this time around I didn't have any ghosts to deal with. Only dogs and humans getting lost or straying from their appointed places. I was the finder and at the same time, from Crane's point of view, the lost.

"My husband may be looking for me," I said.

"I'm glad I don't have anyone to answer to."

"I just don't want to worry him."

Ahead the shortcut path loomed, narrow and twisted and dark with interlaced branches meeting overhead. It was still slightly ominous, but this route could shave precious minutes off our trip home.

Annica had a similar thought. "It's been real interesting, Jennet, but I've had enough adventure for one day. I want a hamburger and a Coke and some major downtime."

"You can have dinner with us," I said. "I made a casserole."

"Sounds good. Let's take the shortcut back. Nothing happened to us before, and it isn't so windy now."

Why not? With nothing to show for our quest except an empty Clovers bag, I was ready to stop and regroup, to make dinner for my husband and start all over again tomorrow.

~ * ~

But the shortcut path had changed. Above the woods the sun still shone, but here, under the trees, it might as well be dusk. And there were sounds, some of them typical forest noises, others not so readily identifiable.

Swishings and scamperings and slitherings. Twigs crunching under inhuman feet, cries that must originate in the throats of birds.

They were birds, weren't they?

Annica shuddered. "I don't like these woods."

"It isn't exactly Shakespeare's enchanted forest," I said.

"No, and we won't be coming across fairies anytime soon." Annica started at a particularly loud swish. "Was your husband serious about snakes?"

"Oh, yes. Crane knows the woods."

"I thought he was trying to scare me." She paused. "He was talking about garden snakes, right?"

"Michigan has the Massasauga rattler too," I said. "It's poisonous, but chances are we won't see one."

"Candy keeps sticking her head in bushes," Annica said. "Don't they like to hide in greenery?"

"You're right. I'll keep her on the path. I hate snakes," I added.

But it wasn't snakes I feared as much as the nameless villain I'd fashioned out of tunnel shadows and rational fears. He was in the woods, following us. Whenever I turned around, he ducked behind a tree. Whenever I heard an inexplicable noise, that was the villain.

I was suddenly certain we weren't alone in the woods.

"Crane?" I called. "Mac? Brent?"

No one answered.

"This wasn't a good idea," Annica said. "Could we cut through the woods and get back on the lane?"

"And chance meeting up with a snake?"

"I guess that idea's even worse. Are there black bears in these woods?"

"I'm sure there aren't. There've been cougar sightings nearby though."

"I wish I had my meatballs," Annica said.

"Or a shotgun."

"Let's go faster, Jennet. Let's run!"

Suddenly Candy froze. She growled, a low warning meant to intimidate the bravest of souls.

"Something's there!" Annica whispered.

Something heavy stamped down on rotting leaves and broken wood. The sound was close and coming closer.

With a furious cry, Candy yanked herself free of her leash and charged into the woods.

"Candy!" I cried.

The deafening blast of a gun discharging cracked through the air.

Thirty-seven

"Candy!" Annica cried. "Oh my God."

The gunshot echoed in my mind. It drowned out all thought, all surrounding noise.

Then I heard Candy's vigorous angry barking.

I plunged into the vine-entangled opening through which she had disappeared. I saw her. Very much alive. She stood over a young woman whose fall of jet black hair wrapped around her face. I didn't see the gun.

Fear for Candy and white-hot anger drove away my customary civility. "You fool! What are you thinking, firing a gun in these woods? You could have killed my dog."

The response was like a bullet, swift and sure. "Better than have it kill me. Aren't you going to ask if *I'm* hurt?"

The woman swept her long hair back to reveal a sullen expression and a remembered face enhanced with bold, heavy makeup. She was Anne, the trespasser in the woods across from Camille's house.

She was as angry as Candy who continued to growl at her. "I thought it was a cougar. What business is it of yours anyway? Do you own the woods?"

"As a matter of fact, I do, and those 'No Trespassing' and 'No Hunting' signs you must have seen are mine."

We'd had this same conversation before in another wood. On that occasion, Candy had slammed into her. This time Anne had come prepared.

"Are you all right, little girl?" Annica gave Candy a pat on the head. Her voice trembled as she took hold of the leash and handed it to me.

I ran my hands over Candy's body. She wasn't even grazed. Her growls subsided into little put-upon whimpers. She didn't like loud noises. She'd been startled. And she was lucky.

We were in a small clearing that allowed sunlight to stream through the overhead branches. Vines crawled on the ground, leaves and debris from past seasons quivering in their creeping tentacles. This was an ominous place, quiet and vaguely frightening. In this close space, the wind was more a whistle than a howl.

"What happened to the gun?" I asked.

Anne surveyed the immediate area. "I don't see it, but I remember you."

"You should. A few weeks ago, you were trespassing on another part of my land."

That wasn't strictly true, but I had led Anne to believe that I owned the woods across from Jonquil Lane. A few more lies, and the many acres stretching from the new construction to Squill Lane would belong to me.

Well, she couldn't prove otherwise.

Awkwardly bracing her weight on a large boulder, she raised herself to a sitting position and brushed a layer of forest debris from her vest. It was green, like her slacks and turtleneck, all three garments different shades of the color.

"Suppose you tell me who you are, really?" I said. "And what are you doing here?"

"Like I told you before, my name is Anne. I'm looking for someone."

"I see. Not a doll this time?"

She ignored that. "I need to find a couple of children, a boy and a girl. Both are light-haired, and they're both real cute. Maybe you've seen them?"

"I haven't."

"They ran away from home. It's my job to bring them back."

"Are you a law officer?" I asked.

"Not exactly."

"You're related to them then?"

"That's right. I'm their aunt. I promised their mom I'd find them. We don't want the police involved. The reasons are personal. So please forget you saw me."

I didn't believe a word of this disclosure. It was too glib, the tone too conciliatory. And what woman goes in search of her niece and nephew armed with a gun?

But who was she? A private investigator like the missing Scott? Obviously she wasn't going to tell me.

"Well, Anne," I said. "You can't wander around my property. If something were to happen to you, like a snake bite or a fall, I'd be liable."

She'd just fallen, I realized, possibly knocked down by my dog. But neither of us mentioned that.

"I'll take full responsibility for my safety," she said. "Just go on your way and leave me alone."

"It doesn't work that way. I don't know what your problem with the law is, but I suggest you report the missing children to Lieutenant Dalby of the FCPD. He'll help you."

Her answer was a shrug. "I'm going." She stood and swiped at her clothing again. Then she fixed me with a cold stare. Sarcasm dripped like venom from her cherry-red lips. "And thank you so much for your cooperation. I appreciate it."

At my side, Candy began barking. She was looking up to the treetops and beyond, at the sky where fleecy white clouds glided to the north.

I waited. The next moment a hot air balloon drifted into view.

"Look!" Annica cried.

Wide bands of red, yellow, blue, and green splashed brilliant color against the sky. Crane and Brent rode in the balloon's basket. Candy leaped high, intent on catching the wondrous object, not caring if she yanked me off my feet in the process.

"Crane!" I called.

Brent waved. "Wanna ride?"

Crane shouted, "See you at home."

And the balloon sailed away, but the glorious colors seemed to stay behind, solidifying into a single burst of realization.

I knew where I'd seen Anne, even before she'd appeared in the Jonquil Lane woods looking for an Indian doll. In spite of her glistening too-black hair and all my preconceived notions, she was the female in the seemingly happy family group in the Sky Princess. Sara, the babysitter, Johnny Holliday's partner, the woman I'd been picturing dead. She'd simply dyed her red hair black.

I turned around, eager to confront her. But like the hot air balloon, she was gone.

~ * ~

"Where'd she go?" Annica stared at the ground where Anne had stood.

In her fall Anne had crushed a patch of ghostly white wildflowers. Even as I watched them, they seemed to right themselves, their stems straightening and struggling to reach the light.

"She took off. Just when I recognized her. Let's hurry back to the shortcut. Maybe we can meet her when she comes out of the woods."

"Then what?"

"Then… We'll play it by ear."

"I didn't hear a sound. How could anyone move so quietly?" Annica peered into the green darkness beyond the clearing. "Do you think she's one of your ghosts?"

"Good heavens, no. That was Sara Hall, the suspect in the Cooper kidnapping."

Annica gasped. "I was wondering why you wanted to see her again. She's so unpleasant."

"She's a dangerous woman," I said. "I thought Holliday had killed her. That'll teach me to jump to conclusions."

Because Johnny Holliday, whether he be villain or victim, was dead. His companion was alive. I had to abandon my neatly crafted scenarios and deal with reality. Perhaps Sara had killed Holliday. I'd been thinking of her as an infatuated young woman, led astray by a charming ne'er-do-well.

Could she be the mastermind of the abduction plot? Could she have been the one who shot Eric before the Sky Princess left on its ill-fated trip?

At this point, reality struck my new theory a crushing blow. That couldn't be right. Hadn't Sara sent down her orange scarf with the words 'Help me' on a torn napkin? That innovative plea for help had prompted my thinking of her as a victim.

And where were the children? By now, they must be accomplished at getting away, but they were still young and vulnerable. Sooner or later, their luck would run out.

Suddenly Anne's gun took on an alarming new significance. Perhaps she thought that by erasing the victims, she could erase the crime. Fortunately, she didn't seem to know where the gun was.

Still, she might have another one.

We left the clearing and found the shortcut path. Candy, her experience already behind her, led the way, prancing jauntily ahead of us, tail wagging as she investigated a new world of smells.

Strangely the sounds of the forest had returned, all the chirrupings and swishings and crunchings one would expect in a woodland. But I didn't have time to be leery of them. Anne might already have reached Jonquil Lane. Our chances of intercepting her were rapidly dwindling.

She must have a car, although no vehicle had been found at Skyway Tours office or the launch site, and she must have a place to stay in Foxglove Corners. Another vacant house, perhaps. I couldn't see anyone moving from place to place in the country on foot.

"Do you think she knows the children were in the cottage?" Annica asked.

"Probably. Let's pray she doesn't find them before we do."

In the distance, the tops of the unfinished houses broke through a curtain of green-leaved branches. These skeletal structures afforded many places where a child or a puppy could hide. Children *with* a puppy, I corrected myself. I had no doubt that the three runaways were together.

So should we stop to search the new construction or pass on by, hoping to connect with Anne? As Annica had said, *What then*?

The children would almost certainly hear us and take off again.

I was definitely out of my league. The best plan was to head straight home.

"We have to call the police," I said.

Thirty-eight

After a while, the woods grew thinner, the darkness gave way to light, and the shortcut path gradually twisted its way out to Jonquil Lane.

"At last!" Annica said. "I've had enough hiking in the woods to last me a lifetime."

The prospect of treading the last mile home on a level roadway had an energizing effect on all of us. Even Candy walked faster, only stopping when she spied a muddy puddle. She tried to lap up a fast drink before I pulled her away. I wished I'd brought fresh water for her, but I didn't know we'd be gone so long.

"It's been quite an adventure," I said. "Even though nothing major happened."

"Candy found that harvest doll in a tunnel and we met up with a kidnapper. We're pretty sure where the twins have been staying. I wouldn't call that nothing."

I had to agree with her, and something she'd said set off a faint alarm bell, something about a kidnapper. Sara… Danger? That was it.

"I don't believe it," I said.

"That we did all those things?"

"No."

My mind had taken me back to the day I first saw the Sky Princess. It had been flying low enough for me to see details: comic book characters etched on the children's shirts, Johnny Holliday's rakish moustache, Sara's orange scarf.

And myself on the ground with Gemmy and a black collie, the dog whose leash I still held.

"Why am I just realizing this? Crane reminded me that if I saw Holliday he must have seen me. So would Sara. She changed her name and her appearance. I look the same."

"Why is that important?" Annica asked.

"Because she's taken pains to disguise herself. If she knows I can identify her as Sara Hall, she might want to get rid of me."

"Me too because she figured you'd tell me. Which you did." Annica was silent for a moment, gazing at the spindly blue wildflowers that grew along the lane. "On second thought, I don't think I'll take you up on your dinner invitation, Jennet. I should do some studying for tomorrow's classes."

"I'm sure we're safe," I said, sure of no such thing. "Remember, my husband is a deputy sheriff."

"Still I think I'll call it a day. The wind is picking up."

It was blowing dusty clouds of dried leaves and twigs across the graveled lane. We were coming to the abandoned development. Bleak chateau walls, glowing in the day's last light, seemed to beckon to me. Walls without roofs, gaping apertures left for windows, a toppled 'For Sale' sign almost buried in the leaves of a long past autumn. Silent secret places.

Briana and Bennett could be huddled within its shadows with Sandy. But how could they keep a puppy quiet?

I ignored a fleeting desire to stop and investigate the site. Mac could do it more safely and efficiently. Besides, it would soon be dark, and I didn't think I could take another step.

But I did. Several steps, several yards. The last mile home can be the shortest or the longest, depending on circumstances.

Finally Camille's yellow Victorian came into view, along with my green Victorian farmhouse. How beautiful it was, how soft and elegant, borrowing its grace from the surroundings. This was the place I wanted most to be.

As we drew near, I could hear the dogs barking from inside. Candy's tulip ears blew back in the wind as she lunged ahead.

But something was wrong.

Annica's car was parked in the driveway behind mine, but I didn't see the other vehicles that should be there, Crane's Jeep and Brent's blue Mustang.

I glanced down the lane, but there was no traffic at all. "Didn't Crane say he'd be right home?"

"No. He said something like 'See you at home.'"

"Same thing. I wonder where he is. He had plenty of time to get here. They were flying, for heaven's sake."

"He'll be along," Annica said. "Maybe he found someone breaking the law. Or maybe he and Brent decided to go for a longer ride. Wouldn't they have to take the balloon back to the balloon port or its hanger or whatever they call it?"

"Back to the Skyway Tours launch site, I suppose."

Still, it had taken us far longer to trek through the woods than it would to fly over them in a balloon. I tried to brush off a nagging twinge of apprehension. A deputy sheriff's wife has to deal with erratic hours and unpredictable happenings or be forever on edge.

"Are you sure you won't stay for dinner, Annica?" I asked.

"I'm sure. You'll want to wait for Crane, and I'd like to be home before dark."

She was already heading for her car, keys jingling in her hand.

"Goodbye, then. I'll let you know what happens."

"We'll have to think of another way to find that puppy," she said.

I took my own key out of my pocket. The collies were still barking, three inside the house, one outside. In addition, Candy was jumping on the door, raking its surface with her nails. And the wind had picked up. It set the wind chimes on the porch into merry motion and my nerve ends tingling.

I pulled Candy away from the door with one hand and slid the key into the lock with the other. As much as I love following a mystery to its conclusion, I was ready to turn to another activity.

~ * ~

Once Halley, Gemmy, and Sky completed their welcome home ritual and Candy drained the dogs' water bowl of its contents, the quiet of the house seemed to close in on me. Even the wind had died down. Automatically I checked the cabinet in which Crane kept his gun. It wasn't there. He hadn't been home then. It was no use looking for a note, but I checked the voice mail on my cell phone. Nothing.

I couldn't imagine where he and Brent had gone, could only hope they hadn't run into some kind of trouble. But who was better able to handle trouble than Brent and Crane?

After alerting the police to the presence of Sara Hall in the Jonquil Lane area and suggesting they look for the abducted twins at the cottage at Lane's End, I set about tearing lettuces for a salad and heating the casserole. I'd make baking powder biscuits. Brent could smell them from a mile away. What about dessert? I opened the freezer and decided to defrost a pound cake.

The minutes raced by. With dinner prepared, I washed the woodland debris away, brushed my hair, changed into a red knit dress and added the gold heart Crane had given me last Valentine's Day.

The day was rapidly fading. I turned on the light in the dining room. Instantly a duplicate room appeared beyond the windows, a duplicate Jennet smoothing the tablecloth. Reflections, all, but the illusion had haunted me when I was a little girl.

Was there a whole new other world out there in the night? Another dimension?

One touch of the light switch and it would all vanish—that duplicate other world. But I left the light on.

I wandered over to the window and watched the trees moving in a sinister fashion against the darkening sky. At the edge of the Jonquil Lane woods, a poplar snapped with an earthshaking crash and fell into a line of young evergreens.

Candy, who had been watching through the bay window for a white Jeep, jumped off the loveseat and ran to the door, whimpering. Sky made a dash for the safety of her den under the mahogany table, while Halley rushed to my side. Gemmy took Candy's place at the window.

I turned on the radio just as the announcer was booming out the forecast. 'High wind advisory until ten. Gusts up to forty miles per hour possible…' Nothing more worrisome yet.

"It's just the wind," I said aloud, more to convince myself than the collies, who would react to my tone but not the words.

It was tornado season. Still, for a Michigan dweller to experience three tornados in a lifetime would be too much of a coincidence.

Just the wind.

Straight-line winds could do as much damage as a tornado. They could wrench roofs from houses, topple trees, send cars careening off the road.

What if the Sky Princess had crashed again with Crane and Brent aboard?

Something had happened, or was going to happen soon. Why else were frost needles pressing into my skin?

Get busy. Quit thinking.

I set the table for three because I knew Brent would join us. Unless something happened to prevent it.

Don't think that way.

Carefully I arranged the plates, the silverware, and three snowy white napkins. Salt and pepper shakers, sugar bowl, creamer. Then I reached for Rebecca Ferguson's candlesticks, in their usual place on the mantel. It was a night for a candlelit dinner, a night to tell stories of adventures in the woods over steaming coffee and pound cake.

A night for quiet pleasures, even while the wind blew. Except it was suddenly, eerily quiet.

I struck a match and held it above the first tall taper.

A face swam into focus in the silver surface of the candlestick's stem. A pretty woman with fair, thick curls falling forward on her shoulders looked gravely back at me. She wore an old fashioned shirtwaist with a brooch pinned at the throat. I knew her.

Rebecca!

The burning match fell out of my hand onto the hardwood floor.

As I bent down to pick it up, the sound of a gunshot blasted through the night.

Thirty-nine

The gunshot reverberated throughout the silent house. It mixed with the crash of shattering glass and the dogs' frantic barking. On the floor, the match flame burst open, an unholy orange and yellow blossom. The smoke alarm went off.

Don't try to pick it up.

The fire was inches from the rug, leaping into a terrible life, reaching up to engulf my hand. Like the flames, images flashed in my mind. *Fire extinguisher. Kitchen. Cupboard. Vase.*

I grabbed the vase on the table, doused the flames with water, and watched them die in a spill of yellow daffodils. And I felt faint. Holding onto the edge of the table, I took deep breaths, willing my heart to beat at a normal rate. I couldn't stop shaking.

The bullet?

A quick glance told me it had torn through the window and pierced the dining room wall, breaking a china teapot on the what-not shelf. A chunk of the handle had landed at my feet.

I couldn't continue to stand frozen at the table, making a clear target of myself.

Then move.

Where are the dogs?

My mind registered four agitated collies. They appeared to be all right, and I was still in one piece, but they couldn't stay in this room with shards of glass and pieces of china scattered on the floor. Quickly, belatedly, I turned off the dining room light, plunging us into darkness.

One of the dogs pressed her body to mine. Halley, I knew, when she licked my hand. Candy must be the one pawing at the side door, her impervious barking demanding that I take immediate retaliatory action. A furry body brushed past me. Gemmy or Sky. No, not Sky; she would be under the table.

The bullet hadn't even grazed me because I had seen Rebecca's face in the candlestick's stem. The apparition had startled me into dropping the match. Which I'd stooped to pick up. Which had removed me from the assassin's line of fire. Just in time. One more second, and I would have been hit.

Why not give the assassin a name? Sara Hall.

Was she still out there, lurking in the darkness that enveloped the house, waiting for another chance to take aim and fire?

Get away from the window! Out of the room!

Calling the dogs, taking the haunted candlesticks with me, I stumbled into the kitchen. There was my cell phone, where I'd left it on the counter with my schoolbooks. Quickly I dialed nine-one-one and waited. The dispatcher's voice was cool and efficient, and I managed to tell my story in spurts. "Somebody just shot at me. I was in my house, setting the table for dinner…"

Irrelevant. Don't babble.

"One shot. It missed me. I'm still there. Here, I mean. I think I know who did it."

I gave her my address and slammed the phone shut. Three dogs gathered in the kitchen, staying close to me, but Candy ran excitedly from side door to front door and back again.

I tried to keep my thoughts on track. I'd had a close call, but help was on the way. Sara wouldn't be likely to strike again so soon.

I'd been right about her intention. She wanted to keep her new identity a secret—until she'd dealt with the twins. Then she'd disappear with dyed black hair, a new name. and all ties to the past eliminated. No one would be able to tie her to the kidnapping.

A sound broke through the stillness. Almost like a rap on the door, it was very soft, very distinct.

Crane and Brent? It couldn't be. Why would Crane knock at his own door? And who would venture out in a windstorm? On the fairest of days, drop-in company in the country was rare.

The dogs were in a frenzy of excitement. Candy ran back and forth, sending my school papers tumbling to the floor.

The rapping came again.

I hesitated. An assassin doesn't try to gain entrance to her target's home. She shoots from the safety of the shadows and runs.

Should I take a chance and open the door?

Not without checking first.

From the window above the sink, I had a partial view of the area beyond the side door, enough of a view to see there was no one there. It was the wind, then, making all sorts of odd and deceptive noises, intent on luring me outside.

"Settle down," I told the collies. "There's nothing there. It's just the wind."

They didn't believe me. I was barely convinced myself because at the moment the wind seemed to have died down again.

Moonlight streamed through the window, bathing familiar objects in an alien half-light. I could barely make out the gables of Camille's house across the lane. A single light on the first floor was on. Were Camille and Gilbert home? I could call them, but I was the one whom Sara wanted to kill. Besides, I'd never want to put them in harm's way.

I pushed the chair away from the window and sat down to listen for the siren.

A feeling of calm descended on me as I hugged the candlesticks to my breast. Aunt Becky had told me their legend. How on occasion Crane's Civil War ancestress, Rebecca Ferguson, had been known to appear to her descendants, always in a time of peril.

I had married into the Ferguson family, becoming Rebecca's great-great-great niece, but for a long time I'd been aware of a connection to her. I'd even seen Rebecca once on the morning of my wedding to Crane when time seemed to stand still for a moment. Well, I'd almost seen her. Let's say I sensed her presence, a warm spring breeze in a room with the windows closed.

The candlesticks had come into our house as a wedding gift from Aunt Becky. In all the time they'd been in my possession, all the times I'd dusted and polished them and moved them from room to room, I'd never seen Rebecca Ferguson's face in their stems.

"One day you will," Aunt Becky had promised me. "When it matters. Mark my words."

She was right. It had mattered tonight, and I'd seen more of Rebecca than her face. She'd appeared in her clothing with a brooch pinned to an old-fashioned shirtwaist. Or had I seen her entire form, a floor length skirt? And how could I see all of that in a slender candlestick stem?

It had been like looking in a mirror and seeing another's reflection.

I gazed into the candlesticks' surface now, held them up to the moonlight. They were simply cherished antiques again, neither magical nor haunted. Rebecca had accomplished what she'd set out to do.

Jennet Ferguson, standing at the table in her dining room, was gunned down by a bullet fired from outside her property. She died instantly, a classic example of being in the wrong place at the wrong time.

That hadn't happened, thanks to Rebecca. Thanks to the dropped match. Once again I'd dodged a bullet, literally this time. Holding the candlesticks, one in each hand, gave me comfort.

In a time of peril, Rebecca would always come.

But how much otherworldly intervention could one person expect? My enemy was still at large.

Out in the lane, I heard the siren's wail. Light arced through the kitchen, and the siren died. The police had arrived in record time.

Candy led the dash to the front door, ears back, still and forever barking.

I stood on unsteady legs and followed the dogs.

~ * ~

Lieutenant Mac Dalby and his young partner, Jim Madison, were both tall men. They filled the living room with their presence and their power. Everything was going to be all right now.

But where was Crane?

I grabbed Candy's collar and steered her toward the crate. She was too startled to do anything but comply. At my command, Sky and Halley sank into a Sit, and while Gemmy poked at the crate with her nose, I leashed her. Candy started growling.

"They won't bite," I said.

"Are you hurt, Jennet?" Mac demanded.

"The shot missed me." I saw no need to launch into a narrative of the face in the candlestick and the near fire, although a smell of smoke lingered in the air. "I think the shooter was Sara Hall. I ran into her today in the woods. She shot at Candy."

That, too, was a separate story.

"Sara Hall? The kidnap suspect?"

"The killer. She might have shot Eric Morrow."

Mac strode to the side door. "Why would she want to kill you?"

"Because I saw her in the hot air balloon with the twins. She looked different then."

I realized that didn't make sense. There was more to tell, but Mac was going through the door, apparently satisfied with a half answer. "Stay here," he ordered. Whether he was talking to his partner or to me was unclear.

Jim offered Halley his hand to sniff. She wagged her tail. "Nice collies," he said with a sidelong glance at Candy who was trying to break out of her crate. "I had a collie when I was a kid."

I smiled. "Everyone did."

Mac came back in, slamming the door. "There's no one out there now. The lane is clear. She must have taken off through the woods."

At night? I didn't think so.

"Where's Crane, Jennet?"

"I'm not sure. He went somewhere with Brent Fowler."

Skyriding? I thought. And then? He should be home by now. Because nothing had happened to him.

"Do you have a friend you can stay with?" Mac asked. "The lady in the yellow house, maybe? The dogs should be okay on their own."

"I'm not going to let Sara Hall drive me away from my home," I said. "And I'd never leave the dogs alone with her unaccounted for."

"Just until Crane gets home," Mac said. "You'd be safe. Doesn't the lady have a new husband?"

This was the man I'd known for so long, as condescending as ever, even though I'd proved that I could cope with any villain. Eventually. Sometimes with a little help.

I said, "I'll be all right. If I just knew where Crane was."

Sara had no reason to want to kill Crane. He hadn't been outside the day she'd gone floating over the lane with her victims.

Unless she realized that I'd recognized her and thought I'd told him about my discovery. He and Annica, widening the circle of people who knew that Anne was really Sara Hall and that Sara had kidnapped two children.

"I'll find him for you," Mac promised. "In the meantime, you sit tight."

Good advice, but it might prove impossible to follow.

Forty

When the officers left, the silence came back. I could hear every tick of the clock and every click of a collie nail on the floor as Gemmy and Halley circled around the kitchen table in a mindless game of Chase-the-tail.

Until I let Candy out of the crate. She rushed to the side door and began jumping on it again. Her bark had a high-pitched note of desperation.

"Down!" I told her. "You're not going with them."

She yelped her protest.

"And you're not going out. You don't have to go out."

But she did and she conveyed her wishes in every manner known to the canine race: pathetic whimpers, whines, and lunges at the door. She nudged me with her nose, laid her paw in my lap, took the hem of my dress gently in her mouth, and fixed me with the most soulful look in her repertoire.

How could a mere mortal resist her?

"No! Quiet!" I eyed the crate again.

You had to let her out, Jennet, I thought.

Sometimes being crated quieted her. Sometimes not. But she was food-motivated. Luckily they all were. I handed out peanut butter heart treats to three collies and threw a handful into the crate for Candy.

True to her nature, Candy bounded in after them, and I latched the door. Peace! If only for a while.

They all had to go out before bedtime, but I couldn't shake the feeling that Sara might be outside. She would have seen Mac's cruiser arrive—and leave. Knowing the coast was now clear, she'd find a hiding place and wait for another chance to kill me.

I could almost see her, crouching behind a tree, the moonlight shining on her gun.

Why worry about taking the dogs outside, though? Crane would surely be home before bedtime, maybe with Brent.

With a sigh I checked my casserole, still in the oven on 'Warm' where it might as well stay. The biscuits lay unbaked on a cookie sheet. The salad was still chilling, the table set. With nothing more to prepare or bake or heat, I sat down where I could see the stove clock.

Candy had already gobbled the heart treats and began to paw the crate's door. Halley and Gemmy tired of their game and lay down to lap water. I debated the wisdom of sweeping up the glass and china in the dining room and decided to wait until later.

I lit the cinnamon-scented pillar candle in the middle of the table, hesitating only a moment before striking the match. I would *not* be afraid of fire. I would not think about my brush with death. Every few minutes I looked at the clock.

How could time go by so slowly while the evening seemed so long? I'd packed a lot of activity into a four-hour time span. The trek through the woods with Annica, the search of the cottage and tunnel, followed by the shooting incident, the fire, and the arrival of the police.

It was seven-thirty.

Sky emerged from under the kitchen table and padded into the hall, and Gemmy lay in front of the crate occasionally whining to keep Candy company. Only Halley stayed closed to me. I kept my hand on her silky head.

I'll go mad if something doesn't happen, I thought.

Then everything changed.

~ * ~

The cell phone's rippling notes sounded like little alarm bells. I snapped it open. "Hello?"

"Jennet? It's Mac."

I pressed it close to my ear to hear every word over Candy's incessant noise. "Did you find Crane?" I asked.

"He's on his way home. He'll tell you all about it. And we found Anne Jackson, also known as Sara Hall."

"Can you hold her?"

"We were trailing her. She was driving seventy down Spruce Road when she collided with a deer. She doesn't have a driver's license. We ran a check on the car. It was stolen two weeks ago, and we found a gun in the glove compartment. She doesn't have a permit. Yes, I'd say we can hold her."

"Is she hurt?" I asked.

"She says she wrenched her neck, and she *does* have some nasty looking cuts, but it didn't stop her from trying to get away. Jim nabbed her. The lady is in the hospital."

Although the danger was over, my heart still pounded at unbidden thoughts of the what-might-have-been's if the deer hadn't leaped out into the road, delivering Sara into the hands of the police.

"Just like that?" I said. "You make it sound so easy."

"Police work is never easy. The Hall woman fought like a wildcat trying to break loose. Madison ended up with some bad scratches and bites. He's going to need a tetanus shot."

Thank God I'd never had to tangle with the demented nanny.

"But you subdued her," I said.

"Right always prevails."

Still, I had to ask. "And you're sure she isn't going to escape from the hospital?"

It was all too easy to imagine her face in the window. Evil, framed by that long black hair, determined to make the next shot count.

"We have a guard on her," he said.

I had to accept that, then, had to let paranoia go.

Anne had had a bad day. A fall in the woods, a rush to escape the scene of a murder attempt, and revenge in the form of a leaping deer. And a bed in the hospital, under police guard.

But I couldn't feel sorry for her as long as the twins were missing.

"How about the deer?" I asked.

"Not so lucky."

"Thank you for letting me know," I said. "Thank you."

Thank you, thank you. For finding Crane.

Who had better have a good excuse for being late to dinner.

I went back into the dining room and, sidestepping the broken glass, looked out the shattered window.

If Sara was in the hospital, then I could take the dogs out without fearing for our lives. I'd do it now. How wonderful it all felt—the euphoria, the knowledge that everything had turned out so well without a hands-on conflict with a villainess, and, best of all, Crane was coming home.

Even though the twins were still missing. I hoped they'd found shelter from the wind, perhaps gone back to the cottage where'd they be safe although they wouldn't know why.

Candy was sitting in her crate, head tilted, eyes alert, as if she were trying to read my thoughts, as if that were possible.

"All of you," I said. "It's okay. We're going out."

Out into the banshee wind which had made a sudden comeback. But if that was the worst the night could serve up, I would manage admirably.

I tossed on a jacket and tied a scarf around my head. Then I leashed Gemmy. As usual Sky and Halley would be good off leash. As for Candy…

Seeing preparations for an outing in progress, she was once again pawing impatiently at the crate's door.

Leash in hand, I opened the crate. She sprang out, sixty pounds of determination and sheer canine power. Almost falling backward, I grabbed her choke chain, quickly attached the leash, and pulled up on it sharply to get her attention.

"Settle down," I ordered. "Or it's back you go."

She sank into a grudging Sit. I remembered my vow to take my wayward girls to obedience school. After tonight there'd be no more procrastination.

As soon as I opened the door, Candy bolted. The leather leash cut across my palm as she wrenched it out of my hand and dashed into the gusting wind. Across the wildflower meadow, out to the lane—where there was rarely traffic. Please God don't let there be any tonight.

I should have known this would happen.

"Candy!" I screamed, and in a lower voice added, "Come back."

She'd never come.

This was like the last time, the day we'd seen the hot air balloon materialize above the woods. Candy, entranced at the sight, trying to catch it. Failing that, taking off with Gemmy into the woods across the lane. And they'd stayed away all day. Now it would soon be dark. Gemmy was frantic to join her.

Holding fast to her leash, I scanned the area. There were no cars in the lane, and thank God for that. None I could see or hear anyway. Camille's first floor light was still on, but the car was gone. The house of my other neighbor, Doctor Linton, was dark and quiet.

I was alone. I might as well have been alone in a wild, wind-whipped world with three collies at my side and one miles away.

My Candy. So contrary at times, so endearing at others. She had come to me as a stray with a rope around her neck, brought by a boy who hoped to claim the reward I'd offered for my lost Halley. I didn't want Candy then. I only wanted Halley. But I took her. She was, after all, a stray, and I could find her a home.

My feelings had soon changed. Candy was part of my life now.

Why was I thinking of her in the past tense just because she'd run away to the woods? She'd done it before, often getting in serious trouble that I'd always managed to get her out of.

Why did I feel I was going to lose her tonight? And was this night going to go on forever?

There was still a little daylight left, but it was rapidly fading. I couldn't follow Candy into the woods at this hour any more than I could have followed her on the day of the hot air balloon.

A crash reverberated through the shrieking wind. Tons of wood splitting the ground open somewhere in the woods. Another tree sacrificed to the wild weather, its branches capable of crushing a dog or a human.

I saw her then, a graceful black form running out of the woods. A smaller animal, lighter in color, ran at her side, like a shadow. I squinted, trying to see clearly.

Coyote? All the times Candy had been restless, had she wanted to go run with the coyotes?

Into the high gusts, across the lane, they came closer, never stopping, never slowing down. Candy and her shadow looked like two canine companions running in play. They crossed the lane.

And I recognized that shadow. It was the puppy, Sandy.

Forty-one

The lost one. Lost no more. If I could only coax her into the house.

The two dogs swerved onto the walkway, and I saw them clearly. Definitely, no doubt about it, Candy's companion was the runaway puppy.

Sky and Halley ran to greet Candy and the wonderful surprise she'd brought with her, and Gemmy pulled on her leash, desperate for freedom.

I realized I'd never set eyes on Sandy before except from a distance at the Memorial Day barbecue. I gazed at her now. She looked like a wilder version of Brandy and Mandy. No wonder I'd mistaken her for a coyote. She was pitifully thin and rangy, a creature that ran on long, spindly legs and seemed to carry all the burrs and crushed leaves of the forest in her matted coat.

But her color underneath was butterscotch gold, and she had an elegant collie head. She was running toward me, not away. Sometimes, as I'd always known, miracles do happen.

Now to make sure this miracle didn't slip out of my grasp.

"Sandy," I said softly.

She didn't respond. As I'd thought, without a human to call her by her name, she wouldn't recognize it. Still I repeated, "Sandy." I held out my palm for her to sniff. She took the bait and wagged her tail slowly. Then, mouth open and a mischievous collie gleam in her dark eyes, she grabbed the sleeve of my jacket in her teeth.

Startled, I tried to pull it free only to realize that Candy had a portion of my dress, above the hem, in her mouth.

Caught by the two creatures I'd set out to catch! Everything about this night was upside down.

"Candy, drop it!" I ordered and tried again to regain the use of my arm only to hear an ominous ripping. My sleeve now had an unsightly tear in it.

"You little devil!" I said.

She sprang back and looked at me, pure puppy innocence.

Candy dropped the end of my skirt and gave an impatient little yelp.

My nerves, worn thin by collie antics, began to fray. "What's gotten into you?" I demanded.

Candy closed her jaws gently around my hand. Her eyes communicated a message I couldn't decipher. But I didn't have to understand it. Having seen my share of Lassie movies as a child, having lived with Candy, I listened to my dog.

"Do you want to show me something?"

Her answer was a burst of frantic yips.

"To take me somewhere?"

She released my hand and dashed out to the end of the lane where she turned once to look at me. With two more yips, she swung her head back in the direction she'd just come from. In the darkness where the woods began and the wind, a powerful, primeval force, set the trees into motion. Where a falling branch could impale me.

"Not on your life," I said.

In answer, she ran back and grabbed my dress again.

Are you listening to your dog?

"All right," I said. "I surrender. But only to the woods' edge. No farther. And we're not all going."

That last was for the benefit of my collie contingent and the newcomer in our midst.

Opening the door, I shooed Halley, Sky, and Gemmy inside. Then I glanced at Sandy who sat on her haunches, puppy fashion, returning my look somberly. Without a collar or leash, getting her in the kitchen would be difficult. But hopefully Sandy, like my own collies, would prove to be food motivated.

In the kitchen, I opened the Lassie tin and spilled out the peanut butter hearts. My dogs converged around me as I scattered the treats on the far side of the kitchen floor. To my surprise, Sandy rushed inside to join them. While they pounced on the feast, I picked up Candy's leash and hurried out the door.

"This had better be good," I said, wrapping the end of the leash around my wrist. She wasn't going to break free again.

The two of us set out toward the woods. Candy pulled me along. My hair blew in my face and the scarf, tied in haste, came undone. A gust carried it across Camille's foxglove bed and out of sight.

Watching it disappear, I tripped on a fallen branch but caught myself before falling over on Candy.

You'd better have your head examined, when this is over, I told myself.

Candy led me a short way and pulled me behind the line where the lane melted into the woods' edge. Here a stand of spruces growing too close together obscured the view beyond. We passed them, and I sank into soft earth, uneven and mushy with rotted leaves.

A fallen tree lay on the ground ahead, a massive oak whose doomed leaves quivered convulsively in the wind, making eerie rustling sounds. Death rattles. Caught in the trap of branches I saw a small white form.

Candy leaped over the downed trunk and came to a sudden stop.

I gasped. The form was a child. There were two children.

"It's okay, Bri," said a tremulous little voice. "Help's come. Told you so."

Candy nudged me toward the speaker. In a state of high excitement, ears flattened against the sides of her head, she fell upon him, licking his face, sending him toppling back onto the forest floor. He laughed and sprang up.

"You're Bennett," I said. "I'm Jennet."

Good grief! That rhymed. I'd never realized it.

He nodded. "That's my sister, Briana. She's hurt bad. I can't move her. Can you help us?"

"Let me see."

I climbed across the trunk and approached the little girl. My short-lived euphoria sank. Briana was trapped under the tree. The heavy limb of one of its forks lay across her leg. I could never lift that heavy wood, not even with Bennett's help.

Briana was wearing the shirt with the face of a Disney princess, now filthy and ragged. Her fair hair hung in strings, and her face was tear-strained.

"I can't get up," she said and began to cry. "I can't do it."

"Help me get the tree off her," Bennett said. "Please, miss."

"We can't. Not even with two of us."

Candy couldn't help; she'd done her part. Standing beside me, she was whining, like any movie Lassie, challenging me to finish her rescue.

"I'm so cold," Briana said. Her teeth began to chatter.

I hesitated. There was only one thing to do, but I hated to leave the twins alone out here in the woods with night fast approaching.

"So cold," she said.

I shrugged out of my jacket and settled it over her. The material was lightweight, but it was all I had. I pulled it up to her neck and felt her forehead. It was like touching a burning stove.

"Can you stay with your sister a while longer, Bennett?" I asked. "You'll be safe. I'll leave Candy to protect you."

And she would. She'd protect the children with her life if necessary.

Bennett jumped up. "But where are you going?"

"Just to my house to phone for help," I said.

"But… What if she comes back? She wants to kill us."

"Sara?" I said.

He nodded again. "The witch."

"Don't worry about Sara. She can't do anything to you. She's in another place being watched."

Which I could only hope was true.

"Okay, but can you hurry?"

"I'm on my way. It's just a few steps. On the other side of the lane."

I let the leash fall. "Watch the children, Candy," I said.

Whining, she lay down beside Briana. The rest was up to me, as it should be.

I couldn't help feeling that this latest complication might be my fault. The knock on the door I'd summarily dismissed as the wind. Could it have been the children trying to find a safe haven from Sara and the wind?

If I'd only seen them, if I'd opened the door, they might never have gone into the woods to be in the exact location where the tree was going to fall.

Forty-two

The easy part was turning the rescue over to the police and the paramedics. I stood on Jonquil Lane beside Mac's cruiser with Candy still on her leash and listened to the siren and the dying wind while the ambulance disappeared behind a curve.

Even a novice could see that Briana was gravely ill. I remembered how hot her forehead had felt and how she kept saying she was cold. What had caused the fever? They'd find out and treat it, but she had other problems.

The branch had broken her left leg. My last glimpse of her flushed face had been heart wrenching. How sad to be rescued finally only to be defeated by a fallen tree.

But both Briana and Bennett were strong; they must have been strong to survive for weeks on their own in the wilds of Foxglove Corners, subsisting on borrowed canned goods, cookies, and jam, all the while living in fear of Sara Hall. Now they were in good hands.

Strobe lights flashed red and blue in the darkness. Off and on. Blue and red.

It was completely dark now. As soon as the ambulance had arrived, I'd rushed inside, past the excited collies, and slipped into another jacket with a warm lining and a hood. Then I'd found a jumbo-sized chocolate bar in the cupboard and turned the outside lights on.

Crane hadn't arrived yet, but he would soon. Mac said so. 'Any minute' were his exact words.

"Good work, Jennet," he added. "Those kids were right under our noses, but it took you to find them."

A compliment from Lieutenant Mac Dalby was a rare concession indeed, but I couldn't accept praise that belonged to another. "They'd still be lost in the woods if it weren't for Candy. I think she knew they were there all along with Sandy."

"Good dog." Mac stroked Candy's head. "Would you like to join the Force, Girl?"

She looked at him, tail wagging slowly.

"I think I'll keep her," I said.

When Mac drove off, yet once again, I went inside to check on my long-delayed dinner. Bennett's story played over and over in my mind, the little I knew of it. While Briana had slept and we waited for the ambulance, Bennett told me bits and pieces while chomping on the candy bar. His account was similar to the one I'd constructed, putting together various clues.

Briana and Bennett had called Sara the Witch.

They'd recognized her, in spite of the black hair, watched her from the comparative safety of the cottage at Lane's End as she'd prowled around the grounds, trying to decide if anyone lived there.

Finally she found a way in and searched the cottage, but she didn't know about the secret tunnel Bennett had discovered. She left, not knowing that Bennett and Briana were hiding only a few yards away.

"Why did she want to kill you?" I asked.

"I don't know," he said. "She was always so nice to us. Then one day she was different."

Their mother was away, but Sara had arranged a birthday surprise for them, a whole special day of fun.

With Sara's boyfriend, Johnny, they'd gone to Windemere Water Park and Petting Zoo where Sara had allowed them to select one present each at a souvenir store. Briana had chosen a little Indian doll and Bennett a Hardy Boys book. Then at lunch Sara told them about the greatest present of all, a ride in a hot air balloon.

"You're going to love it," she'd said. "It's going to be like taking a ride on a magic carpet."

After that, things got mixed up. At lunch Sara argued with Johnny about the plan and what to do next. She turned mean with the twins. By then they were tired and wanted to go home, but Sara insisted they all go on the balloon ride. She'd already made the arrangements and paid for it.

"She wouldn't let us go home," Bennett said. "Johnny yelled at us."

But the children were resourceful. After lunch, Sara touched up her makeup and left the lipstick on the table beside her purse. Briana tore a piece from her napkin and wrote 'Help' on it in bright red. Bennett had tucked the message into the label of Sara's scarf when she wasn't looking.

Briana, not Sara. Now that made sense.

At the Skyway Tours office, Bennett tried to tell the man Sara and Johnny weren't their parents, that they wanted to go home, but Johnny had yanked him away and they'd gone up in the balloon. At first it was fun. They'd seen the collies and me down in the road. Sara said they were going to fly all the way home in the balloon.

They didn't believe her.

Then the balloon went down. They thought Sara had been killed. While Johnny fussed over her, Bennett grabbed his sister's hand, and they ran into the woods.

"We just kept running," he'd said. "Wherever we went, there were trees. One day we found the puppy and a house in the woods. And we kept seeing a balloon in the sky with a man in it. Briana and me hung her sweater up in this old tree house. We thought he'd see it and fly down to get us out of the woods."

And they'd apparently never realized that Sara or Johnny might see it? Well, who can think of everything?

He finished his story and the chocolate bar at the same time.

Bennett hadn't mentioned the shooting at Skyway Tours. I started to ask him about it when Briana woke and began to cry. Then we heard the sirens. At last.

There would be time for more questions later, all the time in the world for explanations and reunions when Briana's leg was tended to and her illness diagnosed.

But I wondered why Bennett hadn't talked about the shot.

~ * ~

I knew the exact moment Crane rounded the last curve on the lane before home. Candy left her dinner half eaten and led the pack to the door.

Crane and Brent stormed into the house with a great deal of noise and commotion, most of it caused by the barking of four collies. The scents of the outdoors came in with them and a burst of energy that had been missing from the past hours.

Crane swept me into a hearty hug and a kiss while Brent looked on in amusement.

"He thought he'd never see you again," Brent said. "I wish I had a wife to welcome me home."

"You're late for dinner." I succeeded in keeping the tears back. "What happened?"

"Brent's hot air balloon went haywire," Crane said.

Brent interrupted him. "Hey! Let me tell it if you're going to exaggerate."

"It was the wind," Crane said. "Right after we saw you in the woods…" He stopped and found his deputy sheriff persona, the one I thought he'd left behind long ago. "What were you two doing in the woods?"

It was an admirable attempt to sidetrack me.

"Looking for Sandy. You said you'd see me at home. That was hours ago."

"We got caught in an updraft. It blew us off course—all the way up to Alcona County."

"I know you're exaggerating now," I said.

"Okay. It *felt* like the wind carried us way up north. Our cell phones didn't work. The radio didn't work. I didn't know where we were. All we could see were woods and lakes."

"So we knew we were still in Michigan," Brent added.

"That sounds like a scene from a boys' adventure story," I said, remembering Bennett's Hardy Boys book. "What were you really doing?"

Brent rushed to answer. "It's the truth, Jennet. Did you ever hear that old saying? Truth is stranger than fiction?"

"I'd never lie to you," Crane said, affronted.

"I know. It's just so—unbelievable."

"Then we had to put the Sky Princess to bed," Brent said. "We met up with Mac Dalby, and he told us there'd been some excitement on Jonquil Lane. Said you'd tell us all about it."

"But why didn't you let me know?"

"I tried to," Crane said. "You didn't answer your cell phone."

"Can we eat now?" Brent asked. "I'm starved."

"As soon as the biscuits are done."

I took the casserole out of the oven and placed the biscuit sheet on the rack. "Everything else is ready, but you left a big chunk out of the story, Crane. How did you get out of that updraft and regain control of the balloon?"

"The wind died down," Crane said.

Could I believe that? "We've had high winds most of the day."

Brent winked at me. "Not in Alcona County. That looks great, Jennet. What is it? Roast beef? Potatoes?"

"A casserole from an old family recipe."

"Let's eat," Crane said.

"I have to reset the table in the kitchen," I told them, suddenly remembering the shards of glass and shattered teapot on the floor and the broken window that was letting our warm air escape and the cold air in.

Crane paused at the entrance to the dining room, surveying the damage. His voice was low and steady. "Did a bullet do that? What happened here?"

"I had an adventure of my own," I said and told him about Sara's failed attempt to kill me. "You won't believe this, Crane, but I saw Rebecca Ferguson in the candlestick. Then I dropped the match and almost started a fire. If I hadn't dropped that match, I'd have been shot."

"She's delirious with joy," Brent said in a low aside.

"No, that's what happened."

Crane took me in his arms. He didn't say a word. He didn't have to. I'd already thanked Rebecca for both of us.

Forty-three

Fearing a long jail sentence for multiple crimes, Sara Hall decided to tell all in the hope of trading full disclosure for leniency. Unfortunately her version of all lacked credibility and was rife with contradictions. It was a desperate grab for sympathy.

I read the tale of the devious babysitter in the *Banner* the next morning.

Tale? I should say web of lies. I'd never heard such an outrageous story.

Sara denied that she'd shot Eric Morrow and Johnny Holliday, nor did she know who did.

She claimed the birthday excursion-abduction was Johnny's idea, conceived when he learned the children's grandfather was a wealthy developer. He'd forced her to participate, but he alone had written the ransom note. Then when the scheme fell apart, he disappeared, probably taking the money with him.

As for Bennett and Briana, something spooked them—not her—and they ran away. Of course she wasn't stalking them. Good riddance to bad kids, she always said.

Sara had grown tired of taking care of other people's children, tired of being bored and bossed around and never making enough money to buy nice clothes or put herself through college. She might have forged her references, but whoever read them anyway?

It wasn't fair.

She admitted to being naïve and easily duped and, incidentally, being unable to control her young charges. They were impossible children, and she had never wanted to be a nanny anyway. Pretending to like kids had been so stressful.

When she met Johnny Holliday and they began a relationship, she assumed he'd support her. He always seemed to have plenty of money.

Doing what?

Sara didn't know. It wasn't the first time a handsome, charming man had led a girl astray with promises of the good life.

True, she'd helped herself to free room and board and a few dresses at a couple of vacant houses, but Johnny had left her in the middle of nowhere with neither money nor transportation, still in pain after the balloon crash.

The gun?

It was in the glove compartment of the car she borrowed.

That was all Sara said.

On the same page, in an interview with Bennett Cooper, I learned why Bennett hadn't talked about Eric.

After Bennett had appealed to Eric for help, when Johnny yanked him away from the Skyway Tours office, Bennett heard a shot. Sara warned him never to tell anyone what had happened because he was responsible for getting Eric killed.

Who were people going to listen to? From the resentment that sharpened Sara's voice when she spoke about Johnny, I had no trouble believing that she had shot him and Eric as well.

I searched through the rest of the page for news of Briana. Her condition had been downgraded from critical to serious.

From Mac I learned that Liza Cooper had rented rooms at a nearby bed and breakfast for herself and Bennett until she could take both of her children home. I wondered if she'd be receptive to talking to me.

But first I had to take Sandy back to Josie, who was overjoyed that her puppy had been found.

After settling the dogs for the morning, I led Sandy out of the crate on her new red leash and outside into the car with only one brief stop. She had been restless all morning, and I couldn't take the chance of having her run away again. As a concession I opened her window and mine just enough to catch breaths of fresh air.

On the way to Josie's house, I took a detour to Mallowmere Kennels. I'd brushed Sandy, over her softly growled objections, and she'd had two good meals, several drinks of water, and a restless night in the crate. From upstairs, I heard her crying in the night, no doubt lonesome for her home in the woods.

She looked good, but she would need a real bath and more socialization. Most of all, she'd have to get used to civilization and obeying simple commands. I hoped Josie would be able to manage all that. I didn't want Sandy to be homeless again.

The sun broke through the clouds as I neared the kennels, and miracle of miracles, there was no wind. It was a perfect spring morning, a day for new beginnings.

Marvel came rushing down the stairs of the old farmhouse to meet us. Sandy scampered to the far end of the back seat, observing her overtures warily.

"She's beautiful," Marvel said. "I never thought you'd be able to find her."

"Sandy was in the woods near my house all this time. She's been staying on and off with the Cooper twins who were on the run."

"I read about it in the *Banner*." Marvel said. "That could have been a real tragedy."

"I think Sandy misses them, but she seems to have formed an attachment to my collie, Candy. I think she'll adjust to new surroundings. I just hope Josie's home will be the right one for her."

"If it doesn't work out, I'll take her back in a heartbeat," Marvel said. "I think she's the best pup in the litter, although I didn't realize it when she was a baby. I guess I have a lot to learn."

I took Sandy out on her leash, and she tugged her way over to the run where her brother, Andy, was eagerly pawing the gate. The lone male, he still hadn't been sold.

They touched noses through the chain links. Did she remember him? Maybe. Who knew what went on in a dog's mind?

"At last every puppy is where she should be," Marvel said. "Thanks to you, Jennet. You broke the curse."

I bent to fluff the fur around Sandy's ears. "There never was a curse."

"The mix-up then. Believe me, with my next litter, I'll be more careful when people come to look at my puppies."

I hoped so.

Saying goodbye to Marvel, I settled Sandy in the back seat again. The next and last stop was Josie's house. For Sandy, it was the end of the line.

~ * ~

A half hour later I handed Sandy's leash to Josie. The puppy flattened her ears and wagged her tail. Behind them, Josie's mother smiled on the sentimental Lassie-come-home scene.

So far so good.

"She remembers me!" Josie cried. "Welcome home, Sandy. I prayed for you to come back."

I didn't think Sandy had any recollection of the house or the excited girl who waved a plush duck in front of her face. But, like most collies, she loved children. Like all dogs, she responded to a friendly tone and a quacking toy.

"All's well that ends well," I said.

Josie stepped back to get a better look at the puppy. "She's different. What's wrong with her knees? They're so knobby."

"Nothing. That's the way a dog grows."

She tried to pick Sandy up, and the puppy wriggled out of her grasp.

"At this age, puppies change every day." I glanced at the spacious yard, still unfenced. "Keep her on the leash at all times, and enroll her in a puppy obedience class. It'll do both of you a world of good."

"Take Sandy out in back," Josie's mother said, still smiling. Could this be the same woman I'd met before? She must be. The pink striped shirtwaist dress and string of pearls were familiar.

"Won't you come in, Mrs. Ferguson?" she asked. "We're having sandwiches. There's plenty."

"Thanks, but I have four collies of my own who've been neglected lately. Could I have a rain check? I'd like to see how Sandy's doing in a week or so."

"Sure," she said. "Come back any time, and thanks for bringing our dog home."

Home. That had to be the most glorious word in the English language.

~ * ~

I hadn't been home ten minutes when I spied a silver car moving slowly up the lane. It turned in our driveway, and the dogs set up their usual clamor. Company! Friend or foe?

We'd soon see.

Bennett Cooper jumped down from the car. He held an enormous bouquet with both hands. Candy ran to the front door as he started up the walkway. In his wake came a willowy blonde woman in white slacks and a lacy beige top. She wore as much gold jewelry as Lucy Hazen. Bracelets, chains, and an ostentatious watch. The paper shopping bag she carried looked woefully out of place with her outfit.

Liza Cooper. I recognized her from her pictures in the paper.

I opened the door and told the dogs to Sit. Only Sky obeyed.

"Hi," Bennett said, shoving the flowers at me. "These are for you. Thanks for finding us and saving my sister's life."

"Why, thank you," I said. "That's so thoughtful."

Suddenly I felt as if I were holding spring in my arms. Pastel colored tulips and lilies with fern and crisp baby's breath. Lots of pink and yellow. "But don't forget. Candy did that."

"Thank you, Candy," he added.

She was prancing around his feet, and Gemmy had joined her.

I shooed the dogs back and invited our company to find seats in the living room.

Liza pulled a giant rawhide bone out of the bag. "We didn't forget Candy," she said.

"Oh dear."

Four eyes burned bright with desire. Four collies licked their chops.

I set the bone as far back on my desk as possible. "There's sibling rivalry even in a collie pack," I explained.

"I didn't think. I should have brought more."

"There's no need. Candy knows all about sharing."

Or she will.

How's Briana?" I asked.

"Better. She developed pneumonia, but the doctor tells us she's going to make a full recovery. We're on our way to the hospital now." She opened her purse and handed me a check. "I want you to have this little token of my gratitude."

I glanced at the amount. It was fifty thousand dollars. The reward money.

"Oh, no," I said, giving it back to her. "I can't take this. A lot of people were looking for the children."

Brent and Annica, the police, volunteer searchers. People whose names we'd never know.

"Everybody helped, and in the end it was Candy who found them," I said.

Her hand froze in mid-air above the check. "I realize that, but there's no way I can divide the reward among everyone who helped bring my children home, and a dog can't spend money. You were there to call the ambulance," she added.

I didn't say anything.

"Besides the money has been in a special account for this very purpose. Take it. Please."

"No, but you can donate it," I said. "There are so many worthy causes in Foxglove Corners. The Lakeville Collie Rescue League, the animal shelter, the police… You could make life more comfortable for the police and the sheriff's deputies."

You'd better stop, I told myself. *These are all your own causes.*

She brightened. "That's a marvelous idea. I'll let the twins decide who gets what. When Briana comes home."

~ * ~

That evening after dinner Crane and I sat on the porch with our collie family. We talked about Rebecca's well-timed appearance. He told me about his day patrolling the roads and by-roads, and I told him I'd turned down fifty thousand dollars. As the sun began to set, we drifted into a friendly argument about hot air balloons.

"I don't think I want to go on a color tour after all if you're at the mercy of the wind," I said. "*Terra firma* is a lovely concept."

"You'll enjoy it, Jennet. We'll pick a nice fall day without even a breeze."

"We have a whole season before we have to decide," I said. "All summer."

Crane didn't have to know yet, but I'd already made my decision. There'd be no hot air balloon rides for me. They were far too dangerous.

I told myself it wasn't the dreams, after all these days still so vivid and frightening.

When fall came, I'd stay on the ground and look up at the panorama of changing leaves from the first hints of color in the woods to the glorious peak days when Foxglove Corners turned a hundred shades of red and gold.

But I remembered Brent had already reserved an October date for us, one I'd arbitrarily selected. Well, we had plenty of time to cancel, or Bent might tire of his new business. Or Crane could go alone.

Did I really want that?

I remembered how lost I'd felt when I didn't know where he was. That was only yesterday. And before, when I feared he had been killed in the tornado. And all the times before that, before our wedding, when I wasn't sure he loved me. When I worried he was seeing another woman. And back farther, after our first chance encounter at the Mill House when I wondered if I would ever see him again.

So long ago.

I reached over Halley's sleeping form and took his hand in mine.

"Does that mean you'll go, honey?" he asked.

"Yes," I said. "Wherever you go, I'll be with you."

Meet

Dorothy Bodoin

Dorothy Bodoin lives in Royal Oak, Michigan, with her collie, Wolf Manor Kinder Brightstar (Kinder). After working as a secretary for Chrysler Missile Corporation, which included a two-year assignment in Italy, she attended Oakland University where she received Bachelor's and Master's degrees in English literature. For several years she taught secondary English in Michigan, eventually leaving education to write full time. Her most recent books are *The Dog From The Sky* and Spirit Of The Season. She is currently working on the twelfth book book in the Foxglove Corners series.

Made in the USA
Middletown, DE
21 June 2018